DUET OF DEATH

Hilda Lawrence is the pen name of American author **Hildegarde Kronmiller** who published her first book in 1946. She began to write from her home in Baltimore when she had divorced her husband and had nothing else to do. She started with a detective story because, she said, 'no one expects perfect construction. To begin with a novel is fatal unless you are a genius. The detective story doesn't ask too much.' **Hilda Lawrence** also wrote *Death of a Doll* and *Blood Upon the Snow*, both now part of the *Pandora Women Crime Writers Series*.

DUET OF

Death

HILDA LAWRENCE

First Published 1949

PANDORA

LONDON SYDNEY WELLINGTON

First published in 1949
This edition first published in Great Britain in 1988 by Pandora Press, an
imprint of the Trade Division of Unwin Hyman.

Pandora Press
Unwin Hyman Limited
15–17 Broadwick Street, London W1V 1FP

Allen and Unwin Australia Pty Ltd
8 Napier Street, North Sydney, NSW 2060, Australia

Allen and Unwin New Zealand Pty Ltd with the Port Nicolson Press
60 Cambridge Terrace, Wellington, New Zealand

British Library Cataloguing in Publication Data

Lawrence, Hilda, 1906–
   Duet of death. – (Pandora women crime writers).
I. Title
813'.52[F]
ISBN 0–86358–294–X

Printed in Great Britain by
Cox and Wyman Ltd, Reading, Berkshire

Pandora Women Crime Writers

Series Editors: Rosalind Coward and Linda Semple

In introducing the *Pandora Women Crime Writers Series* we have two aims: to reprint the best of women crime writers who have disappeared from print and to introduce a new generation of women crime writers to all devotees of the genre. We also hope to seduce new readers to the pleasures of detective fiction.

Women have used the tradition of crime writing inventively since the end of the last century. Indeed, in many periods women have dominated crime writing, as in the so-called golden age of detective fiction, usually defined as between the first novel of Agatha Christie and the last of Dorothy L. Sayers. Often the most popular novels of the day, and those thought to be the best in their genre, were written by women. But as in so many areas of women's writing, many of these have been allowed to go out of print. Few people know the names of Josephine Bell, Pamela Branch, Hilda Lawrence, Marion Mainwaring or Anthony Gilbert (whose real name was Lucy Malleson). Their novels are just as good and entertaining as when they were first written.

Women's importance in the field of crime writing is just as vital today. P. D. James, Ruth Rendell and Patricia Highsmith have all ensured that crime writing is treated seriously. Not so well known, but equally flourishing, is a new branch of feminist crime writers. We plan to introduce many new writers from this area, from England and other countries.

The integration of reprints and new novels is sometimes uneasy. Some writers do make snobbish, even racist remarks. However it is a popular misconception that all earlier novels are always snobbish and racist. Many of our chosen and favourite authors managed to avoid, sometimes deliberately, the prevailing views. Others are more rooted in the ideologies of their time but when their remarks jar, it does serve to remind us that any novel must be understood by reference to the historical context in which it is written.

Some of the best writers who will be appearing in this series are: Josephine Bell, Ina Bouman, Christianna Brand, Pamela Branch, Sarah Dreher, Katherine V. Forrest, Miles Franklin, Anthony Gilbert (Lucy Malleson), Hilda Lawrence, Marion Mainwaring, Nancy Spain . . .

Linda Semple
Rosalind Coward

To
Maggie Cousins

COMPOSITION
FOR FOUR HANDS

———

Part One

THEY wheeled her chair to the big bay window in her bed-room. She'd been fed and bathed. She'd had what they called her forty winks. They said it was a beautiful afternoon and wasn't she lucky to have such a nice window? Then they left her. It was Saturday. She knew it was Saturday, because school-children were playing in the little park across the way and the florist had come with her weekend roses. She'd bought the house because of that little park. Nice for a child. The park and the big, rambling gardens. For swings and play-houses, later for tennis courts ... It was Saturday. Ralph, her husband, was home from the bank, and he'd helped with her lunch, spooning the broth so carefully, call-ing her his little baby. Not speaking to her, though; to the nurse. He'd said: 'Miss Sills, she's all I've got now. She's my little baby girl, and she's all I've got.'

Miss Sills had looked as if she had wanted to cry. Her hand had gone out as if she had wanted to touch his beautiful white hair. She had said: 'You mustn't brood, Mr Manson. No matter how miserable you are, you must make yourself look happy for her sake. She's terribly sensitive, she feels things.'

She could hear things, too. Sometimes they forgot that. When they spoke directly to her, they raised their voices and made gestures, as if she were deaf. But when they talked among themselves, they acted as if she weren't there. They seemed to think she couldn't hear unless they put their faces close to hers and waved their hands. That was all right; she wanted them to talk among themselves. The more they talked like that, the better. When they left the room, she wanted to know where they were going. She wanted to know where they were every hour of the day. And the night. The night.

They left her, and she heard their footsteps going down the hall; Ralph's turned at the rose guestroom. That was where he slept now. She'd heard the doctor tell him to sleep there, to be within call. Whose call? Not hers; she couldn't open her mouth. She could open it, but she couldn't make a sound. The nurse's call. Miss Sills'.

Miss Sills had a cot at the foot of her big bed. If Miss Sills called to him in the night, he could be there in less than a minute, down the hall or across the sleeping porch that ran along that side of the house. I suppose they talk among themselves, downstairs, and say that I may die in the night, she thought. I wonder if I can smile. I don't know, they never bring me a mirror. They never put my chair anywhere near a mirror. But if I can smile, then that's what I'm doing now inside. Careful. Be careful.

MISS SILLS' footsteps went beyond the rose room to the head of the stairs, went down, and were lost in the thick rugs of the lower hall. Going for her afternoon exercise. Soon I'll hear the front door close, and then she'll wave to me from the garden. Then I'll see her across the street, in the little park, walking with long, easy steps, swinging her arms. Beautiful, beautiful motion. And pretty soon Emma will come in to sit, chirping and smiling and talking. Talking, talking, talking. But I'm used to Emma. She's been with me so long she's almost like a member of the family. She will tell me about the prices of things, pretending I still keep house. The butcher, the fruit man, the farmer with his wagon – robbers all, but what can a person do? And Emma will say: 'My, but you look fine to-day. There's colour in your cheeks.'

Rouge. Miss Sills had put it on. You couldn't stop her. Rouge and curling irons and manicures. She said it was good for morale. *Morale.*

Emma would sit in the low chair, neat as a pin in her

afternoon uniform, and talk about tea and dinner. And she'd have her tatting. Emma did tatting now. She used to knit, but they made her stop – because of the needles. The needles were the right shape, as nearly the right shape and size as anything could be, anything you'd be lucky enough to get your hands on. Lucky enough if your hands, if only your hands –

Hands. Emma's old hands, worn and rough because she made her living with them, but strong. Emma's old hands that didn't need strength, gripping the lovely needles. Rolling them between her fingers, turning them over and over; beautiful, beautiful motion, wasted on Emma.

Emma must have seen her watching the needles; she must have seen a look in her eyes, because she'd said, 'No, no, Miss Nora, you mustn't think of such a terrible thing.' Emma couldn't possibly know what she really was thinking, nobody could know. Nobody except – no, that wasn't possible. Or was it? She'd wondered and worried, driven herself half-crazy, until she overheard them talking when they thought she was asleep. Miss Sills said: 'She wanted Emma's needles to-day. Emma saw the look. I don't like that, Mr Manson, I don't like it at all. She couldn't hold them even if we put them in her hands – she can't even hold a hankie, not yet, not now. But I don't like it. In these cases you sometimes get a sudden change – temporary, of course, like a muscular spasm. She could do herself a serious injury if she got hold of anything like that, anything with a point. So I told Emma to stop the knitting and work on something else. Like tatting. You can't hurt yourself with a little celluloid bobbin.'

He said: 'Hurt herself? How dreadful! But I'm afraid you're right. I saw her watching your pencil when you were writing the drugstore list. She wanted it, she craved it. A pencil! What could she do with a pencil?'

'I don't know. We can't get into her poor mind. But really, Mr Manson, we've got to be alert every minute. We've got to prepare ourselves for a physical change. You know she could put her – I hate to say this – she could put

9

her – well, she could hurt her eyes. In the state she's in, I mean her emotional state, she may think of herself as useless, a burden to you. A self-inflicted injury – oh, it's too awful, the poor thing! Maybe she doesn't even want to *see*!'

His warm hands covered her then. He said: 'Guard her, Miss Sills, don't let anything happen. She's all I have. Those lovely eyes, have you noticed how they – follow? They're the only thing about her that's alive.'

THAT was why Emma gave up knitting for tatting, which she hated. That was why Miss Sills no longer wore pencil and pen clipped to her apron bib. A self-inflicted injury ... Don't think about it, she told herself. You're lucky, you're very lucky, because they guessed wrong. Think of something else, make yourself think, hard, hard. Think of your hands, your fingers: think of a substitute for a pencil. Anything, anything that will turn and roll between useless fingers, turn and roll and give them strength. Secret strength that must be kept hidden. If you were a soldier in a hospital, they'd put something in your hands and help you turn and roll it. In a hospital they'd help you. That's why you're not in a hospital, that's why you're home. You heard them: 'She'll be more comfortable in her own home with the people she loves.' Self-inflicted injury; you heard that, too. You're lucky again because you can't laugh. You're lucky because if you once started, you couldn't stop. You'd give yourself away. Self-inflicted injury, when all you want to do is to keep your life, not lose it. Keep it, such as it is, keep it until – Why, I'm crying. Those are tears on my hands. I didn't know I could cry. Think of something else. Quick ... Bruce will be coming on the four-fifteen. Better not think of that, either. Every afternoon, bending down to look into your face, kissing your hands, telling you how well you look, teasing, pretending ... Stop that. Stop that.

Look at the fringe on your steamer rug. Old, happy rug; kind, thick fringe. Thick! Almost as thick as a pencil! Try it, try it while you're alone, hurry before – before Emma comes. Before anyone comes. Before they all come tramping back from their walks, their exercise, from the station. There, you almost did it that time. Almost. But don't worry because it seems impossible now; some day you'll make it. Try. Try again. There's a good thick strand, lying across your left wrist. See if you can touch it with your other hand. See if you can move your wrist, your arm, your arm, try ... No. No, but don't cry again, that's getting you nowhere. Keep trying, and thank God your mind is all right. That's what they aren't sure of, your mind. That's where you're ahead of them; that's how you'll win in the end. One of these days one of your hands will reach the fringe and close over it. One of these days you will take the fringe in your hand and open and close your fingers. Roll the soft, thick fringe between your fingers, endlessly, over and over, until they are strong enough to hold a pencil. Pencil. You'll never even see another pencil. You know that. But your fingers will be ready for whatever comes. It doesn't matter if you never walk again, if you never speak again. All you need is two fingers. Two? No, one, one will be enough, one finger can point. You can pretend to be writing with one finger, a pantomime. You can make it clear and unmistakable if you are ever alone with the right person ... But how will I know which person is right? I'm not sure even now. How will I know which one is both right and safe? Now, now, don't cry. It takes away the little strength you have. Now, now, don't be a baby. 'My little baby girl,' he said ... There's Emma.

MILLY SILLS crossed the park and hurried to the Larchville station. The four-fifteen from New York was pulling in, and the platform was filled with families and dogs. She had time only to set her beret becomingly awry before George Perry and Mr Bruce Cory came shouldering through the crowd. Milly and George, who lived, with his father and mother, next door to the Mansons', had been friends for some time. She eyed Mr Cory rather hostilely, but had to

11

admit he was a handsome devil for – what was it, fifty? Emma had told her that the other Mr Cory, Mrs Manson's first husband, had been about ten years older than Mrs Manson, and she was forty-two. And Bruce Cory was that Mr Cory's twin. Well, handsome devil for fifty-two or whatever it was. No fat, not an ounce. He made old George look like a puppy.

'Damn,' Milly said under her breath, 'it looks as if George and I can't be alone for even five minutes these days.' She waved, and they waved over the other commuters' heads. She made rapid plans for the evening. Maybe a movie, maybe dancing, maybe both. 'I'll work on him,' she decided. 'I don't care if he does look grim. He'll have to get over that. I, for one, won't have it. I, for one, am having too much as it is.'

However, she noted, there was nothing grim about Bruce Cory, with the polo-field skin and the squash-court figure. She watched his approach with admiration and appropriate distrust. He walked as if he had oiled hinges.

'Mr Perry, I believe,' she said to George when they came up to her. She hooked an affectionate arm through George's and gave him a pinch, but he didn't seem to feel it. To Bruce Cory she gave the smile she kept in reserve for patients' relatives.

'Hi,' George said. 'I ran into Mr Cory in the smoker.'

Cory returned her smile with a look of approval that travelled from her white canvas shoes to her white beret. She felt herself liking it. George had given her one look, a quick one, with absolutely nothing in it. But nothing.

They moved across the platform. 'Cab or walk?' George asked.

'Walk,' she said. 'This is my airing.'

Cory was instantly solicitous, looking down with a worried air. 'Are you having any fun?' he asked. 'Or is it all perfectly deadly?'

Having any fun, she jeered silently. What a thing to say! I know you, my friend. To date you've given no trouble, but there's one of your kind on every case ... She gave him the smile she kept in reserve for that kind, the one that said: 'When I go downstairs at midnight in my bathrobe, I'm going for hot cocoa – get it? Cocoa.' Aloud, 'Everything's fine, Mr Cory, thank you,' she said.

'Anything happen after I left this morning? Any change?'

'No change. No change is considered fine in cases like this. We can't ask for more than that for a while. But she had a good lunch – good for her, I mean – and she seems to be making an effort in other ways, too.'

'Splendid! What kind of effort?'

'Well, she seems to notice things. I haven't said much about it except to Mr Manson, but I do feel encouraged. I think she's trying to concentrate. You know, listen. She seems to realize that she's helpless, and her eyes –'

Cory spoke sharply. 'What about her eyes?'

'Oh, nothing like that, Mr Cory!' He did love her, they all did. In her way she was lucky. Some people had no one, had to go to city hospitals and wear dark, shapeless robes all day long because they didn't show the dirt or the food that got spilled. Mrs Manson had real silk and fine wool, and there wasn't a single minute when somebody wasn't trying to anticipate her wants, read her thoughts. Read her thoughts – if she had any. That was something they weren't sure about.

'Oh, no, Mr Cory, there's nothing wrong with her vision. I only mean she notices more and tries to watch everything we do, although she can't turn her head, not yet. But I'm pretty sure she'll be able to do that soon. I even told Mr Manson so.' Then, because Mr Cory still looked unhappy and unconvinced, she added: 'Cheer up. It could be worse. Think how poor Mr Manson feels.'

Cory nodded. 'Good little Sills,' he said, 'We were lucky to get you.'

They walked on in silence.

TO-NIGHT she would be free from eight to twelve. Once a week she had a night like that. Sometimes she went home, a fifteen-minute walk across town lugging a suitcase of laundry for her mother to do. It wasn't necessary, but her mother liked to do it. Her mother always met her at the front door and took the suitcase before she kissed her. She dumped the clothes into the washing machine as if she were fighting a plague. Then she sat in the rocker she kept in the kitchen and double-dared anybody to come within a yard of the machine. The washer was a Christmas present from Milly, and the capable, elderly maid was a present, too. But Mrs Sills chose to regard the washer as her own invention and the maid as an indigent relative, not right in the head. 'Maybe I ought to go home,' Milly thought. 'I missed last week.' Then she looked at George. Still grim. A face like granite. Jealous, she gloated. What do you know! Her heart suddenly warmed. 'Movies to-night, George?'

'Not to-night.'

'What's the matter with you?'

'Toothache.'

'Of course you've seen the dentist?'

'No.'

'Well, of course you will, won't you?'

'Maybe.'

Fool, she thought. Why do I bother? Suit yourself, lie awake all night and suffer. See if I care ... Later, when she remembered that, she felt as if she'd been daring an axe to fall on her neck. Because George didn't go to the dentist, and he did lie awake. He got up at three in the morning to spit a poultice out the window, and she cared a great deal.

Now Cory was saying something and she turned with elaborate interest. 'I beg your pardon, Mr Cory. I didn't get that.'

'I asked you what you thought of Doctor Babcock,' Cory said carelessly.

'I have every confidence in Doctor Babcock,' she said primly. 'So has Mr Manson.'

'I know he has. Babcock's the only one who's lasted. I understand you've worked with him before?'

It was a question, not a statement. She was pleased. He doesn't know how green I am, she thought. I must be doing all right. Maybe none of them knows ... Her reply was short but lofty. 'Oh, my, yes.' One tonsillectomy.

She remembered the night, a little less than two weeks before, when Doctor Babcock had routed her out of bed. He didn't tell her what the case was, and she turned it down, because she'd just wound up six weeks with a simple fracture, age twelve, who slept all day and demanded comics all night. She said she needed sleep. But he told her he was desperate, his patient was unhappy with her present nurse. He was perfectly frank; he admitted the woman was difficult and would probably be unhappy with Florence Nightingale. It was like Babcock to drag in Nightingale. Then he'd said the patient was Mrs Manson. At that, she'd gone with him, at once, at one o'clock in the morning.

She'd been glad of her decision ever since, and it had nothing to do with the fact that good old George's house was practically in the Manson backyard. Mrs Manson liked her, she could see that. And Babcock looked pleased. That meant a lot. Her first really important case. If she made good, there wouldn't be any more spoiled kids and old women. If she made good, she could stay with Mrs Manson until the end. The end? Well, stay until something happened one way or another. Or until Milly herself couldn't take it.

'What did Babcock say this morning?' Cory was pressing her arm.

'He didn't come, Mr Cory. He called up right after you left. He said he'd drop in this afternoon. I don't like to be away when he comes, even when Mr Manson and Emma are there, but if I don't go out at my regular hours, I get dopey. And that's not good for Mrs Manson.'

'What about another nurse? I don't know why we haven't insisted on that.'

'Not a chance, I suggested it myself, and if you'd seen the look in her eyes – She's terrified of people, even old friends who come to inquire. We've had to stop all that. We have to be awfully careful, even with the people in the house. Like Hattie, the cook. The cook's all right when she keeps her mouth shut, but the other day she burst into tears and talked about Mrs Manson's son.'

'About Robbie?' At her nod, Cory looked away. 'Bad,' he said.

'Bad? It was criminal. George was there; he saw the whole thing. But we didn't tell a soul. No use getting Hattie fired. We simply gave her – we laid her out. She won't do that again.'

'You can tell me about it, can't you? Forget that I'm Robbie's uncle.'

She answered eagerly, appealing to George, forcing him into the conversation. 'Of course we can tell Mr Cory, can't we, George? You do it; you know the background better than I do. You see, I didn't know about Robbie's birthday, Mr Cory. How could I? If I'd known, I'd have got Hattie out the minute she started. Tell it, George.'

George complied, slowly and reluctantly. 'It isn't much,' he said. 'But it was a nuisance. You know I'm in and out of the house a lot these days, at odd hours. And you know I practically lived in the place when I was a kid. Mrs Manson never let them fill in the hedge.'

Cory said, 'Yes, I know.' He knew that the Perry cottage backed on the Manson garden, and that the dividing hedge still showed gaps made by small boys in a hurry. He knew all about the childhood friendship and that George was a few years older than Robbie, and that after they outgrew the swings, the play-houses, and the gym apparatus, they didn't see much of each other.

'We went with different crowds when we grew up,' George said. 'Naturally. You know how that happens. This last year I hardly ever saw him. He was twenty-one and I was twenty-six – that makes a lot of difference. To say nothing of Robbie's unlimited money.' In spite of himself he emphasized money.

'Forget that,' Cory said. 'Go on with your story.'

ACCORDING to George, his mother said it would be nice if he began to hang around the Mansons again – second-son stuff. And Mrs Manson seemed to like it. At least, he said, she didn't have a relapse. Not until the Hattie episode. He'd been dropping in for several weeks when that happened, having drinks in Mrs Manson's room, talking about anything that came into his head, never mentioning Robbie. Nothing ever upset her when he was there alone, even though he was pretty sure she didn't hear half he said. She just looked at him, accepted him, and that was all anybody hoped for. Then the cook business happened.

'Small thing in its way,' George said, 'but a fine example of the chances you take when you don't control the people who go to see her.'

He said he'd been doing his usual routine that afternoon, rambling on about the weather, the pretty sky, and see how the leaves are turning, Mrs Manson. Thanksgiving on the way, Hallowe'en before you know it, and so on. Then Hattie came in with a lamb chop and a piece of chicken on a plate. Raw. A custom of the house, a scheme to coax Mrs Manson into thinking. Emma's idea. Here are two pieces of meat. You may have one for your dinner. Which? Emma swore it worked; she said Hattie could tell which one Mrs Manson wanted by the way she looked.

George said he had reached Hallowe'en in his therapeutic travelogue, pumpkin faces, and so on, when Hattie burst into tears and started to babble.

'I was sunk,' George said. 'I'd forgotten that Robbie's birthday was all tied up with pumpkins. But Hattie hadn't. She carried on about the jack-o'-lanterns they used to put in his room on birthdays. They did that from the time he was three until he was eighteen. Then he made them stop it. Did you know that?'

17

'Yes,' Cory said. 'They all babied him.'

'Exactly,' George agreed. 'Well, that's all, but it sent Mrs Manson right up to the taking off place and turned me into an old man. Hattie still comes in with her plate of raw meat, but she doesn't talk.'

The little park was straight ahead, and across the park the big house stood in its bright fall garden. Milly thought of the motionless figure she had left by the window, and her steps dragged. She listened half-heartedly to the conversation. They were getting along all right without her; George was warming up, for him. Giving out information instead of hoarding it, treating Cory like an equal. Now he was saying something in a soft voice about a dreamy kid.

'Always was,' George said. 'Always lived in another world. Robbie had his mother's features, but he didn't have her – excitement. Of course, I never saw his father; but taking you as a model, I'd say Robbie wasn't like a Cory, either.'

It was an obvious compliment, George's voice was deferential and admiring, and Cory flushed. Milly said to herself, 'Good old George, he'll get a job out of Cory yet.'

'When my brother died,' Cory said quietly, 'I rather hoped she'd remarry. I was glad when she did. No, Robbie wasn't like my brother. Robbie was – himself.'

George said: 'I don't like to think about it. I don't even like to talk about it.'

BUT Milly thought about it as they entered the park and crossed under the yellow maples, between flaming beds of scarlet sage. The maple leaves were gold, the gold of new coin. A boy with all the money in the world, with anything – 'Do you think they'll ever find out what he did with it?' she asked vaguely.

Cory didn't answer. He said, 'Is she in her window?'

'She should be,' she told him. 'We put her there as usual, Mr Manson and I, just before I came out. She likes to watch the park – at least, I think she does. I told Emma not to

touch her, to wait until I came back. It's sort of queer –'
She stopped to challenge her own words and to wonder
why they suddenly asked for challenge.

'What's queer?' Cory was smiling. 'The window? Or
Emma?'

She answered slowly. 'Neither. I only mean she's funny
about being touched. I don't think she likes it, and we're
pretty sure it isn't a question of pain. But when I get back
from my walks and go to her room, I always feel as if she's
been waiting for me. For *me*. Almost – well, anxiously. And
I've only been on the case a little while; it isn't as if I were
an old friend. I guess it's the uniform. People seem to trust
nurses.' I've said something idiotic, she told herself instantly.
Cory had given her a quick, sharp look, and George was
rolling his eyes to heaven. As if I'd pulled a boner, she
thought, as if I were feeble-minded. I'll show them.

'And the more fools they,' she said briskly. 'I mean, for
trusting nurses. I can count cases on all ten fingers that
would curl your hair. Helpless patient plus renegade husband, son, brother, doctor, lawyer, friend. Take your choice.
Willing female confederate, uniform from a theatrical place.
Object, money. And believe me –' She stopped again,
appalled. Why don't you pack up and get out before you're
fired? she mourned to herself.

'Brilliant girl,' George said to Cory. 'And simply crazy
about Mill Sills, R.N.'

They turned in at the gate.

Mrs Manson was still by the window. She'd seen them
turn into the park and cross, talking.

Emma had seen them, too. 'There, now,' Emma said,
'there's Mr Brucie and George Perry with Miss Sills. I'd
say she went to the station to meet them, wouldn't you?'
Emma smiled and nodded and waved. She looked as if she
were glad to see someone who could smile and wave in
return. And talk. Poor Emma. Talking, talking, talking, and
never being quite sure that she was heard.

'You're lucky, that's what you are,' Emma insisted. 'And I want you to remember it, and appreciate it. A nice young girl like Miss Sills to look after you. A daughter couldn't do more. And Mr Bruce Cory, giving up his beautiful New York apartment to come out here and cheer you up, for old times' sake. Giving up his gay city life, when we all know he hates the country. He's popular, too, he is. In the gossip columns nearly every day, but in a nice way. No café society for Mr Brucie; he runs with the cream dee lah cream.'

She stopped listening to Emma. There were other things to listen to.

The front door opened, and they walked across the strip of floor that was bare. Then they walked on the rugs. Then the sound of their voices. Ralph's voice, low, greeting them. Then another door, the library. They were going to have a drink before they all came up, trooping in full of smiles. 'How wonderful you look! You keep this up, and you'll be out for Christmas!' Out? Out where? Out beside Robbie.

Doctor Babcock encouraged them to talk like that. He himself talked like that, rocking back and forth on his strong legs. They all did that, rocked; they thought it made them look as if they had nothing on their minds. But she'd seen the look Babcock had given Ralph the day before. She'd been keeping her eyes almost closed, as children do when they pretend to be asleep, looking between her lashes. Babcock had looked at Ralph and shaken his head. Hopeless, the look had said. And he'd shrugged and raised his eyebrows in answer to an unspoken question of Ralph's. The shrug and brows said, 'Hopeless, except for a miracle.'

They were all watching for a miracle, for a sign of change. She saw it in their faces, heard it in their voices. They knew what to watch for; they discussed its improbability as if she were already dead. And one of them knew how much that kind of talk meant to her. One of the people who came to her room was quietly alert lying in wait for a sign that showed she understood. She had read the speculation in one

20

pair of eyes. She was much cleverer than that; she was careful to let her own eyes show nothing. If the miracle came, she knew she must hide it. The first sign of a twitch, the first small movement, one finger, one muscle in her body, and the news would go all over the house, over the town. And that would be the end of her. 'Have you heard about Mrs Manson? Too bad, just when she was beginning to show improvement.' Maybe it would happen before that. In a panic, in a sudden panic –

She looked at the rug, at the fringe lying across her knees. She looked at it until her eyes burned. 'Emma,' she implored silently, 'Emma –'

'Now, what's wrong with your nice rug?' Emma scolded. 'I declare, you're looking as if you wanted to eat it up! Could that mean you're cold? No, your face is nice and warm. Let Emma feel your hands. So that's it, hands freezing. Well, we'll tuck them in a little wool nest. There you are. Oh, my poor Miss Nora. Oh, my poor lady.'

The hands were covered, that was luck again. Or was it something else? Was she projecting her thoughts, making Emma think what she wanted her to think? Good, simple, childish Emma and her good, simple mind. Could her own mind possibly direct Emma's? Concentrate! If you can do that, who knows what may happen? If you can will Emma to come and go, you may have a minute alone. A minute alone when you need it. A minute alone when the time comes ... Don't think about that now, she's watching you. Close your eyes. Somebody said the eyes are windows of the soul. If that's true, close them.

The thick fringe, the good thick fringe, was in the palm of one hidden hand. She closed her eyes and dreamed about it lying there, afraid to try anything stronger than a dream.

THEY came in, all four of them through the door that was beyond the half-circle of her vision, all four and a fifth. Ralph, Brucie, George Perry, Miss Sills, and another one. A strange one. She closed a door in her mind; she'd been

21

away on a journey of her own, crawling inch by inch, even walking, in her dream world. When they filed across the room and stood in a line before her chair, she saw who the fifth one was. Doctor Babcock. She made herself look down at his feet, she could just manage it, turning her eyes down until they hurt. He was wearing overshoes. That was why she hadn't known his muffled tread. It was raining, then. Yes, it was growing dark outside, there was rain on the windows.

Miss Sills said brightly: 'We're going to have a little party. As soon as George builds up the fire. See, here's George! He says he wants a drink, but we're going to make him work for it. And here's another man – picked me up at the station, he did, claiming he lives here now. Shall we give him a drink, too?'

Miss Sills was flushed and happy. *She's in love with one of them. Which?*

Ralph had a tray, and he put it on the tea cart that held the medicine and rubbing oils, the strong glass feeding tube, the lipstick, the firm, cylindrical lipstick. A tray of drinks. One for her? There was a rattle of coal in the grate, then a sound of smothered laughter. Miss Sills and George. It was George she loved.

Brucie bent to kiss her cheek. 'How's our baby?' He drew her hands from beneath the rug and massaged them gently, smiling down into her face. 'We started to have drinks downstairs, and then Ralph got this idea. Babcock came in and said it was okay. See the glass of milk? Look. Funny colour.' He took it from the tray and held it before her. 'Milk plus. The plus is rum. Good for girls.'

The fringe was lying across her knees, wasting its beautiful potentialities.

Doctor Babcock didn't wait for the others. He took his drink, raised it in a toast to the rest, and gulped half of it. 'Good for boys,' he said.

They laughed. Even Emma. Emma said, 'Doctor, you never give me any medicine like that!' They laughed again, and Emma's shrill cackle rose above the rich, masculine rumbles and the light, applauding ripple that nurses always save for doctors.

Ralph handed the drinks around, Scotch and soda in the hunting-scene glasses. The glasses she'd bought at Tiffany's six weeks before. Only six weeks? Only that? The day she had lunch with Robbie at the Plaza. The day –

RALPH'S strong brown hand held the milk close to her mouth. His other hand held the feeding tube. He said: 'No dreaming, darling, this is a party. For you. Now take a nice long swallow for the old man.'

She closed her lips, made them tight.

He coaxed. 'Come, darling, it's good. Bruce made it himself. See? I'll take a swallow first.'

Brucie's face, full of mock chagrin. His laughing voice. 'What's the idea – testing for poison?'

Awful, awful, awful to say a thing like that. To say it out loud, to make a joke of it. To say it, to say it.

Miss Sills, crossing the room rapidly, coming to her chair. 'Hey!' Miss Sills, rattling off a long sentence, addressing them all, meaningless words ending with the same letters. Pig Latin. Robbie used to – Pig Latin.

Miss Sills was telling them not to say things like that. Miss Sills was all right. Watch Miss Sills closely, make sure. If Miss Sills is all right, then –

They both took her hands, Ralph and Brucie.

'Baby,' Ralph said, 'forgive us. We're clumsy fools. You've always been such a good sport, we sometimes forget we must be careful now. You understand?'

Brucie kissed the hand he held and placed it on top of the rug. On top. He took the milk from Ralph. 'Let me,' he said. He slipped the feeding tube between her lips.

The drink was all right. It tasted good. Rum and milk. Nothing else, simply rum and milk with a little grated nutmeg. She should have known there would be nothing else. Poison would be ridiculous, unintelligent.

23

Emma fussed with her sewing basket and said she was going. 'Going to see that the table's set properly. Doctor Babcock's having dinner with us. He invited himself when they told him it was steak. You're going to have steak, too, a special treat. I'll cut it up myself, nice and fine. Nice and rare, to build you up. What do you want, Miss Nora? Oh, dear, tell Emma what it is you want? I can feel you asking.'

Concentrate. Hard, hard. The rug, the rug over your hands, both hands. The fringe.

They all watched, they crowded her chair, looking at her, at Emma, at one another.

Doctor Babcock said, 'Emma, I'm afraid you'll have to go unless you –'

Emma crowed. 'I know! Don't tell me what I'm to do and what not to do! It's her hands! See how she looks at them? She likes them covered up, wrapped up in that old rug. I found that out this afternoon, and I'm no doctor. They get cold, no activity, you might say. It stands to reason – you don't need college to know that. There you are, my pretty girl, my smart, pretty girl!'

She closed her eyes because the relief was almost unbearable. It works, I can make her do what I want her to do. The fringe was thick and firm between her hidden fingers. Look as if you were sleeping, look as if you were sleeping, and concentrate.

'Wheel her chair to the fire, and leave her alone for a bit.' Emma, firm and arrogant with success. 'She'll be happy by the fire and knowing you're all with her. No loud talk and laughing, mind you, none of your wicked jokes. Surrounded by her loved ones, all cosy and warm, that's what she needs.'

Miss Sills: 'Who's the nurse around here? Let me see your credentials, madam.'

Soft laughter. Her chair moving forward, the warmth increasing, the door closing on Emma, the hushed regrouping of other chairs, the crack of coal in the grate, the ring of ice cubes against glass. Low voices talking about football. She didn't have to listen to that. She could travel back and pick up the threads. The threads would make a tapestry, and the tapestry would show the figures.

THE day she bought the glasses with the hunting scenes, Fifth Avenue was all the world's great streets in one; the day was all September days together. She remembered to put a bag of cracked corn in her purse for St Patrick's pigeons, and she sent her car to a garage, because she wanted to walk. Once she saw her reflexion in a window and preened like a girl. 'I look thirty,' she said to herself, 'and why not? All the other women have only painted faces and lovers, but I have Ralph and Robbie.'

It was too early for lunch. Robbie couldn't make it until one. That was ridiculous, and she'd told Ralph so; when a bank is practically a family business, it ought to make concessions to the young squire. But Robbie wouldn't have it that way. She'd asked him once why he worked so hard, and he'd said it was because he hated it. 'You have a frightful conscience,' she'd said. 'You got it from me, you poor thing, but I'll make it up to you.'

Walking up Fifth Avenue, she planned a surprise. She'd tell him he needn't stay at the bank after the first of the year. By that time Ralph and Brucie would know he wasn't lazy. She'd tell him he could go abroad and write. These youngsters who wanted to write! It was the Left Bank or sterility. No good telling them they were wrong, no good telling them that a kitchen table in Brooklyn and a stack of paper are all a writer needs.

McCutcheon's. Dinner napkins. Big heavy, luscious dinner napkins with fat, rich monograms. She didn't need them, she had too many, and hardly anyone used them any more. But square, solid piles of damask carefully wrapped in muslin and reaching to the top of the closet shelf, that was a beautiful sight. And practical in case you felt like giving a buffet supper for a couple of hundred people. You might feel like that. For instance, you might have a wedding. She ordered two dozen.

Tiffany's. Just to look around, that's all. Everybody did that. Look around like a tourist, ogle the diamonds. Beautiful diamonds, solitaires, very practical in case you had an – She hurried to the floor where the glassware was, struggling to keep her face straight, and ordered three dozen highball glasses with hunting scenes. Practical if you felt like giving a hunt breakfast. No, that's champagne. Or doesn't it matter? It does. She ordered the champagne glasses, too.

The Plaza. The hacks, the coachmen, one old fellow with a wilted orchid pinned to his coat. Some girl last night, some pretty young thing with her best beau, jogging through Central Park. Maybe the girl got engaged; maybe she gave it to him and told him to wear it for luck.

The waiter captain. Robbie had phoned that he'd be a little late and she wasn't to wait. The captain gave her the message. 'Mrs Manson, Mr Cory said you were to go ahead. He suggested a nice old-fashioned.'

SHE ordered the drink. One-fifteen, one-twenty. Then she knew he was there even before he bent over the back of her chair and kissed her neck. Demonstrative, for Robbie.

'Toper,' he said.

'Robbie!' He looked dreadful. 'Robbie, what have you been doing to yourself?'

'Working for your living. Why?' He rubbed a hand over his face. 'Maybe I forgot to shave.'

'You did not! Robbie, if I positively didn't know you were in your own bed at ten, I'd say you'd spent the night in sin. Tell me what's wrong. Don't lie to me, tell me!'

He said he was tired, that was all. Tired, so help him. 'Do you want me to cross my heart in a joint like this?' He wouldn't look at her. He ordered his lunch without the menu; shirred eggs, black coffee. Drink? No, no drink.

She talked, talked her head off, told him about the new napkins, the new glasses; but he wasn't listening. He was sick, he must be dreadfully sick. 'Robbie, where does it hurt? Now, don't be childish. You've got a pain somewhere, and I want to know. It can't be your appendix, that's out. What *have* you got left? I always forget which of yours came out and which of mine. No tonsils, no appendix, no – no – Robbie, your heart!'

'I still have that,' he assured her. And he laughed; too loud, too sharp. He parried every personal allusion and kept the conversation on her weakness for linen and crystal, her transportation of cracked corn from Larchville in a Bergdorf bag, when she could buy a paper sack of it from a little man who hung around the cathedral for that very purpose.

She gave up. She'd get him alone that night; she'd go to his room whether he liked it or not; she'd make him tell her what was wrong. 'Home for dinner, Robbie?'

'You bet.'

That was all. He phoned for her car and waited until it came. He handed her in and strode off, across the street, into Central Park.

'NORA, we're going down to dinner, darling. Miss Sills will stay until Emma comes.' Ralph.

'No roller-skating in the halls, baby. It's bad for the carpet.' Brucie.

'Lucky Mrs Manson, to be able to sleep so gracefully. You're better, my dear lady, I know it, I can see it, I've been waiting for it. I think I'll speak to the masseur. Perhaps we can lengthen the treatments. If I had your fine spirit and this charming room, I wouldn't mind a touch of invalidism myself!' Dr Babcock.

'Thanks for the drinks, Mrs Manson. Good-night.' George Perry.

'Thanks for getting out of here, all of you, and quick.' Miss Sills.

'That's right, slam the door. Deliver me from men in a sickroom!' Miss Sills again, patting her shoulder. 'I thought they'd cheer you up, but you don't look too cheery. Hear me tell Babcock to get out with the others? I don't know the meaning of fear. I'll say anything. If he fires me off this case, I'll come straight back. I'll climb the ivy and crawl through the window. Baby this and baby that. Don't you make any mistake about whose baby you are. You're mine.'

Miss Sills was all right, she must be, she had to be. When the time came, Miss Sills would stand fast. She was young – how young? Twenty-four or -five? But she was physically strong, and she'd been trained to think and act fast. Stand fast. Stand. At bay? No, not at bay. It wouldn't come like that. It would come in the dark, on silent feet, as it had come before. Come when she was alone. But if there were no time to lose, if minutes, even seconds, were precious, it would strike without waiting, without warning.

If it came like that, Miss Sills would have to die, too. Not Miss Sills, not a young girl who'd done nothing!

'Isn't that rug too hot now? Mrs Manson, I think the rug's too hot with the fire going full blast. Here, let me take it. You're roasting. You look like a little red beet.'

Take the rug? Take the fringe away? No! No!

'Now what have I said that's wrong? Don't you like being called a little red beet? Golly, honey – I mean, Mrs Manson, I wish I knew what you wanted. You do want something, don't you? I wish I – say, has it something to do with your rug? Emma said you'd taken a sudden fancy to it. Did I guess right? Right! Well, then, it's yours. You keep it. I'll just move your chair back from the fire. That's better, isn't it? You know something, Mrs Manson? One of these days you're going to smile at me, and that's the day I'm waiting for.'

Dear Miss Sills. Be careful, Miss Sills. Don't be too good to me . . .

At nine o'clock that evening Alice Perry walked into her son's room. George was reading in bed, and he looked up at her without speaking when she entered.

'Sulking, George?' Alice Perry's hair was like cotton

28

batting, and her round face was fresh and firm. Her voice was firm also.

'No. Toothache.'

'You've seen a dentist?'

'No. It'll go away.'

'Sometimes you act like a child, dear. You'll find a package of those small poultices in the medicine cabinet. Use one to-night, and see a dentist in the morning. I shouldn't have to tell you that.' She walked about the small room, rearranging chairs, replacing books on shelves, frowning at a bowl of yellow chrysanthemums. 'Who brought these in here? You?'

'Yes, I like the colour. Nothing wrong with that, is there?'

'No, of course not. But you're clumsy with flowers. These are much too stiff, and the bowl's all wrong. Never mind that now, I'll do them over to-morrow. George?'

'Yes, Mother.' He put his book aside.

'You stopped there on the way home, didn't you?'

He didn't need her half-look at the windows that faced the Perry backyard, the gaping hedge, and the Manson garden. 'Yes, for a little while.'

'How is she?'

'Tut, tut. I can remember when you gave me the devil for saying "she". Like this: "If you mean Mrs Manson, say so." Sure I stopped. I had a couple of drinks.' He was entirely good-humoured and smiling. 'Mrs Manson is the same.'

'Still helpless? I mean, still dependent?' She added, 'Poor creature.'

'Still all of that. No speech, no movement.'

'Ralph Manson tells me nothing. Bruce Cory is just as bad. I ask every day, by telephone or in person. I knew Nora Manson when she was Nora Cory. I took you to call when she moved here and Robbie was a toddler and you weren't much more. Ralph and Bruce know that as well as they know their own names. Yet sometimes I think they don't want me in the house.'

'No.' He answered carefully. 'You mustn't make it a personal issue. I think they feel it's better for her to see no one outside the immediate family. If she's beginning to be aware of her condition – and they think she is – why –'

'Why what, George?' She laughed. 'Talked yourself into a corner that time, didn't you? *You* see her, don't you?'

'Yes. But luckily for me, my connexion with the family is on a different plane. I represent bicycles in the hall, peanut butter on the piano keys, stuff like that. All very wholesome and nostalgic in the right way.'

'And exactly what do I represent, you silly?' She ruffled his hair.

'Now, Mother, use your pretty little head. You're another woman, and you're healthy, and you haven't had any trouble. Also, and very important, you were there that day; if she sees you, it's bound to – upset her. They don't want that. They want her to live as she does, from hour to hour, in a sort of merciful stupor, segregated from the past. Because if she ever does get well, she'll have plenty of time to mull things over. She'll have a whole lifetime to look back on, and she won't see a pretty picture. Let her have this, whatever you call it, hiatus. If she gets well and looks back on *this*, it'll seem like heaven.'

'George, you get more like your father every day. You treat me as if I didn't have good sense ... I don't think she's going to get well.'

'Why not?'

'Those specialists from town. They came and went. If they'd been hopeful, we'd have heard about it. But there hasn't been a word, at least not what *I* call a word. And now there's only Babcock. She's lost her mind, hasn't she? Frankly, she never had much of one to lose.'

He picked up his book and flipped over a page. If he meant it for a signal of dismissal, it wasn't heeded.

'Cat got your tongue, Georgie?' She was amused, standing by the bed, looking down and smiling.

'Toothache. No, she hasn't lost her mind.'

'Then what do they call this – this state?'

'Shock and paralysis, one bound up with the other. Some cases have been cured.'

'Have they? Well, I'm glad to hear it.'

SHE walked to the windows, examined the chintz curtains and admired the design. 'This was a good buy,' she said. 'I'm a good shopper.' The rain fell lightly against the glass. She tapped the pane with immaculate little fingers. 'Your father went to the movies. On a night like this, he must be crazy. Or bored. I asked him which, and he looked as if he couldn't decide what to answer. Funny man.'

'He likes the rain,' George said. 'He likes to walk in it.'

'The ground is soaking.' She hummed and tapped the pane, peering out into the dark, dripping gardens. Then: 'George, the lights are on in her room. Why, at this hour?'

'Masseur. This is the time he comes. She sleeps afterwards.'

'Sedatives, of course?'

'Yep.' He looked up from his book, startled by the sudden sound of curtain rings travelling across the rods. 'What's the idea?' he asked agreeably. 'I like them the way they were. I like to look out.'

'There's nothing to see.'

'Sure there is. The rain. I like it, same as the old man.'

'It's depressing. And there's a draught. These windows never did fit properly. Shoddy building in the first place, but what can I do? Your father's satisfied as long as the roof doesn't leak on his bed ... That girl went out a while ago, George. I saw her from the kitchen window. I think she saw me, too. She came around the side of the house and looked over here. Then she went away in a hurry.'

'Name of Sills, Mother. Miss or Milly, take your choice.'

'Now, George, there's absolutely no need for that frozen stare. You know how I feel. She's not – she's not your type. You've had every advantage, I've seen to that, and you can thank me for it. I honestly think it would kill me if you threw yourself away on an ordinary –'

'Easy, Mater. How do you like the Mater touch? That's my fine education.' He looked contrite at once. 'Listen, Ma, I've got a toothache, I don't feel like talking. Run along now, like a good egg.'

'Don't think you can get around me with that "egg". Are you going to slip out and meet her later?'

'I hadn't thought of it, but since you've given me the idea –'

'George! I can't imagine where a girl like that goes at night. It was nearly half-past eight when she left. I must say it looks very odd.'

'This happens to be her night off. She usually goes home to see her mother. She's nuts about her mother. And her father, unfortunately dead and unable to speak for himself, was an honest-Injun college man. Now you know it all. So how about me bringing Miss Sills over here some afternoon? She has time off in the afternoon, too.'

'Really, George!'

'Well, why not? I'll tip her off to wear the Sophie original, and you won't be able to tell her from a lady.'

He was pleased when the door slammed on his last words. For a while he stayed where he was, stretching his long legs and staring at the ceiling, prodding his tender jaw with a pessimistic finger. Then he got up and went down the hall to the medicine cabinet in the bathroom.

The poultices were there – everything was always where she said it would be. He tucked one of them over his aching tooth, laughed to himself in the mirror, and returned to his room. There he drew back the curtains, raised a window, and stood looking out into the dark, wet night. Far across the stretch of gardens the lamps on the Mansons' street were a chain of dim yellow haloes. There was almost no traffic; an occasional car crept warily over the shining asphalt and was lost in the blur of rain and trees and lights that marked the shopping centre across the park. The rain hung like a veil a few inches before his face; he felt as if he could part it with his hand and look through to something that was now obscured.

Mrs Manson's sleeping porch filled the centre of a landscaped vista. He remembered when she'd had that vista made. She'd said she wanted to watch them while they played. Watch him and Robbie. Two men had put ladders against the trees and swung in the branches like monkeys while she directed them from the ground. A great day for him and Robbie, with branches falling from the air and the servants running around in circles.

Now her room was bright with lights; but, as he watched, they went out, one by one, until a single lamp burned. He knew that room so well that he knew where each lamp was and what it looked like. The one that was left stood on a small table by the glass door that opened on to the porch. The bulb was purposely weak. It was meant to give comfort to sleepless eyes, nothing more.

Two figures came to the glass door and stood there, a slight woman in black and a stocky man in white. He knew their silhouettes and their unvarying ritual; he didn't need their black and white for identification. Emma and the masseur; a last-minute chat, whispered amenities, compliments given and taken by two people in the pay of the same household. The masseur moved like a chimpanzee disguised as a man or a man disguised as a chimpanzee. But Milly said he was good. The best in the business, she said.

George watched the man take his leave. He could count every invisible step, every foot of the upper hall, stairway, and lower hall, and give to each its allotted time. So much for the hat-and-coat routine, so much for the walk to the front gate, so much for crossing the street to the park, for the left turn toward the station, which would bring him into view again.

His bare elbows were on the dripping windowsill and the wet wind was making his tooth jump, but he was too intent

33

to notice. It was the final, hissing exhalation of his breath that startled him out of his absorption. What am I doing this for? he asked himself. What am I breathing heavily about?

The man, whose name was Breitman, had come into view on schedule and was moving in the right direction for the station, head lowered, trunk forward, long arms hanging wide. What am I doing this for? George asked himself again. What's the big idea of keeping tabs? The guy could have stopped for a drink with Manson and Cory – he sometimes does. So what? . . . His eyes returned to the glass door. The single lamp had been moved back. Its light was as faint as the glow of a distant city reflected in the sky, but it was enough to show the passing to and fro of Emma's slight, black figure. She raised and lowered the linen shades that covered the glass panes of the door, then raised them again and opened half of the door. She disappeared and returned with a painted screen, which she dragged into place before the open section. He smiled, because he knew she was making faces and talking to herself. When Emma took charge of things, she always told herself she was the only person in the house who saw that Miss Nora got what was good for her. The screen wasn't Emma's job, it was Manson's or Cory's, even Milly's; but Emma beat them to it when she could. Once or twice he had been in the house at bedtime and tried to lend a hand; but Emma had brushed him aside and tossed him out with a few choice words. Well, he thought, to-night she's having it her way, and to-morrow the family will pay and pay. And so will I, he decided, touching his cheek and preparing to wince. But the tooth wasn't too bad; in fact, it was much better. He returned to his bed and book and settled against the pillows.

The wet wind blew in at the open window, spattering the curtains that were such a good buy. He told himself they could take it. It was good to be under the covers, in an empty room, with thoughts instead of people for company. The upstairs telephone extension rang faintly. It was at the end of the hall, outside his mother's room. He didn't notice how many times it rang; his mind was far away, across the dark, wet gardens, across the little park with its dripping trees, as far away as the Sills' cottage. When he thought of the phone again, it had stopped ringing. The whole house was silent.

EMMA wedged a hassock and a low chair against the screen, settled the backs of her hands on her hips, and quietly dared the result to fall down. The screen stood firm. She examined the remainder of the room, properly darkened for a restful night; the fire banked with ashes, her work; the roses on the windowsill, her work; chairs in place, tables cleaned, also hers. Hot milk in a vacuum jug on the bed table and the bottle of sleeping pills beside it. The milk was Hattie's work. But everything to hand in case it was needed. The milk and the pills weren't needed, not now. Sleeping like an angel, breathing nice and regular. When she was like that, Miss Sills didn't want her to have a pill. Miss Sills had said she was the one to decide whether or not a pill was necessary and nobody but herself was to touch the bottle, either. She had said accidents could happen and sometimes did. 'Not when I'm around,' Emma had said coldly.

The mantel clock said nine-thirty. A good long wait before Miss Sills came back, Emma reflected, unless the rain drove her home early, which wasn't likely. Young people made out like they could walk between the drops.

She rubbed her eyes furtively. She was sleepy, and she longed for her own bed with its overabundance of thick quilts and the paper sack of hard white peppermints under the pillow. But she put them out of her mind, and her heart warmed with a martyr's glow. I'll wash my face with cold water, she told herself. That'll keep me awake. I'll just run down the hall to the lavatory – take me a couple of minutes, no more.

There was a bath adjoining the bedroom, but she obstinately chose to accept Miss Sills' instructions about that. Miss Sills said it was a private, not a public bath. Emma turned up her nose at the gleaming tile and spotless basins. Like a hospital. You could do an operation in it.

She gave a last, quick look at the figure on the bed. So flat, so thin, so still. Dark lashes smudged the pale cheeks; dark hair lay across the pillow. The old rug was spread over the eiderdown – she'd wanted it that way, you could tell. It was too hot, but Miss Sills could take it away later. And that massage, it was a punishing treatment. Those poor thin arms and legs, you'd think they'd break in two.

EMMA went quietly down the hall, stopping once to peer over the stair railing. The lower hall was dim. Her sharp old ears identified and placed the faint sound of music under the hardier sound of rain and vines blowing against the landing window. They were playing the radio down there, in Mr Ralph's little study at the far end of the hall. Turned down low and the door shut. The masseur's report must have been good; otherwise, they wouldn't be playing the radio. If the report had been bad, they'd be glooming in and out of her room, keeping her awake with their talk about how well she looked and how she'd be horseback riding in another month. Not fooling a cat, either. Laughing and smiling all over. That's how they acted when the report was bad. A child would catch on ... And I'm no child, she added, even though they think so. I can read them like a book. That goes for Breitman, too, and I'll tell him the same the next time I see him.

She sent an indulgent smile down the dim stairs and pattered softly to the lavatory at the end of the hall. The afternoon towels hadn't been changed. Her job, and she'd forgotten it. Well, considering the company, and all the extra work, you'd think Miss Sills would be kind enough to – Someone had left a tube of toothpaste on the washbasin. Miss Sills! Her brand and the top not screwed back on.

She studied the tube for almost a minute, then squeezed it in the middle and twisted it awry. That'll show her what co-operation is, she gloated. But when she admired her work, she felt uneasy. The result was so clearly a piece of thoughtful malice that she tried to straighten out the tube. But it broke and covered her hands with paste. She hid it in the towel hamper. The wastebasket was too public.

After that she was wide awake and decided she didn't need cold water on her face. She started back.

Across from the lavatory a closed door stood in a deep recess. Every day she looked at that door and said a prayer under her breath. Now she looked at it again, and her eyes filled. The hall light lay softly on the smooth, waxed panels; but no amount of waxing and rubbing had been able to erase the old deep dents at the bottom or the new scars that bit into the area around the lock. That lock was new, too. It was so new that it glittered like gold.

The deep dents were made long ago by small, stout shoes kicking for admittance to an attic that was always locked a week before Christmas and kept that way until late on Christmas Eve. But no matter how careful they were, little Robbie managed to be around when the bulky packages were carried up the back stairs and smuggled through the attic door. No matter how quiet they tried to be, he always heard them and came on the run. As far back as the first rocking-horse time, when he couldn't run without falling down. The rocking-horse time was the first; then the scooter, then the tricycle, then the bicycle and the sled, not to mention all the other things, like railroads and trucks that cost too much and were big enough to ride in. Well, maybe they did spoil him. What happened later must have been their fault. A child grew up to be what you let him be. Yet –

She raised her eyes to the lock. The scars were deep. Once again she saw frenzied hands working against time with whatever tools they'd been able to find in the cellar chest. Once again she heard the heavy breathing of men doing something they never had done before, heard the hopeless

37

clatter of a screwdriver as it slipped through sweating fingers, heard the loud, insistent ringing of the front door-bell. Above it all, the ringing of the bell ... How long ago? Six weeks ago. Yes, six weeks.

EMMA turned from the door and went back to the room, walking slowly, with bent head. She was more than sleepy now; she was old and beaten, and she knew it. If she woke up dead in the morning she wouldn't care. As she found her way to a chair ·by the banked fire, she told herself she wouldn't care at all. The light from the single lamp found and lingered on the rose-coloured jug and the bottle of pills that stood on the bed table. Before she closed her eyes, she sent a long, compassionate look across the room to the figure lying under the blankets and rug. It was still. Of course it was still. But something that could have been a shadow rippled over the rug at the fold where the hidden hands lay. It could have been the shadow of the ivy that swayed in the wind outside the glass door. She told herself it was the ivy and the lamplight, and that satisfied her.

Emma went to sleep with her hands folded under her neat black apron, sitting upright in her chair. Sometimes she stirred in her sleep, because she was running away from a horror. She was running up the attic stairs, followed by bells and voices. And all the while she knew she was running in the wrong direction, but she couldn't turn back.

SHE heard Emma moan in her sleep like a tired and labouring animal, and the sound dragged her up from the depths of a beautiful dream. She was dreaming that her fingers had wrapped themselves around the fringe at last, had turned and twisted and grown strong. She fought to keep the dream, clinging in her sleep to the heavy strands, because they made a chain that bound her to life. No dream had ever held the ecstasy of this one. She could almost feel pain. She could almost persuade herself that her hands –

It was no use. She was awake. That was wishful thinking, she told herself despairingly; that was childish. She couldn't afford to be childish.

She opened her eyes and looked at Emma. Emma sat in shadow, the fireplace was dark, the corners of the room were darker. She couldn't see the clock, but Emma's presence and the screen, the jug, and the sleeping medicine told her it was still too early for Miss Sills. The screen, with its flanking chair and hassock, was Emma's work. Miss Sills could make it stand without support.

And there were four pills left in the bottle. It was easy to count them, four pills neatly covering the bottom. That was correct. She knew how many there ought to be; every night she counted them. The dose was one, and it was placed in her mouth and followed by a drink of the hot milk. When she couldn't see the bottle, or when the number of visible pills was uncertain, she refused the milk. There were too many opportunities for slipping extra pills into the jug. Sometimes the jug was brought by one person, sometimes by another, all the way from the kitchen, with stops *en route* to talk or answer the telephone. And sometimes there were as many as six people in her room at one time, all talking and moving about. And too often she was in her chair by the window, turned away from the table.

Four pills; that was right for to-night. Unless a new prescription had come and – Stop that. Stop. Don't waste emotion on imagination. Save the emotion for the things you know. Let the things you know feed you and make you strong. Listen to the rain on the roof, on the porch. Faint and clear and clean and measured. Like fingers on the keys of a typewriter in a distant room with a closed door. See how everything falls into place when you make your mind behave? Always make your mind remember the things it must. Try again. Begin again with the rain.

The rain has nothing to do with us, but it seems to belong. Perhaps because it sounds the way the typewriter keys used to sound. Night after night, before that day.

It didn't rain that day. That was the day of sun and St Patrick's, and McCutcheon's and Tiffany's and the Plaza . . .

She didn't go home when she left the Plaza; she shopped for another hour and then drove to the bank. Maybe Robbie would drive home with her, maybe Ralph, maybe even Bruce. There was no earthly reason Bruce couldn't drive out for dinner at least, and she'd tell him so. It was about time he paid them a little attention. A good dinner and a good talk. She'd ask his advice about Robbie. And she'd tell him he could leave early for whatever it was that kept him so close to town. Probably a girl, and a young one at that. He always looked foolish when she asked him what he did in the evenings. A very, very young girl, with plucked eyebrows. Men like Brucie are invariably trapped in the end by girls young enough to be their daughters.

When the car stopped at the bank, she had her own trap set for Bruce. She'd tell him how much she missed the long walks and rides they used to take together. She'd tell him he was almost as dear to her as his own brother had been. No. No, that wouldn't do. That might sound as if – She felt the colour surge to her cheeks. Hussy, she said to herself, what a mind you've got.

She entered the bank and walked briskly to the offices in the rear. I'll simply tell Bruce that I'm worried about Robbie, she decided, that Robbie looks like the devil. Maybe he's noticed it himself. I'll remind him that he's Robbie's only relative and that, while Ralph does his best, it still isn't quite enough. And we'll have something very special for dinner, just the four of us, me and my three men. I'll make it a gala. I'll wear my new dress and that crazy rouge I haven't dared try yet.

SHE was beaming when she went into Ralph's office. Ralph wasn't there.

Miss Harper, his secretary, was doing her nails and looked embarrassed. 'Mr Manson left about an hour ago,' Miss Harper said, 'Can I do anything for you, Mrs Manson?'

40

'No.' She hesitated. 'Do you know where he went? Home or the club or what?'

'He didn't say, Mrs Manson, but I think he went home. He filled his brief-case, and when he does that –'

'Yes, I know.' Ralph and his homework. Ridiculous, but he got a big kick out of being an executive, even after hours. Nice old Ralph, doing his best to act like a Cory and a banker and doing it too hard. 'What about my son? Do you think the bank will bust if I take him home with me? I've got the car.'

'Mr Robbie didn't come back after lunch,' Miss Harper said. 'I believe he – I heard Mr Manson and Mr Cory mention it.' Miss Harper's embarrassment had turned into something stronger. She didn't seem to know where to look.

'Mention it in what way? You mean they needed Mr Robbie and couldn't locate him? They knew he was with me.'

'Oh, I don't know anything about it, Mrs Manson! Nobody said – I mean, I simply heard Mr Cory ask where Mr Robbie was, and Mr Manson seemed to think he – I really don't know anything about it, Mrs Manson.'

She told herself Miss Harper was an idiot, a maladjusted, fluttering, stammering little fool. 'It's all right, Miss Harper, thank you.' She wanted to say that Robbie could come and go as he liked in his own father's and grandfather's bank. 'I'll go in and see Mr Cory. Perhaps he'll ride home with me.'

Miss Harper started to say something about Bruce, discarded the sentence before it was fairly launched, and substituted a noisy and frantic hunt through her desk. 'My bag and gloves,' she explained, waving them as if they were a last-minute reprieve. 'I know you'll excuse me, Mrs Manson, but I've got to rush, I really have. Heavy date, you know, heavy date.' She smiled falsely and scurried out of the office.

She followed Miss Harper slowly, aware of a sudden and unaccountable depression. Perhaps the gloves and bag *were* a reprieve. Miss Harper's pale eyes had shown an absurd relief when she held them up.

Bruce's office door was closed, and when she got no answer to her knock, she went in. Empty. All at once she was too tired to question even herself. She nodded to a clerk, who stopped at the open door with a startled look, and then she went back to the car.

All the way home she told herself she had been too happy in the morning. When that happened, you always ate dust in the afternoon. For no good reason, for no reason at all. Of course there was no reason. She planned dinner all over again, confident that all three would be home when she got there. All three, even Brucie, Brucie, coming out with the others for a surprise. But why, after all these months, why a surprise? Was it a silly anniversary or something? Had she forgotten one of her big-little days? No, she hadn't forgotten.

ON the station side of the little park she saw Alice Perry walking with her head down. Alice looked dejected, not brisk and trim as usual. Poor Alice. Always too ambitious, always expecting too much of her two Georges, husband and son, never satisfied with the small, pleasant comforts of her life.

She raised her hand to beckon, then remembered something Ralph had said. She hadn't agreed with him then, but she dropped her hand now. He'd said: 'Go easy on the indiscriminate lifts, darling. In bad weather it's all right, but you stop for anybody and everybody, and it looks patronizing. Especially to people like Alice Perry. She's apt to think you're rubbing her nose in your fine car.'

She'd been indignant. 'I've known Alice Perry since George and Robbie were children. I like her, and you're crazy, darling.'

'All right, I'm crazy. But Alice doesn't like you. She wants what you have.'

She'd laughed. Maybe Alice did want what she had, but that was only because Alice was born discontented. It wasn't a personal thing. They'd always been friends of a sort, as two women are when their children play together. Now she turned from the plodding figure and pretended not to see it. I don't feel like talking to her anyway, she told herself. I don't feel like talking to anybody. I want to get home in a hurry.

Emma let her in. Emma was wearing her hat, she'd been to the stores, and just got back. No, she didn't know if Mr Ralph or Mr Robbie had come home. She didn't know anything about Mr Brucie. She'd look in the coat closet and find out in a minute.

'Don't bother,' she told Emma. 'I've got something for you to do. I'm going to call Mr Bruce in town and ask him out for dinner. A very special dinner, because I feel that way. I want you to huddle with Hattie. Open all that stuff you've been hoarding, stuff like caviar, use all the eggs and cream and butter in the house, and get more. See if that man has pheasants. And don't tell me anything about it. I want to be surprised.'

She went to her room and, still wearing her outdoor clothing and dialling with gloved fingers, called Bruce's apartment on her own phone. Why am I acting as if this were a life-and-death performance? she wondered. But Bruce's apartment didn't answer. She tried his club. He was expected for bridge, and she left word that he was to call her as soon as he came in.

The upper hall was quiet; the doors were all closed. They weren't home. When they were home, you could hear them through walls and doors. She drew her bath and laid out the new dress. Diamonds? No. Plain gold? Chic. Or sapphires? Yes, sapphires because her eyes – Hussy.

SHE was in the bath when she heard someone come into her room. 'Ralph?' she called.

'It's Bruce, dear. I'll wait here until you come out.'

'How perfectly wonderful! You're a mind reader! I've been trying to get you. You've got to stay for dinner.'

'That's what I came for. Take your time, Nora.'

'What's the matter with your voice? Got a cold?'

'No. I don't know. Yes, I guess I have.'

'I'll fix that. I know the very thing. Is Ralph with you, or Robbie?'

'No. I came alone.'

'Brucie, I went to the bank to-day. Am I screaming too loud? Anyway, I went to the bank after lunch with Robbie. I'm worried about Robbie, he looks awful. But you'd all gone. That crazy Miss Harper – I don't see how Ralph stands her ... See Robbie anywhere around?'

'I haven't looked. How are you anyway, Nora? It's been so long –'

'Your fault.' She left the tub and got into her dressing gown. 'Be with you in a minute. If you want a drink, ring for Emma. This is going to be a party.'

She went into the room and saw him bending over the laid fire. He was putting a match to the paper, and when he turned to greet her, his face was stiff and white.

'You really are sick!' She ran across the room and touched his cheek. 'You are, and I love it. We'll keep you here to-night and take care of you. Brucie, if you want to marry a little fool, go right ahead. She'll be better for you than that creeping, crawling gentleman's gentleman. That man doesn't know the first thing about –'

Bruce was looking over her shoulder, and she turned. Ralph was coming in. Ralph didn't speak; he didn't have to.

They can't both be sick, she told herself. Not both of them, not all of them. Something's happened. They've got bad news, and they're here to tell me. The bank – No, Robbie! I knew it. I've known it all day ... She wrapped the dressing gown close; she was bitterly cold with a sweeping, numbing cold that rushed from all sides. She

44

found a chair by the crackling fire and sat erect. 'All right,' she said. 'Don't waste time. Let me have it. He's run away, hasn't he? He can't be dead.'

'Dead?' Ralph's voice was startled, his face accusing. 'Whatever makes you think – Bruce, will you?'

'Yes,' Bruce said. 'Nora, you haven't seen Robbie since you two had lunch?'

'You know I haven't!'

'Did he say anything to you – about us, about the bank?'

'No, no. But he looked dreadful. Go on, Bruce!'

Then he told her. Ralph stood by the window with his back to the room. As Bruce spoke, she knew it was right that he should be the one to tell her. Bruce and Robbie had the same blood.

He told her that almost two hundred thousand dollars had been stolen from the bank over a period of two years, a job so carefully contrived that no one had known about it until yesterday. There was no doubt about Robbie. She barely heard the damaging phrases, words like 'estate' and 'trustee'; she heard only that there was no doubt about Robbie. The Board was convinced.

Bruce and Ralph had asked the Board for a few days' grace. They were going to talk to Robbie – that was why they were both there. But Robbie hadn't come back from lunch, and that had forced their hands and frightened them a little. They had both looked for him.

'He wasn't at any of his old hangouts,' Bruce said. 'So I came here, because I was pretty sure he'd turn up, if only to see you. I don't think he's made a bolt.'

'I don't believe it,' she said.

'I find it hard to believe myself. But it looks – Apparently it began when he first came to the bank. We're going to give him every chance.'

'He didn't do it.'

'I want to believe that, too. We'll soon know, Nora. He'll tell us; he's no liar.'

45

'He didn't do it. He wouldn't know how. Find him – both of you go and find him. How long have you been in the house, and what have you done?'

Bruce said he had come alone on the three o'clock train, let himself in with the key he always had had, and seen no one. Then he'd gone for a walk and just returned.

Ralph said he had come on the following train, found Robbie's room empty and no one about, and locked himself in his own room to think. Ralph's hands, on the back of a chair, were white around the knuckles.

'Ring for Emma,' she said.

EMMA came. She had a menu in her hand and began to read it aloud the minute she crossed the threshold. 'Turtle soup,' she said. 'I don't care whether you want to be surprised or not, you've got to listen. A good turtle soup with sherry, not too heavy for what comes after and nice for a coolish evening. Then a small fresh salmon –' She stopped. 'What are they saying to you, Miss Nora? What's happening here?'

'Have you seen Robbie?'

'I told you before, I haven't seen a soul until now. I was out from lunch on. But if you want to know if he's home, I guess he is. Or was. Hattie says she heard the typewriter going a while back. Up in the attic.'

Bruce said quickly, 'Attic?'

'Where else? That's where he keeps his machine, that's where he does his writing, the young monkey. Sometimes, when he comes home early, he just slips in and goes up there.'

Ralph said: 'I'll check. I'll go right away. That'll be all, Emma.'

Emma stood where she was. 'It will not be all,' she said. 'It's my right to know what's happening here.'

They stood in a tight little group before the attic door and watched Ralph put his hand on the knob. The door was locked.

'He's taken the key,' he said over his shoulder. He sounded as if he were swallowing a scream.

'Scream,' she cried, 'scream, get help. Scream, scream, or I will. Get that door open!'

Bruce ran downstairs. He was gone for a lifetime, in which Robbie was conceived, born, bathed and fed, sung to in the evening dusk, played with in the morning sun. She leaned against the wall and bore him again with pain.

Bruce returned with the cellar tool chest. The front door-bell rang and rang through the house.

'I'll pay, I'll pay,' she heard herself say. 'Restitution, recompense, I don't know the word. He didn't do it, but I'll pay.'

'Stop that,' Bruce said. 'Somebody go down and send that woman away. Mrs Perry. She's at the door. Somebody send her away.'

Something heavy and metallic slipped through his fingers and clattered to the floor. She went down on her knees before the locked door. They were all on their knees, even Emma, pounding with tools, boring, prying, calling his name.

SHE knew her lips were shaping his name now. She tried to tighten them. Useless. She tried again. Better. Now she had her lower lip between her teeth, holding it fast. The muscles in her face were rigid, under control.

Could I do that yesterday? she wondered. Could I have done that a few days ago? Am I getting stronger or am I dreaming again? Don't dream; don't. You'll know when the time comes. Concentrate on facts, on things that have body and substance. If you don't you'll lose your mind. Concentrate on anything. The bed, the lamp, the jug, the glass bottle. Never take the medicine unless you are able to count the pills. Remember that. Never take it unless you can count, and take it only from Miss Sills. If you could talk, what would you say first? If you could walk, which way would you go? No, no, think of something that is real.

This room is real; it has body and substance. The jug

of milk, the bottle, the painted screen, all real. There are grey clouds and black birds and green rushes on the screen. That's right, that's right. And there's one small bird deep in the rushes at the bottom, sitting on a nest. Find the small bird on the nest. Low on the left, near the floor – you know where it is. Find it . . .

There was a gloved hand lying on the floor under the screen.

It moved along the floor, in the space beneath the frame, a bright-yellow hand with thick, spread fingers. Another hand crept out and moved beside it. They minced to the right and then to the left, feeling their way, like two blind, glutted things.

Her lips curled back from her teeth.

The two hands travelled to the end of the screen and stopped. A few inches above them another hand crept around the frame and curled and slipped and clung. Then another. Four thick, yellow hands close together, beckoning . . .

'I don't know why you want to leave before your time's up,' Mrs Sills said to her daughter. 'It's not half-past ten yet. What do you think I cut that cake for? Not for myself, I can assure you. Stale bakery cake is good enough for me. I made that cake for my only child, who brings me a bundle of messy old uniforms and says it's such a bad night that she'd better be going out in it. Going where?'

Milly was unimpressed. 'Don't give me that cake routine again. You're fifteen pounds overweight from four-layer chocolate fresh out of the oven. And I'll take my laundry to the Steam Hand, if you don't like it. I hate rain, and you know it, and George has a toothache.'

'I begin to see the light,' Mrs Sills said. 'George has a toothache, and Mrs Perry won't let him out. So you haven't any place to go except to see your old mother. When I was your age, I had four or five on the string and glad enough to come running when I called the tune . . . Are you going to marry him, or am I being personal?'

Milly said nothing.

'Don't do it,' her mother said, 'unless you can afford a place of your own. Don't do it unless he can support you. None of this career-after-marriage business, because when the babies begin to come and you have to stop work, they always get mad – because they miss the extra money and won't admit it. And don't economize on cheap furniture; it doesn't pay in the end. No veneers – good solid walnut or cherry. I'll give you half of my silver ... Was that George you called up a while ago?'

'Yes.'

'I couldn't hear, because you lowered your voice. I don't know what you have to tell a man that your own mother can't know about.'

'You couldn't hear because I didn't say anything. He wasn't home – or wouldn't answer the phone.'

'Toothache!'

'Good night, Mother.' Milly started for the door.

'Have I said something wrong?' Mrs Sills wondered wistfully.

'Not a word.' Milly gave her mother a kiss and a hug. 'I'm going to stop at Marge's to return a library book. Then I'm going straight back to my nice, sick baby, and I don't want any other kind for a long while. Now you know, and I'll drop in to-morrow afternoon on my exercise. If I can. Be good.' She closed the front door and went down the short path to the sidewalk.

THE rain fell steadily, evenly, meeting the pavement with a hiss but sinking into the sodden grass without a sound ... You'd think it had a home under the grass, she thought. You'd think it had a special place to go. Worms. Nothing under grass but worms. But under this particular grass, under this very super Mrs Nathaniel-Sills-and-daughter grass, there are also bones. Cat, dog, canary, and goldfish bones, in shoeboxes and matchboxes, all rotted and gone.

I have the soul of a poet ... After that it was too easy to think of another kind of grass, trim and parklike, where the same rain was sinking into the earth and finding –

She ran past the lighted drugstore on the corner, turned and ran the length of a block to Marge Foster's shop. 'Hi,' she said in a breathless voice that she tried to make casual.

Marge, sorting rental cards at her worktable, looked up. 'Put that umbrella in the stand before I drown. What brings you out in all weathers?'

Milly slid her book across the table. 'I make it twenty-four cents due. Here's a quarter, and I want change.'

'You kill me,' Marge said. 'I can remember the day when you patronized Carnegie's Free. Why don't you go back there? Sit down. How are you, honey?'

'So-so.' Milly pulled up a chair. Miss Foster's Lending Library and Gift Bazaar was empty except for the proprietress and Milly. 'Terrible night. George is sick. He says. Mother's going to give me half her silver. She says. What do you know, Marge?'

'What do *I* know? You're the one who lives the life.'

'I'm gaining weight – they feed me swell. On some cases you share a bowl with the dog.'

'You're lucky. You look wonderful.' Marge gave the rain-blurred windows a rapid survey. 'I don't feel like business, I feel like talking to an old school tie. Put your feet up and relax.' She crossed to the door, locked it, and returned. 'And they call me money-mad.'

MILLY settled her feet on the edge of a bookshelf. 'I ought not to stay, honestly. I'm not due back till twelve, but she's acting kind of funny to-night. Got a cigarette?'

'Here.' Marge pushed the box across the table. 'Milly, you know I'm as safe as houses. I wouldn't open my mouth about anything you told me.'

'I haven't got anything to tell. Match? Thanks. What's the matter with you? You look as if you didn't believe me.'

50

'Sure I believe you. George Perry's mother was in this afternoon, looking for "a little love story, nothing modern". The whole time she was here she was talking at the top of her lungs about how her son is the light of Mrs. Manson's life. Is he?'

'Of course not. Half the time he's there she doesn't even look at him. If I know you, Mrs P. said something else and you're working up to it. What?'

'Well, she did want to know how well I knew you. Casual-like. Quote: "Are you very friendly with that little nurse of Mrs Manson's? I believe Mrs Manson has become quite attached to her." I don't think she loves you.'

'She doesn't even know me. I'm taking my time about that. What else?'

'She thinks Bruce Cory is too good-looking. She sort of hinted that he liked Mrs Manson too well before she up and married his brother. To say nothing of marrying Manson, too. And now that he's hanging around again, using her illness as an excuse – Her and her little love stories! Milly, is Mrs Manson going to die?'

'Not if I can help it.' Milly turned and looked at the dripping windows. They showed a strange, new world. But the single, wavering blur of light was only a street lamp that stood on the kerb; the twisted shape that rapped on the pane and sprung away and rapped again was nothing but a branch. 'Not if I can help it,' she repeated. 'I'm a good nurse. I know that. And Babcock must think so, too, or he wouldn't have wanted me. Not for a patient like Mrs Manson.' Milly's voice grew soft. 'She's a darling, she's a pet, and I worry about her all the time. I want her to get well. I want her to get even half-well. The minute she shows a definite improvement, they want to take her away somewhere, a change of scene. Any kind of change ought to help. But I don't know. The other day I dressed her up in her jewellery, rings, bracelets, clips – stuff to knock your eyes out. But she no like, I could tell. Had to take it all off and lock it away. Emma says it was on her dressing table, ready to put on, the day Robbie died. Maybe that's why she doesn't like it.'

'I like the way you say "died". All right, but you don't have to look at me like that. Is Emma nice to you? In books, the servants are terrible to nurses.'

'She's okay. She isn't like a servant; she sort of runs things. She's been there years and years. Emma was the one who found her.'

'I KNOW.' Marge removed her glasses and polished them thoroughly. 'Change of subject coming up. Somebody was in here yesterday asking about you.'

'Who?'

'I don't know. A woman. She looked sort of familiar, but I couldn't place her. This shop is like a railway station. Strangers drop in maybe once or twice a year, motorists and so on, people from New York buying a book for a weekend present. Maybe she was somebody like that, just a face I'd seen once before. Anyway, she didn't know you, didn't know your name. She wanted to know if I was acquainted with the nurse at Mr Manson's.'

'Maybe somebody who used to know them. Didn't like to inquire at the house. You know, tragedy and all that.'

'Maybe. They came from New York themselves years ago. But I got the idea it was you she was interested in.'

'Me? No. You know everybody I know. Funny. What did she say?'

'Nothing much. She just ambled around, bought a couple of Hallowe'en cards, and acted friendly in a pushing way. You know, the great big smile that goes with spending ten cents. First she asked how Mrs Manson was getting along – lots of people ask me that, because they know I know you or they've seen you in here. Then she wanted to know where you lived.'

'For heaven's sake! I'm getting a reputation.'

'Think so? Wait. She said, "Does the young lady live in Larchville, or did they get her from New York?" I said

Larchville. And I also said what do you want to know for, but in a nice way, of course. And she said she thought maybe she knew you and was just making sure. She did a lot of smiling and hemming and hawing and said she thought maybe you'd trained at the hospital with her cousin or somebody. She said she was interested in young nurses starting out who'd trained where her cousin had.'

'Crazy. No sense to it. Who's her cousin?'

'She very carefully didn't say, even when I asked.' Marge lighted a cigarette. 'Know what I think? I think she was a snooper, a busybody, one of those women who try to get the dope on other people's troubles so they can brag to the bridge club. She had a face like bridge-every-afternoon; sharp. Also heavy around the hips, too many of those bridge desserts. So when she said your name had slipped her mind and wasn't it Johnson or something like that, I closed up like a clam.'

'Right. Thanks.'

Marge was thoughtful. 'You know, there could be something behind it, Milly. Something like family trouble, for instance. She might be a relative of the Cory family, still sore about Manson's marrying the money Cory left. Or she might be an old girl friend of Cory's – I mean the first husband.'

'Did she look like the kind of girl friend a Cory would have? They say Bruce is the living image of his brother. Was she the kind of woman a man like Bruce Cory would – look at?'

'From what I've seen of him I'd say no, but fast. Her clothes weren't any better than mine. She was all right, you understand, but she didn't have the kind of manner you expect in a woman connected with a Cory or a Manson. But you can't always tell about boys like Cory and Manson.'

'What a brain,' Millie admired. 'Sensational!' She dragged her feet from the shelf. 'After eleven. I ought to start back.'

'Aw, wait. I've got coffee. It's on the hot plate.'

With the coffee they had bakery doughnuts, which tasted better than four-layer chocolate because they came out of a paper bag.

It was ten minutes to twelve when Marge locked the shop door behind them. They walked to the corner before they separated. Marge stood on the kerbstone and watched Milly cross the deserted street and strike out in the direction of the park. The slight, raincoated figure and the big umbrella were swallowed in mist and fog. The rain had turned into an aimless drizzle.

Marge went home and tried to remember where she'd seen the woman who was interested in young nurses. The woman was beginning to fill her mind ... Not a one-shot customer, Marge decided. I'm sure of that. Maybe somebody who just moved to Larchville, one of those people you stand next to at the grocery store. Maybe. Green coat and hat. Drop a brick out any window this year, and you'll hit that same green coat and hat.

MILLY let herself in. One light was burning in the hall, the one they always left burning when she was out. It was a signal for her to put the chain on the door. It meant everyone else was in. She fixed the chain, turned out the light, and crept upstairs.

The doors along the upper hall were closed. All except Mrs Manson's at the front. Light came from that doorway, a dim, straight shaft on the dark hall carpet, like a path cut through shadows. She stopped in the lavatory and brushed her teeth with just water, because she couldn't find her toothpaste. Her hooded coat and umbrella were dripping, so she hung them on the lavatory door.

Emma was asleep in a chair before the dead fire, but she'd done her usual job on the glass door and screen. Milly grinned at the screen, anchored with chair and hassock. One of these nights Emma would use the bureau, too.

She walked to the bed. Mrs Manson was awake, wide awake. Her face was white, and her eyes were glittering.

54

'Hey,' Milly said softly, 'what's the idea?' She remembered then that the door to the hall was open and went back to close it. We're about to have a little one-sided argument, she told herself, but we needn't let the whole house in on it. 'Hey,' she said again, 'you're bad to-night. What makes you so bad, honey – I mean, Mrs Manson?'

Mrs Manson's eyes met hers.

'Now, wait,' Milly said. 'One thing at a time. You don't like something, I can see that. Well, we'll take care of it, we'll toss it right out, whatever it is. But the pulse comes first.' She drew the cold hands from under the rug and held one limp wrist.

The eyes clouded; then the glitter returned. They gleamed like the eyes of an animal caught in a trap that was imperfectly sprung. Milly had seen a squirrel once –

The pulse was too rapid. She held the cold hands in hers. 'You're frightened,' she said. 'I know. But it's all over now. Milly's here. Still, I don't know why your hands should be freezing, you've got plenty of blankets and the room's exactly right. Nervous about something? Now, now, you mustn't be.' She sat on the edge of the bed and talked softly and persuasively. 'I bet I know what happened,' she said. 'You had a bad dream. And because you're sick and sort of helpless, you couldn't throw it off. Now me, when I have a bad dream, I practically kick myself out of bed and wake up screaming. They're terrible, aren't they? But everybody has them once in a while, pal – I mean, Mrs Manson. I mean, you're not the only one.'

No, that wasn't it. According to Mrs Manson's eyes, it wasn't a dream. They said so, as plain as words. They said they had seen something.

Milly felt a prickle along her spine. Got me doing it now, she thought. Not that I haven't been getting ready for it. Bones in boxes ... For two cents I wouldn't look over my shoulder, even at Emma.

She rubbed the hands gently. They were like ice, but Mrs Manson's forehead was beaded with perspiration. Get busy,

Milly told herself. Get to the bottom of this, but don't let her see that you're worried. She couldn't possibly have seen anything. There's nothing to see. Maybe she heard –

'LISTEN, honey, I'm going to wake Emma up and send her to bed. And maybe Emma can tell me what – what you want.' She went to Emma and touched the old woman's shoulder. Emma was a heavy sleeper. Milly had to shake her awake.

'Well,' Emma said. 'Is it time for you already? I must have dozed off.'

'You must have taken one of Mrs Manson's pills. What happened in here while I was out?'

'Nothing.' Emma was indignant. 'You don't have to glare at me like that, Miss Sills. Everything was as quiet as you please. We slept like a baby, same as if you'd been here.' Emma looked at the bed. 'She's all right. Even I can see that.'

'You're as blind as a bat,' Milly whispered. 'She's anything but all right. No, Emma, don't go over there now. I want to talk to you.'

Emma struggled to her feet, blustering and protesting. 'I'm sure I don't know what you're getting at, Miss Sills! I can see as well as you can, and I say she's all right.'

Milly said: 'Please keep your voice down, Emma. Who was in this room to-night?'

'Nobody. What do you think I am? I wouldn't let anybody in. Mr Manson and Mr Cory stopped for a minute or two before the masseur came, but you know that as well as I do. And that's all.'

Milly observed to herself that the whole town of Larchville could have trooped in and out while Emma was having her doze. Aloud she said: 'Did Breitman say anything while he was here? Did he say anything about her condition?'

'Not a word. He never does. He's very close-mouthed. He and I talked the same as we always do, nothing more. Miss Sills, I –' Emma began to break. Milly's stern young face was full of foreboding. 'Miss Sills,' she wavered, 'if anything's gone wrong, while I – Miss Sills, what's gone wrong?'

'Mrs Manson is frightened, and I want to know why. At first I thought she'd had a nightmare, but now I'm not so sure. I think she may have overheard something. Or she may have been – remembering things again. That's always a bad business when you're alone at night, to say nothing of being sick . . . Exactly what did Breitman say?'

'Nothing. Nothing about her. He never spoke her name once. We talked about the weather. He said the country was nice after New York, and he liked to come out here. That's all.'

'Didn't say anything that she could misunderstand? Mention any names, any names at all?'

'No, Miss Sills. Just the ordinary talk, like we always have. She wasn't frightened then, Miss Sills, I know it. Because after he left, I washed her face and hands and covered her up good, and she was nice and drowsy. I was thinking maybe she wouldn't need her pill to-night and how that was a good sign.' Emma's hands were limp against the folds of her black apron, but her voice said she was wringing them mentally. 'I'd like to stay here to-night,' she besought. 'I could sleep in a chair. If she's going to have trouble, then this is where I belong.'

Milly softened. 'No. You get your regular sleep. But I promise to call you if I need anything.'

'Mr Manson?'

'I'll call him, too, but not now. The fewer people in here the better. Run along, Emma. Say good night to her, but make it snappy and happy.'

Emma hesitated. 'You know that second bell on the wall over there rings in my room, don't you? My own room, not the kitchen. It rings right over my bed, nice and loud. If you should –'

'I will.' She eased Emma to the bed and watched the old hands gather up the younger ones and fold them under the rug.

When Emma looked down at the face on the pillow, she obviously didn't trust her voice. But she covered the staring eyes with one of her hands, gently, as if she were telling a wakeful child it was time to sleep.

MILLY closed the door behind Emma and went back to the bed. The room seemed darker with Emma gone, darker and quieter. Even larger. I'm crazy, Milly told herself. A fine state of mind I'm getting into. Missing Emma, thinking of Emma like the Marines. This is what they told us in training. This is what they said would happen some time, and I thought they were bats. They said there'd come a time in the night, in the wards and in homes, when you were on duty alone and felt as if you were being watched. Not by a patient, by something else. They said it was a natural thing and not to be frightened. That's what they said. But some of the older nurses, the old war horses who'd seen every-thing, they said it was death watching you. Waiting for you to turn your back ... She turned around slowly, looking into every corner of the room and listening. What she saw was luxury and security, what she heard was silence. She bent over the bed. 'Never let the patient know you're nervous,' they said. That's what they said.

She smiled. 'Time for the nightcap,' she said, 'and maybe I'll join you.' She took the bottle of pills and reached for the jug of hot milk. 'I'll get the bathroom glass for myself. I can use some of this milk. I'm worn thin; we had too much company to-day.' She smiled steadily. 'You probably feel worse than I do – you can't tell people to shut up, and I can.'

She knew Mrs Manson was watching her hands as they uncorked the jug and filled the cup. She replaced the jug and shook a single pill into the palm of her hand, talking all the while. 'If the sun comes out to-morrow, I'm going to park you on the sleeping porch. To-morrow's Sunday, you remember that, and old George will be home all day. Maybe he'll hang out his window with his face all tied up like the Robber Kitten. He says he has a toothache. Well, we'll make fun of him and he won't know it ... Here you are. Open wide.'

Mrs Manson refused it. It was more than mutiny; she tightened her lips in a straight, hard line, and her eyes blazed. The muscles in her throat were like cords.

Milly stared, holding the milk in a hand that shook. Her eyes widened with delight. Mrs Manson's throat muscles were the most beautiful things she had ever seen. They were strong, pulsing, and controlled. For the first time.

She exulted. 'Well, what do you know about that! You ought to see yourself! You're still a bad girl, and don't think I'm not mad at you, because I am, but I do believe you've turned the corner! You hear that? You're better! You couldn't make those mean, ugly faces a week ago. You couldn't even make them this morning. Well, am I tickled!'

But there was no responsive smile, and that was what she wanted most of all. Response. Anything that would prove co-operation and receptiveness and settle the question of a clouded mind.

'Mrs Manson, smile. Smile just once, and we'll forget about the nightcap.'

The agony in the eyes that returned her look was almost more than she could bear. Mrs Manson was trying to smile, but she might as well have tried to run.

MILLY said: 'Never mind, never mind, baby. Forget it.'

She rolled the pill about in the palm of her hand; it was a capsule, and it rolled lightly and evenly. What am I going to do now? I can't force her – not when she looks like that. But I've got to make her understand that I'm on her side, that the things I ask her to do are the right things. I've got to find out why she's terrified. She can't go through the night this way. Neither can I. If I try the milk again, if I try selling myself with the milk –

Aloud, she said: 'Mrs Manson, please take the milk. I won't bother you about the pill. I know you hate it even though it's good for you. But please take the milk. This is my job, Mrs Manson, I need it. Doctor Babcock might send me away if he found out that I couldn't – couldn't persuade you. And I don't want to go away. Please, Mrs Manson, just a little milk for my sake.'

Mrs Manson's eyes filled with tears. They gathered slowly and clung to her lashes. Only when there were too many did they begin to fall.

Milly put the milk back on the table and dropped the pill into the bottle. 'I want to help you,' she said miserably, 'but I'm helpless myself. I can't think of anything to do. Can't you give me a sign of some sort? Can't you look at something in the room that will give me a clue?'

Mrs Manson's eyes blazed with hope. It was a look that even a child could have read.

'There, now,' Milly rejoiced. 'You see? We're all right, we're fine. We're getting this thing licked, aren't we? Is it something in the room that frightens you, something I don't know about?'

The eyes met hers and held, like a hand reaching out to take another hand. They directed her to the bed table. There was nothing on the table but the milk jug, the cup of cooling milk, and the small glass bottle. And two linen handkerchiefs, neatly folded. The same things that were there every night.

It couldn't be the handkerchiefs. They were her own, marked with her initials, N. M., in a little circle of flowers. There was nothing frightening about a handkerchief. She shook them out. They were clean, empty, fragrant. She touched one of the wet cheeks and studied the table again, following the direction of the eyes, pinning the look to a definite place. The pills?

'Now, you're not afraid of those pills, Mrs Manson. You've had them every single night. They're the same as always; we haven't changed them.' She turned the bottle between her fingers. 'See? Same druggist and everything. Same old stuff. Four little pills for four more nights ... Well, I'll be! I've hit it, haven't I?'

The look had changed; it was eager, urgent, full of horror. It was almost like speech. It warned and pleaded and prayed. Mrs Manson had been in the depths, she was still there, but she was emerging.

AFRAID of the medicine all of a sudden, Milly marvelled. I'll fix that right now. She got her handbag and put the bottle in it, holding the bag so Mrs Manson could see every move. 'See?' she said. 'Just as good as thrown out. And to-morrow I'll tell Babcock you like it the same as you like poison.' Poison. That crack about poison when they were all having drinks in the afternoon; that might have started it. Lying alone, half-asleep, half-awake, listening to the rain, thinking back. When she returned to the bed, she said: 'Those pills are okay, silly. I'm just humouring you because I think you're nice. All right now?'

No, Mrs Manson wasn't all right. She still looked at the table; her eyes still talked. Her lips, stiff and dry, struggled with the shape of a word. Mrs Manson was seeing something that only she could see, and she was trying to tell about it. It was hopeless, and she knew it, but she was trying.

Suddenly Milly was engulfed and defeated. This was hysteria, this was something she couldn't fight alone. Manson? Cory? She looked at the bedroom door, at the glass door. George? Beyond the glass door and the porch, across the garden, George was safe in his own house. She went to the screen and walked around it, unconscious of the horrified eyes that followed her. It was cold on the porch, and the wind was wet and mournful. It sighed in the trees and the ivy, and touched her face with damp fingers.

George's room was dark, the whole cottage was dark. She looked to her left, along the length of sleeping porch. The porch ran to the end of the house, wide and shadowed, overhung with trees and vines. Mr Manson's room opened on it, so did Bruce Cory's. But their rooms were dark, too.

There were no lights showing in any of the rooms that she could see.

Mrs Manson must have been all right when they went to bed, she thought, or they wouldn't have gone. They'd have waited for her or called Babcock. Then she knew what she wanted to do. Call Babcock. It was only a quarter to one. He wouldn't mind, he was used to late calls. And it was later than this the night he came to her house and asked her to take the case. He was crazy about Mrs Manson.

She went back to the room, smiling easily. 'I'm going downstairs to get you a drink of water. Ice water. You won't mind if I leave you for such a little while.' She didn't wait for an answering look in Mrs Manson's eyes. She wanted to get away, to hear Doctor Babcock's reassuring voice, to hear his booming laugh. He'd tell her that hallucinations were common in cases like Mrs Manson's; he'd say he'd be right over.

SHE closed the door quietly and went down to the first floor, hugging the stair rail, not turning on lights. She didn't want to wake the others. Not unless it was necessary. At the rear of the hall she fumbled for the kitchen door. There was no sound anywhere. And I used to have ideas about Bruce Cory, she scoffed. I had the repartee all ready. He doesn't even know I'm alive.

When she was safe inside, she closed the door behind her and found the light switch. The kitchen phone looked beautiful in the clear, strong light.

Doctor Babcock's housekeeper answered after a long wait. Milly knew the woman slightly, but she didn't identify herself. 'Doctor Babcock, please.'

'He's not here.'

Her heart sank. 'Do you know where he is? It's fairly important.'

'No, I don't know. He got a call around ten, and he hasn't come back. You want to leave a message?'

'No. No, thanks. I – Did he say how long he'd be?'

'He said he didn't know. He said he might be a long time, and I was to lock up. I wouldn't be surprised if it was a confinement.'

'Oh. Well, I guess – well, if he comes in during the next hour or so –' She thought of Babcock ringing the bell, rousing the house, Emma, Hattie, Mr Manson, Bruce Cory. She saw Emma and Hattie peering from behind doors, Mr Manson and Bruce Cory, bathrobed and tousled, stumbling down the stairs. She began to have doubts. They might think she'd been forward, calling the doctor without consulting them. And suppose, after all that, they went to Mrs Manson's room and found her asleep. Asleep in spite of herself, exhausted by her own imagination. That happened sometimes. They'd think *she* was the crazy one.

'Well?' The woman's voice was impatient. 'Are you still there, and if you are, what do you want me to do?'

'Oh, I'm sorry. No, there's nothing, thank you. I'll see Doctor Babcock in the morning.' She hung up. She could call again. In another hour, if Mrs Manson was still awake. She filled a glass with water from the refrigerator bottle and went back the way she had come.

SHE watched the door, waiting for Miss Sills to return. Miss Sills was taking more time than she needed for a glass of water, and that was good. It was good if it meant that Miss Sills had stopped in the kitchen to make cocoa for herself. Sometimes she did that. If she did that to-night, if she drank cocoa that she herself had made, then she wouldn't be thirsty, then she wouldn't drink the milk in the jug. Sometimes she drank what was left of the milk in the jug. Everybody knew that. Miss Sills told everybody about it and laughed. If she drank the milk to-night –

When the hands had come, she had tried to scream. She screamed silently in her heart and soul while Emma slept by the fire. She watched the dark, shapeless mass that crept from behind the screen and cavorted on the floor, dragging its thick, yellow hands. Hands where feet should be. It was

63

big enough to stand alone, strong enough, but it didn't stand. It rose and fell like a strong black jelly and made a sound like laughing. Then it went away.

The clock on the mantel ticked on. Minutes passed, uncounted. She watched the screen.

Then the door to her room opened quietly, and she turned her eyes in an agony of hope. *Emma, Emma. Try to hear me, Emma.*

She watched the silent approach over the soft rugs, the deft opening of two capsules, the addition of their contents to the jug of milk. The refilling of the capsules with her talcum powder, the refitting of the halves, the return of the bottle. She was ignored as if she didn't exist. She might not have been there. She was the same as dead then . . .

'Here you are,' Milly said. 'Did you think I'd run away?' She held the glass of water to Mrs Manson's lips. 'Right out of the icebox. Now, you and I are going to sleep whether we feel like it or not. I'll leave the light on. And I won't go to bed. I'll do my sleeping in a chair, right where I can see you and you can see me. Now, don't look at me like that. It's all right. I've done it lots of times before, and you never knew it.'

She moved Emma's chair to the bed; any chair that Emma selected for herself would be comfortable. Mrs Manson watched. The eiderdown from the cot, an extra blanket for her shoulders.

The chair faced the bed; it was nearer the foot than the head. Its back was to the screen.

Before Milly settled down to what she told herself was a sleepless night, she opened both sides of the porch door. George's room was still dark. She sent him a wan smile across the garden and returned to the chair. It wasn't too bad; it was almost as good as a bed.

Then she got up again.

She knew there was another cupful of milk in the jug, and she was thirsty. She filled the empty water glass with the milk and saluted Mrs Manson before she drank.

Miss Sills was nodding. Soon Miss Sills would be asleep. A deep sleep. In the morning Miss Sills would have a headache.

In the morning I will be dead . . .

How will it happen? It couldn't have been planned for to-night – no one could have known she'd drink the rest of the milk. It was a lucky break. The way had been prepared for a lucky break, and it had come. And it wasn't needed, it wasn't necessary at all. It was simply an extra precaution, a weapon in reserve, devious, typical.

How long will I have to wait now?

Not long. This is too good to miss. It would have been better if there'd been more time for frightening me. It must have been a wrench to give that up. I see the whole thing now, I know the plan. I was to be frightened out of my wits until that grew tiresome and wasn't exciting any more. Then, when the time was right, when I was alone or with Emma only, I was to be killed. How? Perhaps smothered. Smothering will be easy.

Emma left me alone to-night. There was plenty of time then. Emma was asleep to-night, over by the fire, out of sight of the screen. There was time then, too. But I had to be frightened first, because that was exciting. That would have gone on night after night until it got to be a bore. Or until a foolproof opportunity came. An opportunity too good to miss. Like to-night.

WERE Miss Sills and I being watched? Yes, of course we were. But what difference does that make now?

Soon the hands will come back and move along the edge of the screen. The black shape will rise from the floor and stand up, and one of the hands will uncover the face, and I will see it.

The face is being saved for the end, like a big scene. Like a scene at the end of a melodrama; when the audience is supposed to be surprised. It won't be played for my benefit; the face knows that I know now. It will be played for the excitement the actor gets.

I know even about the hands. I know what they are. Moving along the floor, under the screen, close together as if they belonged to an animal.

That is too vile.

Miss Sills is asleep. Her head is bowed. She sleeps like a little girl.

When they find me in the morning, will they say I turned in my sleep and smothered myself? 'She turned in her sleep – the pillow. It's the miracle we've been waiting for, but we didn't know, we didn't think –'

Will the police believe that?

Miss Sills sleeps like a little girl.

Can they do anything to her? Can they accuse her of negligence? Or will someone suggest that she was in love with –

Waiting is dreadful. Why is it taking so long? . . .

At last . . . Miss Sills. Miss Sills. *Miss Sills!*

Part Two

IT was Hattie who screamed. The sound ripped through the quiet house, rose and fell, and left in its wake a deeper silence than before. It dragged Emma from the refuge of sleep.

Emma's room was separated from Hattie's by the bath they shared. She knew where the scream came from, but the hush that followed it was endless and shocking. She told herself that everybody was dead. There was no breath in the house; when people are sleeping and breathing in a house, you always know it. She sat up in bed and turned on the light. She wanted to see the clock, although she was convinced she had no more need of time.

It was three o'clock. She covered her mouth with a thin, gnarled hand, to keep herself from screaming, too. Then she heard other sounds, doors opening and closing, feet on the floors above and on the stairs. Feet on the kitchen floor, a chair overturned. Voices. Someone knocked on the door to the kitchen. 'Emma?' It was Mr Cory.

She managed to say, 'Yes, sir?'

'We want you out here.'

She opened the door. 'Mrs Manson, Miss Nora –'

'We want you in the library,' he said.

She put on her robe and slippers and pinned up her scant braids, taking her time because the next few minutes would tell her something she didn't want to hear. When she reached the library, Hattie was already there, alive, and wrapped in a blanket. She looked for the others – Mr Cory, Mr Manson, Miss Sills. Mr Cory was standing by the fireplace, Mr Manson was telephoning, Miss Sills was absent.

'Miss Nora?' Emma faltered. 'Miss Sills?'

'Miss Sills is all right. Everybody's all right except Mrs Manson.'

'Not –'

'We're trying to get Doctor Babcock. Mrs Manson is unconscious, and Miss Sills quite rightly refuses to accept the responsibility. We don't know what – Emma, can you do anything with Hattie? Nothing she says makes sense.'

Emma turned on Hattie. Hattie's shrill, wailing voice rose above the telephone conversation, but they heard enough of the latter to know that Doctor Babcock wasn't home.

SHE hadn't slept well, Hattie said; the ivy had kept her awake. All night long it had been making noises at her window, scratching against the wooden shutters, and she'd listened to it for hours before she'd made up her mind that she couldn't stand it another minute. She'd got out of bed then, not turning on a light, and found the scissors in her work-basket.

'I was going to cut it off,' she said. 'The ivy. I could see it moving back and forth, a long, black, ugly-looking thing out there in the dark. Like a snake. So I was going to cut it off. And then –' She stopped short when Manson left the phone.

'I got hold of Pleydell,' Manson said. 'He's younger than I like, but he's the best I could do. Get on with it, Hattie.'

'Yes, sir. So I was going to cut it off. I was half out the window and had it in my hand when the arm came down.'

Cory looked at Manson. Their faces were white, but they smiled and shrugged. 'There's no reason you should listen to this again,' Cory said to Manson. 'Why don't you wait at the door for Pleydell? He hasn't far to come. Emma and I –'

Manson left gratefully.

Emma said: 'I don't want to hear the rest of it. She's crazy. I want to go upstairs. I want to see Miss Nora.'

'No,' Cory said. 'We've got to kill this thing right now. Your window is only a few feet from Hattie's. You may be able to persuade Hattie that she –'

'Nobody's going to persuade me, now or ever!' Hattie wailed. 'And not Emma Vinup either! I tell you I saw an arm, a long arm, six feet long if it was an inch. It could've choked me to death and would've done it, too, only I frightened it away!'

'Away where?' Cory's voice was soft.

'Don't ask me. Away, that's all. I think up.'

'Up where?'

'How do I know?' Hattie thought it over. 'If it went down, it would've gone down to join its body. And I'd've seen a body if there was one, because it would've been standing on the ground right in front of me. There wasn't a body. There was only this arm, hanging down like the ivy, right in front of my face. Six feet long if it was an inch, with a yellow glove on.'

'Yellow! Hattie, listen. It was dark, it was –'

'A yellow glove, Mr Cory. There's some light out there, you get a little light from the street lamp. I saw that glove like I see you. It swung sideways, like it was looking for something to hold on to, and it hit me in the face.' Hattie touched her cheek with a fat finger, and her eyes rolled. 'Not hard, but I felt it. Like it didn't know I was there.'

Cory turned to Emma. 'Doesn't that sound like some kid warming up for Hallowe'en?'

'Not,' said Emma, 'at three in the morning. This is a nice, residential district. It was something she ate. Go back to bed, Hattie. I'll come in and see you later.' The look she gave Cory said that she was in control and he was less than nothing.

WHEN Hattie had gone, trailing her blanket and sniffling, Emma made sure the door was closed. Then she said: 'Mr Brucie, what happened upstairs? What happened to Miss Nora? Was it Hattie screaming like that?'

'It must have been.'

'But could she hear it? Her door's always closed at night. I've heard Hattie many times before. She did break her record to-night, but that's a long way off. I don't know, I –'

'The porch door was open,' he reminded her. 'And Hattie's window is on that side of the house. I think we can assume it was Hattie's work.'

'Unconscious.' Emma was thoughtful. 'I never knew her even to faint. Never. Even when Robbie – you know that as well as I do! She never was the kind to faint and carry on.'

'But she's sick now, Emma.'

'Are you telling me? And there's something else, too.' Emma frowned. 'She was upset to-night, what you might call wild-eyed. Miss Sills thought she'd had a nightmare.' She told him about Miss Sills' return at midnight. 'Miss Sills was sharp with me, too, as if I'd done something. Me! I'd lay down my life, and you know it. Miss Sills said Miss Nora was terrified, that's what she said.'

Cory walked to one of the long windows. 'Lights on over at Perry's ... How terrified? When a woman can't speak, can't move –'

'It was the way she looked. She looked awful.' Emma faltered. 'It could have been a bad dream – but it wouldn't go away when she woke up. She couldn't shake it off. Miss Sills sent me down to my room. She said she could handle it better alone. I don't know what she did, though.'

'That was midnight?'

'Yes. Twelve or a little after. Mr Brucie, what does Miss Sills say?'

'Miss Sills seems to know less than anyone else. She didn't hear Hattie. She didn't know anything was wrong until I woke her up. She wasn't easy to wake, either. And Nora –' He prowled about the room.

Emma fought for patience. 'If it's a cigarette you're looking for, then for mercy's sake, sit down and let me get it.' She found matches and cigarettes in a table drawer. 'Here. You heard Hattie yourself, didn't you?'

70

'Of course. My door was open and the back stairs – I went to Mrs Manson's room at once.'

'I'd have thought you'd have gone to the place where the scream came from.'

'You'd have thought nothing of the sort. You'd have done as I did ... What are you listening to?'

'Somebody came in the front door without ringing the bell. Can that be the doctor so soon?' She opened the library door. Voices came down the hall. 'George Perry, wouldn't you know it, and the new doctor, too. He looks too young. I'm going upstairs. I can be useful.' She was gone before he could stop her.

GEORGE wore a raincoat over his pyjamas and goloshes on what he said were bare feet. He breathed as if he had been running. 'I saw your lights go on,' he said to Cory. 'I was looking out my window. If you're going to search the grounds, I can help. That's what I came for.'

'Do you know what you're talking about?' Cory asked mildly.

George said: 'I think I'd better sit down. I'm winded. Sure I know. If you're trying to keep this thing a secret, you're out of luck. I met Pleydell on the porch, and he told me, but I didn't need that. I got an eyeful myself, and I'm not surprised that Mrs Manson passed out.'

Cory studied George closely. 'Exactly what do you think you saw?'

George coloured. 'I don't know,' he admitted. 'Listen. I'm far from being the kind of guy who hangs out of windows spying on the neighbours, but –'

He told Cory he'd gone to his window to spit out a dental poultice, and he looked ridiculously young when he said it. 'I looked across the grounds to this house because – well, there it was and there I was, and I saw something moving. Back and forth, under the porch. I thought it was a dog, a big dog, maybe a collie. But there aren't any big dogs around here. So I kept on looking.' He said the dog prowled close

71

to the house, as if it were stalking something, and that was all right, because the place was full of moles and so on. Then it disappeared. By that time he was wide awake and he went to get a cigarette. When he returned to the window, the dog was on the sleeping porch. 'No wonder Mrs Manson fainted, big brute like that, strolling around the porch, walking in her room, place half-dark.'

'Do you have a theory about how a dog could climb that porch?'

'The tone of voice is all right with me,' George said agreeably. 'I didn't see him go up, but I saw him come down. He came down like a monkey. Maybe he was a monkey. I saw him swing over the railing and hang on the vines. Come to think of it, I didn't actually see him hit the ground. By that time I was falling around my own room, looking for my shoes. Maybe he was a monkey or maybe he was the Hound of the Baskervilles. I don't know or care, much, except that he ought to be found and shot. He gave me the creeps . . . How's Miss Sills?'

'There's nothing wrong with Miss Sills.'

'I'm glad to hear that.' George's voice was faintly chiding, and he looked as if he had more to say, all of it censorable. But when he continued, he was mild enough. 'And how come Pleydell instead of Babcock? Not that I don't think Pleydell is good. I do. My mother had him once, and he saw through her like a window. But I thought Babcock had this house staked.'

'Babcock's out on a case.'

'Pleydell says Hattie woke the dead.'

'Yes. Now see here, George, don't talk about this to anyone but me. You'll have us in the papers, and there's been enough of that. To say nothing of demoralizing the neighbourhood. You know our Hattie.'

'I sure do. I used to help Hattie set traps for non-existent mice. This time, according to Pleydell, she saw an arm six feet long.'

'Pleydell talks too much. So, apparently, does Manson.'

72

'So, and I'm not kidding, will my mother. Wait till she hears this one! I slid a note under her door, telling her where I'd gone. In case you wanted me to stick around for a while and help search. You know, in case we decide to take it seriously.'

'Now, George – '

'In case we found something that looked like paw marks. The ground is soaking, so they'd show. Or something like torn leaves, broken twigs, and so on. Or footprints. It could have been a cat burglar, you know. Man instead of dog; object, Mrs Manson's jewellery.'

'All insured.'

'But not enough to pay for being frightened out of your wits. I'd feel better if you and I slipped outside and took a look around. We could take a quick look and satisfy ourselves.'

Cory was indulgent. 'Stop romancing, George. I'm satisfied now.'

'I'm not,' George complained. 'Some of the porch ivy is hanging loose, and it wasn't like that this afternoon. I saw it just now by Hattie's window.'

'It's too dark to see anything like that, and you know it.'

George put his hand in his pocket. 'Not with this,' he said. He played his flashlight around the room. 'I used it when I came across the garden. I saw what I saw, all right.'

'Put it away, George, and grow up.'

'That's what my mother always says,' George agreed. 'Grow up. Oh, well.'

They sat on without talking. The doorbell rang once, and Cory answered it. When he came back, he said it was Babcock. Babcock had finally returned to his house and found the message Manson had left.

George ambled about the room. He showed a mild interest when Pleydell, young, red in the face, and clearly unrecovered from a snub, came to the door and asked to be taken to Hattie. Cory led him away. After that, George's wanderings took him to the garden windows. He whistled softly. His father and mother, armed with flashlights, were picking their way across the wet grass, turning into the path that led to the front door. His father was only half-dressed, but his mother was gloved, hatted, and veiled. He went back to his chair and waited for the bell to ring.

MILLY said she didn't need anything. Mr Manson said: 'Yes, you do. Come downstairs for a drink when you're through in here.' Then he left to answer the doorbell.

Milly stood by the bed with Emma and Doctor Babcock, touching the smooth covers to reassure herself, talking softly, although there was no need for that now. Mrs Manson was mercifully asleep.

Babcock listened, one plump hand embracing his chin. When she finished her story, he said: 'Absurd. And dreadful.'

'I didn't hear a thing,' Milly said. 'It wouldn't have frightened me if I had. I've heard Hattie give out before – she does it when she thinks she sees a bug. But poor Mrs Manson –'

'There, there,' Babcock said. 'It's all over now.'

Milly looked at Mrs Manson's closed eyes. Pleydell had been wonderful. He brought her out of the faint, or whatever it was, and talked as if he gave her credit for being adult and sensible. He described what he called Hattie's nightmare as if he'd dreamed it himself, and he made Emma laugh with him. Mrs Manson listened, her eyes never leaving his young face. Then he gave her a sedative, but not from the bottle on the table. His hand went toward the bottle, but her look stopped it in mid-air. So he took a bottle from his very new bag and held it for her to see. Even then she refused; she looked at Emma as if she were talking to her. And Emma said: 'I'll sleep here, I'll sleep in the same bed. And it won't be the first time, either.' After that it was all right; now Mrs Manson was asleep, and Emma was sitting on the bed and yawning and all but telling them to get out.

Babcock touched Milly's arm. 'Come, Miss Sills, there's nothing more for you to do here. You heard what Mr Manson said. A small refresher – you've earned it, and I need it. A long, trying day, a miserable night.' He led her from the room and guided her along the hall as if she were ill.

She was relieved, she'd been afraid he'd blame her for sleeping. He was being fair and understanding. Two wonderful men, Pleydell and Babcock. She was lucky.

ALL the doors along the hall except two were open; there were lights in the rooms. On the right, the rose guest-room adjoining Mrs Manson's bath – the room Mr Manson used now. Rose blankets thrown back, rose sheets dragging on the floor, the porch door open and the curtains not drawn. Mr Manson had left that room in a hurry. A funny-looking room for Mr Manson to be sleeping in.

Robbie's room on the left. That one was locked. It was always locked. It would be dark and dusty if you could see inside. Were the sheets still on Robbie's bed? Plain white sheets, wrinkled where his body had lain; soft white pillows showing the print of his head? No. No, that bed would be smooth, because he hadn't slept in it.

Beyond Robbie's, the room Bruce Cory used. A brown room, an English-looking room, like those you saw in English movies. Plain dark furniture, heavy and handsome; brushes and jars on the big chest, tortoise, ebony, and crystal. Expensive. Mr Bruce Cory got out of bed like a Boy Scout, no matter who screamed. No matter what. Sheets folded back, dark-brown blankets neat and tidy. The lavatory next door. Then the stairs that went down to the kitchen.

Across the hall from Bruce Cory's, Mr Manson's suite that he wasn't using. But someone had been in there. Lights in the bath and in the dressing room. Drawers pulled out of the dressing-room chest. As if somebody wanted something in a hurry. Handkerchiefs on the floor, a dark-blue scarf trailing from an open drawer. Everything dark blue and cream ... Wanted what in a hurry? A revolver in the handkerchief drawer? That could be. A scream in the night ...

The second closed door was next to Mr Manson's suite. The attic door. Doctor Babcock's hand pressed her arm. 'My arm must be shaking,' she decided. 'My knees are. And my head aches.' She smiled at Doctor Babcock, to let him know she was grateful. The wide stairs to the first floor were straight ahead.

'Take things easy to-morrow,' Babcock said. 'Don't worry about your patient, she's in good shape. Take long walks, think of pleasant things. We can't have *you* cracking up!' They went down.

She had seen George's father before, puttering in his flower beds, a greying, gangling replica of George. His old tweed topcoat, worn over pyjamas, was wet and wrinkled. He looked cold and unhappy as he huddled by the fire. Alice Perry was a familiar figure, too, and also from a distance. Alice Perry was complete, from pearls to corset. No one introduced them.

Milly went to a chair by a window, out of the circle of light. Cory brought her a drink. When she had time to look around, she saw Pleydell in a far corner, making himself small in a huge chair, looking like a choirboy waiting for words from a bishop.

It was after four o'clock; it could have been four in the afternoon except for the dark windows, the lamps, and the assorted clothing. George looked like a perfect fool. She'd tell him so when she got the chance. And he was grinning. There was nothing to grin about.

ALICE PERRY was laughing, a brisk, efficient, party laugh. 'Ordinarily I sleep like a baby,' she declared, 'but to-night I was restless. Of course, I heard George prowling, but I thought it was his poor tooth. Then I heard my big George, also prowling. Such men! That was when I got up and found little George's amazing note. Of course we came at once –

the neighbourly thing to do. Dear Mrs Manson. I'd cut Hattie's wages if she were mine.'

Everyone laughed.

'The villain was the wind,' Cory said. 'George says the ivy's down. Of course that's what she saw.'

'Oh, naturally, the wind,' Alice Perry agreed. 'Our poor chrysanthemums, absolutely beaten to the ground. I showed you, dear, as we came over. George dear, *big* Georgie, didn't I show you?'

Mr Perry nodded.

'The wind was pretty stiff,' Manson said. 'Frightful racket in those old trees, almost human. So human that for a minute I thought Hattie was a particularly big blow.'

Everyone laughed again. Hattie is a very comic character, Milly thought. All you have to do is mention Hattie's name, and everybody howls.

Babcock took it up. 'The wind was bad in town, too. I didn't like it at all.'

'The wind, the wind,' George chanted. They all looked at him. He was playing with his flashlight, turning it on and off.

'Put that thing away,' Alice Perry said. 'It looks silly, and your hands aren't clean.'

'The wind, the wind,' George said again. 'I am forcibly reminded of a little blue-and-gold copy of *A Child's Garden of Verses*. Robbie and I each had one; we learned some of the stuff by heart; we were very, very cute. I quote. Title: *The Wind*. Line: "And all around I heard you pass – like ladies' skirts across the grass." Did it sound like that to any of you, or am I just being sentimental?'

They laughed at George almost as much as they'd laughed at Hattie. Even little Pleydell made a co-operative sound, but he kept it up too long.

Milly looked at him with sudden anger, and he coloured. Why do I always get interested in fools? she asked herself. Why am I down here, anyway? Why doesn't George introduce me to his parents? Why do I stay, like a dope? Because

77

I am a dope. She got up. 'Excuse me, everyone,' she said. 'I belong upstairs.'

They began to talk again before she left the room. She heard Babcock say something about the masseur. His report had been a good one. Babcock had called him in town. They were going to try the treatment every night. Mrs Manson was responding. George said something about Hattie and the masseur.

Milly closed the door on a fresh burst of laughter. George had started them off again. He had an I.Q. of six.

She was halfway up the stairs when George came after her. He didn't say anything, but he put his arms around her and held her close. It was better than putting a ring on her finger. It was the first time he'd ever done that. His I.Q. rose to the height of heaven; exactly heaven.

'Be over in the morning,' he whispered.

THAT light is the sun. The Sunday-morning sun. That is Emma over there. Emma, coming out of the bathroom with the vacuum jug, the cup, the glass. All clean, dry, sparkling, everything washed away. No traces left. Nothing.

Watch Emma through your lashes. The old trick.

Emma is rubbing the damp places on the carpet, blotting out the prints of four hands. She is brushing dried leaves from the floor and talking about the wind. Soon nothing will be left of the night. She is destroying me.

There is a crack in the bowl of the lamp. Will she see that? A new crack in my fine lamp. She won't like it, she'll be angry, she'll talk about it. Emma or Miss Sills, either will do. Emma or Miss Sills, bending over the bed, saying: 'What a shame. Something happened to her lamp, and she liked it so much. Does anybody know what happened to her lamp?'

My lamp was knocked to the floor by two thick yellow hands in a hurry. And after that there was not enough light. Not enough to see in, not enough safely to kill in. No sound,

78

except the thud of the lamp and the breathing of two people. Not my breathing. I held my breath in the dark, and it was the same as hiding. Two people breathing. Miss Sills in the chair and the other at the head of the bed. Slow, drugged breathing for Miss Sills; rapid, frightened breathing for the other.

She waited for Miss Sills to wake. Miss Sills hadn't heard the lamp go over, but she'd heard something. Or felt something. She'd stirred in her sleep and moaned. Poor Miss Sills. No, rich Miss Sills. Rich, powerful Miss Sills, who had given her the gift of another day.

The four hands had scrabbled over the floor to the screen and safety. Frightened off, but playing the part to the end. If Miss Sills had waked, she'd have seen a shapeless mass on all fours. She would have screamed as Hattie screamed. Then: 'My dear Miss Sills, you are not yourself. It's been too much for you. A few weeks' rest –' Then there would be no more Miss Sills. Then there would be no more.

Will the lamp be taken away before someone sees the crack, someone who is all right? And if so, what excuse will be given? ... Never mind that, you know the lamp will go. Forget the lamp, try to remember the rest of it. There may be something, some small thing.

Hattie. How much later was that? One minute, two minutes? Who thinks of time in that kind of dark? The new doctor that Ralph called in was too young, too inexperienced, but kind and instinctively wise. He'd known at once that it was useless to offer the pills from her own bottle, but he didn't try to find out why. His bottle was a new one, and he'd let her see him open it. A safe, new bottle, and with Emma in the room all night as well as Miss Sills ... That's enough, that's enough, go back to Hattie. Maybe Hattie –

The new doctor said Hattie screamed because she had a nightmare. But Miss Sills said Hattie had been frightened by the ivy outside her window. They believed what they said; it was what they'd been told. But Hattie knew every leaf on that vine, every loop and tendril. What Hattie had seen was a black shape with four hands, but she would be talked out of it. If only Hattie would talk first, talk everywhere, to everybody. Even to tradesmen. Tradesmen gossip and pass things along. Had there been light enough for Hattie to see the hands? If Hattie talked about the hands, and it reached the right person – Who is the right person this time? Who knows about the hands?

Who knows? You do. You saw him making them. It was a secret, a joke. He told you he was making them for a present. He said, 'Who's always asking for two pairs of hands?' He laughed when he said it.

Think, think. There was someone else who knew, someone who came into the room and saw. Who? Who came in? ... Now, now, you're doing it the wrong way again. You're letting your mind wander, you're seeing his face. That's bad for you. You're hearing his voice again. Stop for a minute and think of something else. Call yourself the nice names Miss Sills calls you. It isn't a foolish thing to do. Go on. Call yourself a good girl, a honey, a baby ... I'm a good girl, a honey, a baby.

Now go back to last night. Maybe you've overlooked something, something that will talk for you, point a finger for you. Soon. *Soon.*

The lamp that rolled to the floor. The darkness. The waiting. The scream. Then nothing. Nothing, nothing, nothing. Give up.

'YOU'RE awake,' Emma said. 'That's fine. And Miss Sills has brought your breakfast. You slept like an angel, and that's because you knew I was beside you.'

Emma fed her, using a spoon and the glass tube, chirping and fluttering, full of importance. 'Telephone ringing like mad – everybody heard about your fright and wants to say they were sorry. Only ten o'clock, and people come to call already. Doctor Babcock, the Perrys, and that nice little new doctor. But he went away again. Mrs Perry brought a lovely jelly for your lunch and a bottle of sherry. Now eat this egg, and I'll let them all come in to see you.'

Miss Sills arranged her chair. 'Too cold for the porch,' Miss Sills said. 'I think we'll sit in the window. All cosy in the sunny window, and you can doze like a little cat. You need more sleep, you know ... Look, Emma, she wants that old rug. All right, you can have it when we get you settled. You're spoiled, that's what you are. Next week I'm going to use discipline.'

Emma put the breakfast tray in the hall, and they wheeled her to the window. She heard the others coming, walking softly as befitted people who knew she had weathered a bad night.

'Let me see your feet, the lot of you,' Emma said: 'I saw you out in the garden, and I'll have no more things tracked in on my clean floor.'

'Things?' George Perry.

'Leaves and grit all over. Tramping in and out of here last night, and I had to clean it up on my knees.'

THEY surrounded her chair, smiling, paying their compliments. She was brave, she'd behaved like a soldier. She was a fine woman, getting better every day, no doubt about it. She was good-morning, Mrs Manson; she was dear Mrs Manson, who frightened them so. She was okay, Mrs Manson, okay ... She closed her eyes, because she didn't want to see their faces. The voices told her where they stood and sat.

Miss Sills, on the window seat, spoke to someone. 'No, don't take the rug away. I know it's hot, but she wants it.'

'Is she asleep, Miss Sills?'

'Only relaxed. It's a good sign. She's always like this when you come in. Don't stop talking, go right ahead. She likes to hear voices around her, doesn't she, Doctor Babcock?'

'Oh, quite, quite. And what, may I ask, is the immediate future of the good neighbour's sherry?'

Ralph, doubtful, hesitating. 'Well, I suppose we might –'

'It's eleven o'clock,' Doctor Babcock said. 'We had a hard night.'

'You men! That's a *special bottle* for Mrs Manson!'

'Emma, do you think –'

Emma, full of pleased complaints at the social turn of affairs, brought the house sherry from the dining-room. The voices murmured on. Emma rattled glasses, rustled back and forth, and finally subsided. 'I'm thankful to sit down. My legs ache. I'm an old woman, but nobody thinks of that. A person needs two pairs of hands around here.'

Listen! Listen! All of you listen! Emma's quoting someone, Emma's teasing – can't you hear? Watch Emma's eyes, watch where Emma's looking. Say it again, Emma. Emma, say it again!

'Thank you,' Emma said. 'I don't care if I do. I'll get as giddy as all get out, but I iike a nip now and then.'

'You may have anything your heart desires, Emma. The house is yours.'

'I'm glad to know that,' Emma said, 'because I want something this minute.'

Then it came.

Emma said, 'I want your permission to get rid of that lamp by the bed.'

'What's wrong with it?'

'It's awkward, that's what. The shade's too big. It gets in the way.'

Emma. Look at the lamp. Look at it.

Is Emma – no, wait, don't open your eyes. They're moving about; someone has come to stand behind your chair. Careful. Someone is waiting to see if you – *Take your hand away from my neck. Can't you wait for the dark?*

'Hey!' Miss Sills was beside her. 'Hey, what goes on here? What have you got to shiver about? You're as warm as toast. Easy, honey, easy. All right now?'

'Lamp,' George said. 'That reminds me. Say, is it all right to talk about last night?'

'Why not?' Doctor Babcock. 'Last night is already forgotten. Lamp, did you say?'

'Yeah. At what I figure was a crucial moment, somebody turned it out.'

'What are you talking about?'

'The lamp Emma doesn't like. I was hanging out my window, and suddenly this room went dark. For about two or three minutes. The little one by the screen was already out. But the big one by the bed went out, stayed out, and came on again.'

'YOU'RE crazy,' Miss Sills said. 'It was on when I went to sleep, and it was on when Mr Cory woke me up. Wasn't it, Mr Cory – or am I the crazy one?'

'Nobody's crazy, and George is right. The lamp was on the floor when I came in. I fell over it.' His voice was rueful. 'But I got it back on the table, and it worked, thank God. That was a bad minute.'

'Floor?' George was puzzled.

'Floor?' Miss Sills repeated. 'Well, I didn't hear it fall. I didn't hear a thing. I ought to be fired. All I know is that Mr Cory nearly shook my teeth out trying to wake me up and Mr Manson was running around in circles. Excuse me, Mr Manson.'

'My dear Miss Sills, that's libellous. I ran in a very straight line, in the wrong direction. Straight down the back stairs, because I'd recognized Hattie's clarion call. Then, halfway down, I heard Cory begging you to show signs of life at the top of his lungs.'

Doctor Babcock was torn between grief and laughter, sighs and chuckles. 'Dreadful, dreadful, but not without an amusing side.'

'I didn't hear a thing,' Miss Sills repeated. 'I ought to be fired, but please don't.'

'You ought to have more sherry.' Bruce, walking to Miss Sills. 'Here, all's well that ends well. And speaking of Hattie, have any of you good people ever heard a moose?'

83

They seized Hattie's name, hugged it and tossed it about. Hattie was a moose. She looks like a moose. The left profile? No, silly, the right! And isn't there a wart, too? On the nose? Stop, stop, I haven't laughed so much in years. Dear Mrs Manson would love this, we must tell her when she's better. Hattie is a moose with a wart. Hattie –

Emma called from across the room. She sounded happy. 'Look! Look here! This lamp's got a crack in it. It's not fit to use; it's not safe. This lamp's going to the White Elephant Sale at All Saints'.' The cord and plug struck the carpet softly.

'Emma, how perfectly wonderful!' Mrs Perry said. 'Mr Manson, do let us have it. I'm chairman this year, and it's simply dreadful the way people won't give us things.'

'I don't know, but I don't see why not.'

'I can't tell you how grateful – George dear, will you carry – George, stop whistling. Not nice, when poor Mrs Manson – George!'

George said: 'All right. But how do you suppose a heavy lamp like that managed to fall over? Could that be the wind again?'

'Wind? Oh, undoubtedly. She couldn't do it herself, poor lamb.'

'Blowing leaves and little sticks, not to mention grit and mud. My nice clean floor. We'll have to keep that porch door shut,' Emma said.

'By all means keep it shut,' George said.

'George, what are you mumbling about?' Alice Perry asked.

'I'm quoting poetry to myself. My little blue-and-gold book.'

'Well, stop it. No one's interested.'

'I am. Listen. Still the pretty one about the wind that rips the ivy off the porch and blows a fifteen-pound lamp around. "I saw the different things you did, but always you yourself you hid." . . . I think we ought to go home.'

Chairs moved at once, quickly; glasses were set down on tables and mantel; voices mingled; sentences overlapped.

84

Mr Perry, you haven't said a word. George darling, no more sherry. The lamp, Mrs Perry, don't run off without your white elephant! Lovely, lovely, and all for foreign missions, it means so much. George, I said no more sherry, it gives your eyes a funny look. Thank you for calling, thank you. Yes, we're on our way, Miss Sills. Don't look so pleased, we're all going. These little sherry parties are good for all of us. George? George, I'm not going to speak to you again.

GONE. Everything gone.

Emma collecting the glasses. Emma washes everything, the fingermarks, the muddy prints. Emma gave the lamp away. Nothing left, nothing, and the prints on the floor were clear, even I could see what they were ... Emma saw the crack in the lamp, and they said it was the wind.

All but George! There was something in his voice, wasn't there, wasn't there? He knows there was no wind, not enough for that, doesn't he? George, remember the wind; you made a joke of it, but you know it isn't a joke, don't you? Keep remembering the wind, remember the little book with the poems in it. I gave you that book, George. I gave one to you and one to Robbie. Robbie and George, George and Robbie. They were always together ... George!

George is the one who knows about the hands, George saw them when I did, George is the one I was trying to think of! George is the right person, the safe person!

Emma knows the phrase about the hands, but that's all. Stop, go slowly, make a list like a shopping list. What do you need?

You need Hattie to have seen the hands; you need Hattie to talk. You need George to hear. You need Emma to use the phrase again. You need George to hear. You need – you need George to remember ... But if Hattie –

That hand on my neck. I thought my heart would stop then.

Listen. Emma.

'You can carry these glasses down to the kitchen on your way out,' Emma said to Miss Sills, 'but don't you go waking

85

her up to say good-bye. I'll sit right beside her all the time. She won't lack for anything if she wakes, and if she looks hungry, I'll see to her lunch. No need for you to hurry yourself. The doctor says you're to take it easy. And don't stop in the kitchen gossiping with Hattie. If you want the truth, that woman hasn't got all her buttons. That's a pretty coat. I always favoured red. Get along now.'

'Yes, Matron,' Miss Sills said . . .

Miss Sills is going for a walk, wearing her red coat. Watch for Miss Sills. Open your eyes and watch for Miss Sills. No matter which way she goes, you can see the red coat. Look at the children in their Sunday clothes. Dark blue and brown for the big ones, pale blue and pink for the little ones. Nurses, parents. Young parents, full of pride. Who is that woman in the green coat and hat?

Emma, don't talk. Emma, be quiet! Emma, that woman in the green coat and hat!

'So you've decided to wake up and take notice, have you? I'll set my chair right here beside you. I know you – you were playing possum for the others, but the minute you knew you were alone with old Emma, you decided to wake up. That Miss Sills, there she goes, over to see her mother, I expect. Well, bless my soul, look at that rug! What happened to that, I want to know! I tucked it in myself, as tight as tight. You can't have – bless my soul, you're all tied up with fringe. A person'd almost think – but no, you can't do that . . . There, that's better. That won't hurt my girl again. Such an ugly, big red mark . . . Miss Nora, you aren't even listening to me. What are you looking at? What's out there? Same old thing that's there every day, unless it's Miss Sills. Of course, if you can't even listen to your old Emma . . . Well, I hope you're satisfied. There she is, traipsing along like she didn't work for a living same as the rest of us!'

IT is! It is! Miss Byrd. The nurse I had before Miss Sills. She wore that green coat when she went away! She came back! She came back, she had to come back. She knew something was wrong, she couldn't hide it, I could see her trying to hide it. She knew, or saw, or guessed; she watched everybody; she was uneasy. She showed it in the way she watched and listened. So she was sent away ... The patient is unhappy, Miss Byrd; we'll have to make a change. You understand that this is no reflexion on your work. There's no criticism of you, Miss Byrd, none at all, but the patient isn't happy, and we can't have that. Mr Manson thinks perhaps an extra cheque – we're very grateful ... She hadn't looked surprised; she'd almost smiled. She'd looked as if she'd expected it.

Miss Byrd. Everybody laughed at the Byrd because she looked like a hawk.

Miss Byrd, Miss Byrd, I'm up here in my window. Listen. That girl in the bright red coat is my new nurse. Stop her, Miss Byrd, say something, anything. Make friends with her. Her name is Sills, Milly Sills. She's a nice child, she'll be courteous and kind. Talk to her – you'll know how to do it. Tell her what you know. What do you know, Miss Byrd? What did you see or hear? She's almost there. Miss Byrd, the girl in the bright red coat and no hat. She's there, see, she's there! In front of you, in front! Say good morning, say it's a lovely day, ask her the name of the park, ask anything. Stop her, Miss Byrd. *Miss Byrd!*

Now, now, close your eyes again. Don't cry ... You're a good girl, you're a honey, you're a baby. You're my good, good girl.

The lamp is gone; the tracks on the floor are gone. Miss Byrd – forget Miss Byrd. You have another day, this day. How much of this day do you have? Six hours? Six hours until dark. Spend them to the last minute, not on hope, not on fear. Spend them in preparation for to-night. To-night you will be going –

This is the time to climb the attic stairs again. Climb the attic stairs the way you did before, and raise your head when you get to the top. The way you did before. That is a preparation of a kind ... Climb.

ALICE PERRY circled her living room with the lamp in her hands, measuring the table tops with speculative eyes. 'Nobody but Nora Manson would have cupids and a ruffled shade. At her age! For a young girl's room, yes; rather sweet for a young girl, but Nora Manson! Cupids!'

'That thing's Dresden,' George said mildly. 'Bruce Cory gave it to her last Christmas, and she bawled him out. It cost like the devil.' He went to a window and looked across the hedge. 'Emma's too open-handed with other people's property when other people can't talk ... Did you happen to see Cory's face while that was going on?'

She said: 'I wasn't watching him then. George, this crack won't show when the lamp is properly placed. It might look rather fine against the right kind of wall. A soft, grey wall. You know, if I thought people wouldn't – George, don't you think it will be perfectly fair if I –'

'Sure,' George said. 'Give the White Elephant Sale a buck and tell the All Saints' ladies you took a piece of junk off their hands.'

Alice sat down with the lamp in her lap and gave her son a bright smile. 'Where's your father, dear?'

'Upstairs, lying down until lunch. I think I'll do the same.'

Alice smiled again. 'What's wrong with you, dear? Toothache, too much sherry, plain meanness, or are you in love with Nora Manson, too?'

'God help me,' George said, 'and I'm not swearing.' He took the chair opposite his mother. 'Say some more. Don't stop.'

'Well, Bruce Cory's in love with her. I've always thought so, and I made up my mind to watch him this morning. Ralph Manson must be blind. Love, hate, sometimes you can't tell, but the way Bruce Cory looked at her! If Ralph Manson would come off his high horse and pay a little attention to his wife and her brother-in-law, he might see what I did.'

'What did you see?'

'Well – oh, nothing. I simply mean – oh, you wouldn't understand.'

'I might.'

'No. You've always made a heroine of Nora Manson. I've often thought you cared more for her than you did for me. But I never interfered. I've always wanted you to have the best.'

'This,' George said, 'gets crazier and crazier. I haven't been in that house a dozen times in the past year. At least, not until Robbie –'

'Now what have I said that's wrong?' Alice sighed. 'Such a long face. Don't you like to talk to your own mother?'

'Robbie, I was thinking about Robbie. Sure I like to talk to you, but when Robbie's name popped up –'

'Morbid, dear.'

'No. I have a conscience about Robbie. I didn't know he – Listen, there's something I've always wanted to ask you. Did you see Robbie that last day?'

'I? Certainly not.'

'But you went there to call that afternoon for the first time in months. You got as far as the front door, and they stopped you. I've always wondered how you happened to choose that particular day and hour.'

'I have an idiot child,' Alice mourned. 'I did *not* choose that particular day and hour, and I was *not* stopped. I simply had a feeling that I wanted to see Nora Manson, so I went over. But when I was told it was inconvenient, naturally I went away.'

'Not far, though.'

'Not –'

'I was coming down the street from the station when you left their porch. You walked around to the side of the house and looked up at the attic window.'

ALICE flicked the ruffled shade with a careless finger. 'Very well then, so I did. And the explanation is childish, so you ought to understand it. When they opened the door, I heard Nora Manson crying, and it worried me. Although we'd grown away from each other, I never once let myself forget that we both were mothers of sons.'

'You didn't have a hunch about what was going on? You didn't see anything? That little trek to the attic window was unadulterated mother-for-mother instinct?'

'George dear, I don't expect you to understand my feelings. Wait until you have a child of your own. I hardly knew what I was doing. I don't even remember now.'

'I can help you out there. You looked up at the attic window and then you got down on your knees and hunted in the grass. I was practically enchanted. Four-leaf clovers?'

She said, 'Why haven't you mentioned this before?'

'It never came up before. That day, Robbie's day, is shrouded in a black cloud that seems to cover everybody. The way people act, you'd think the world stopped then and everybody stood still.'

'All right, but don't look like that.' Her eyes shifted from George to the garden window. 'I did see him. Robbie. I was sitting in that window, and I saw him run up the path to the house. "He's home early," I thought. "What a pity Nora isn't there." I'd seen her drive off in the morning, all dressed up for town. Then after a while I went to my room to change for my little walk, and quite by accident I noticed that their attic window was open. Robbie, I thought, working at his writing when he ought to be out in the sun. And then the most extraordinary thing happened. I saw something fly out the attic window and fall in the grass. Something shiny. I was really agog. But I didn't do anything about it. I took my little walk, and then I felt like seeing Nora Manson. And I call this a silly conversation!'

'It was the key.'

'What?'

'The key to the attic. Robbie locked himself in and tossed it out.'

90

She didn't speak at once. Then: 'You didn't see me pick it up.'

'No. I saw you get up and go home. You're right about this conversation. Why are we having it? It's ancient history, dead and buried. Like Robbie. Who started it, anyway?'

She said, 'You started it.'

'Maybe I did. Well, nobody ever found that key. Manson had a new lock put on.'

'I saw it this morning ... Here we sit as if I didn't have a thing to do. I ought to be getting lunch, and I don't feel like it. Look at my hands – disgusting! Dish-water! I don't know why other women can afford maids and I can't. There's no better manager in Larchville than I am, yet I never have a cent left over. Money! It makes me sick.'

'Maybe you think too much about money.'

'Well, if I do, it's because I'm the only one around here who thinks at all. Look at you and your father. Look at Ralph Manson. Look at this house and look at theirs. I knew Ralph Manson when he was nothing but a clerk in that bank, and now he practically owns it. All a man needs in this world is a little ambition to get ahead, a little common sense about the future, like –'

'Like what?'

'Like not falling in love with a penniless nobody, and you know what I mean ... If she dies, he'll be rich.'

'No,' he said easily, 'if she dies, Cory will be richer. It's Cory money. And with Robbie gone, too –'

She fretted. 'I really must do something about lunch. George, how rich is Bruce Cory?'

'Rolling.'

'More than Ralph Manson?'

'Manson has a damn big salary, and he's in with the moneymaking crowd. It all helps.'

'That's what I thought ... George, what's out there, what are you looking at?'

He was at the garden window. 'That's Milly's red coat. She's going for a walk. She doesn't usually go at this hour.'

'You heard them pampering her, didn't you? Rest, drink this, eat that, take care of yourself, you're precious. Manson, Cory, and Babcock. Men!'

'What do you think of Milly, Mother?'

'I'll do my thinking about that when the time comes. George, are you sure you really –'

'I'm sure.'

MILLY picked up the gold-and-scarlet ball that rolled between her feet and tossed it gently to the fat blue reefer with brass buttons. It came back at once, this time to her stomach. She returned it again. 'You're an apple dumpling,' she said, 'but that'll be all to-day.'

She had reached the far end of the park; there were no more benches, but across the street, where the buses stopped, the Larchville Women's Civic League had built a circular seat around the trunk of a spreading maple. Home was a few minutes away, with possible roast chicken and certain chocolate cake. And talk. But she wasn't hungry, and she didn't want talk. Not the kind she'd have to give, and take.

I won't be able to hide a thing, she told herself. I never can. Her mother would worry and say it wasn't safe. She'd try to make her leave the case. I won't go home, she decided.

Hattie was bats, pure bats. Washing the sherry glasses and rolling her eyes toward her bedroom. 'You can go in and see for yourself, Miss Sills. That ivy's still hanging there, a fresh break in the vine. A long, thin piece like a snake, not like an arm. The arm was an arm, not ivy.'

She'd listened to Hattie with amazement and disbelief. She'd said, 'What's all this about an arm?'

Hattie had described, explained, and re-lived the night. The arm had a hand on the end of it, a six-foot arm and a yellow-looking hand. Or light-looking. A big hand, all spread out. A starfish-looking hand, like in the aquarium. 'It came down and swung in front of my face, and then it went up.'

'Up?'

'Up where it came from. I don't know where that was, but that's where it went. I wasn't asleep, Miss Sills, I wasn't dreaming. And what's more, I heard feet over my head. But nobody listens to me, not even the doctors. "Don't let Mrs Manson hear you talking like that, or we'll have to give you a bad-tasting tonic." If I hadn't waked up when I did, we'd've been robbed.'

'By a starfish hand, yellow-looking?'

'I hope you never have to laugh out of the other side of your mouth,' Hattie had said.

Now Milly walked to the seat under the tree and sat down. When she thought of what her mother could do with Hattie's hand, she quailed. No, she couldn't face that. She'd rest a while and then go back. Nobody knew what Emma would do next. She might let the Perrys in again. That had been too much. Mrs Manson had looked dreadful ... Mrs Perry, saying, 'So you're Miss Sills?' And turning away. Mr Perry, patting her shoulder and saying nothing. George –

A voice beside her said, 'You have a good heart.'

A woman in a green coat and hat was smiling at her. 'I hope you don't mind if I sit here, too. I was watching you in the park. You're nice with children – that's what I meant by a good heart.'

Milly flushed. 'Thank you.'

The woman was familiar in an indeterminate way. Sharp, thin face, thickly powdered, and a spotted veil. The rouge and powder were like a mask.

'You're Mrs Manson's nurse, aren't you?'

'Yes, I am.' She looked at the woman again. Nervous hands, roving eyes. Hypochondriac, following nurses around? She'd change her clothes the next time she came out. The uniform showed under the coat, the white shoes.

'I saw you leave the house. I was sitting in the park ... I used to know Mrs Manson slightly. How is she?'

Hypochondriac with curiosity bump. 'She's much better,

thank you,' Milly said. 'Now run along,' she added silently. 'You make me feel as if I were under a microscope.'

'I'm glad of that,' the woman said quietly. 'I heard somewhere that she'd had a bad relapse. I'm glad it isn't true.'

'Oh, no. She's much, much better.'

'I know them all,' the woman went on. 'Not intimately, but I know them. The Mansons, Bruce Cory, and those people next door, the Perrys. And Doctor Babcock.'

Milly shifted uneasily. There was too much emotion under the quiet voice. Is she trying to tell me something? she wondered. Or does she want me to tell her? Suddenly she remembered the anonymous customer in her friend Marge's book store, the woman who'd tried to buy information about Milly with a ten-cent greeting card. Finish this as soon as you decently can, she told herself, and move on.

'I'm sorry I don't know your name.' The woman's smile was stiff and strained. 'It seems rude to be talking to you without knowing. But mine is Byrd. B-y-r-d. I live in New York, but I often come out here because it's so pretty.' As she talked, she watched Milly's face. 'Byrd,' she repeated. 'Miss Byrd.'

Milly smiled and said nothing.

'Is Emma well? I know Emma, too.'

'Emma's fine.'

A bus lumbered to the stop, and Milly looked at her watch. 'Glendale bus, that means it's – golly, I've got to run.' She got up.

Miss Byrd took her arm. 'I'd appreciate it if you'd – what I want to say is – Miss – Miss – if you'd give me just a minute of your time!'

'I'm awfully sorry, Miss Byrd, but I'm due at my mother's. See you again some time.' She ducked into the crowd that surged toward the bus, crossed the street, and walked rapidly in the wrong direction for home. Miss Byrd looked like the kind of woman who'd compromise on a nurse's mother.

Marge's apartment was a few blocks farther on. She rang the bell, but there was no answer. After that she walked on small, empty side streets and bought herself a chocolate bar and a tube of toothpaste in a shabby store that smelled of kerosene ... If Miss Byrd washed her face, she might look human. But then, she might not, either. She might look –

She told herself to stop thinking about Miss Byrd. She walked on, eating the chocolate, killing time, putting off her return. What am I stalling about? she wondered. Why don't I go back where I belong?

CLIMB. You'll have to climb.

The attic door was open, the last tool clattered to the floor. Her hands were aching, they were all she could feel. Emma was behind her. Ralph and Bruce were crowding ahead of her.

'My hands hurt,' she said. 'Give me your hand to hold, Ralph. Brucie, give me yours. Don't leave me.'

Ralph said, 'Here, darling, but I wish you wouldn't –'

Bruce said, 'She can't stop now.'

There was a draught on the attic stairs, coming down to meet them, blowing her robe, lifting the hair from her forehead. She thought: We're wrong about this, we'll have champagne to-night in celebration of being wrong. He's writing up there, he locked the door because he hates to be interrupted, and he's dead to the world in some silly plot and can't hear us. She called his name, laughing, but no sound came out of her mouth.

Ralph said, 'There must be a window open.'

Bruce said: 'There is. I saw it from the street.'

She answered them in her mind: 'You fools, of course there's a window open. The boy has to have air. It's always suffocating in that place.'

The climb was endless, there had never been so many steps before. It was years before they came to the turn half-way up. Emma panted behind them. It was hard on Emma. What was? Only the stairs, that's all, the stairs. Emma was old.

Ten to one he went to sleep, she wagered silently. They give him too much to do down there at the bank, he hates figures, they wear him out. He was exhausted, and he came home early and went to sleep on that old sofa he won't let me throw away. Ten to one – Why are you saying ten to one, even to yourself? You never talk like that . . . You're talking like that because you don't want to think. Well, you'd better think. Think hard, and be ashamed of yourself for even listening to their monstrous story. Monstrous? Criminal! You could sue, you could easily sue the whole lot of them for saying the things they did. Ten to one.

'Bruce,' she said, 'you're going too fast.'

'We're crawling, Nora. You're holding us back.'

'No, no! Ralph, Bruce, keep my hands!'

The attic floor was level with her eyes now. It was washed with gold from the western windows. She raised her eyes.

'What's the boy doing?' Emma's head appeared beside hers. 'Robbie, you stop whatever you're doing and come straight down here!'

Robbie's shoes, above the sunny floor, were swinging in space. His brown shoes, his – he –

She went the rest of the way alone and stood before him. When she wanted to see his face, she had to raise her head, because he was hanging from the rafters.

EMMA looked up when she heard the clatter of the lunch tray. 'You didn't have to bring that,' she said. 'I was going to ring for one of the others. You're back too soon.'

'I got bored.' Milly put the tray on the table.

'It looks good,' Emma said. 'That jelly looks good. She's a fine cook, Mrs Perry. Maybe she'll teach you one of these days.' Emma's eyes had the mating look.

'Move your work-basket, Emma. No tatting in the soup, please. Thanks. Why don't you ask me to save you a piece of wedding cake? You're slipping.'

'What are you so high and mighty about?'

'I'm not.' Milly slid out of her coat. 'Yes, I am, and I don't

know why. I hate everything. Maybe I need sleep.' She
walked around to the front of the chair. 'Hello, there.
Haven't I seen you somewhere before?'

'Bless my soul, is she awake? Must have just happened.'
Emma joined Milly at the chair, and they smiled steadily.

'We look nice and rested after our little nap,' Emma said.
'And we're going to eat every crumb and spoonful of our
lunch, because if we do, then maybe we can have our lovely
sherry before dinner. Can't we, Miss Sills?'

'I wouldn't know about that. I'm only the night nurse. I
don't come on until seven.'

Emma chortled. 'Isn't she a one, Miss Nora? Aren't you
a lucky girl to have Miss Sills around? I never thought I'd
laugh again, not in this house. I never –' Emma caught
her guilty tongue between her teeth. 'Miss Nora, I – I'm
going to get another lamp, and I'm the only one who knows
how to do it.' She hesitated at the door. 'What about you?
Did you have lunch at your mother's?'

'I'm not hungry. And hurry up. It'll be dark in about five
hours.'

Milly unfolded the heavy napkin, spread it carefully, and
admired the lavish monogram. She patted the thin, still
hands under the steamer rug. 'Don't get wrong ideas about
Emma and me,' she said. 'We're crazy about each other.
And now let's eat whatever Hattie felt like sending up. This
is beef broth, as if you couldn't see for yourself. And this is
a sweetbread, as if you couldn't see that, too. And here we
have the madam's jelly, shaking in its shoes. Want to start
with dessert and work back, just for the – for the fun of it?'

Mrs Manson's eyes looked steadily into hers.

She returned the dessert spoon to the tray and dropped
the prattle and the professional smile. What she saw in Mrs
Manson's eyes filled her own with dismay. Mrs Manson
was looking at her from the bottom of a pit.

'Mrs Manson?' she said quietly. 'Mrs Manson, I haven't
given you what you need. I've tried, but everything I've
done is only what anybody else could do. You need more

97

than that, every day you seem to need more. It isn't only that you're sick and unhappy. I'm not very old, Mrs Manson, but I've seen a lot of sick people, working in wards with the kind of people you never even passed on the street, never even dreamed of. And now, in the last few days, I'm beginning to see a resemblance between them and you. That's awful, Mrs Manson, but I have to say it. You and I are friends, we both know that, and friends tell each other the truth. You're more than sick and unhappy. All day and night you live with your eyes on death, watching, waiting for – the nod. That's not right. You don't have to die. There's no medical reason for it. No reason at all unless you want to, and if that's the case, then I can't stop you. If you want to get well, you can. You're better than you were – they're not kidding when they tell you that. And you know me, I wouldn't kid you ever, not if they paid me for it. Not you, I wouldn't. You're my friend. Mrs Manson, I want you to stop looking like that. I won't let you die if you'll help me.'

Mrs Manson's eyes closed for an instant, and her breast rose and fell as if she were climbing.

'That's better,' Milly said. 'And it's all right to cry. You'd been crying when I came in, but I didn't want to say anything before Emma. Golly, Mrs Manson, I wish I knew someone who was an old friend of yours, like someone you went to school with. Someone who's your own kind. A person like that might be able to help me. A person like that could tell me what your mind is like and how you used to act when things went wrong. I've got a feeling you always act the right way, no matter what. And that scares me. It means that whatever is wrong is terribly wrong, and acting right and thinking straight can't change it.'

MISS SILLS, Miss Sills, don't let anyone hear you say that. Not to-day, not to-night. To-morrow you'll be safe, but not to-day or to-night. Don't talk to anyone until to-morrow. To-morrow you'll be interviewed, that's when you must talk. To-morrow, to-morrow morning ... Miss Sills, Miss Sills, there was a woman in the park. I know she could help us both, I know it in my heart. But she didn't speak, I watched and she didn't speak, and you walked by.

'I told you it was all right to cry,' Milly said. 'Take a look at me, it's getting to be like the common cold. There now, I'm getting fresh again and that's all right, too. No more sad talk until to-morrow. What do you want first, jelly or soup? Soup? Oke.'

Emma came in with a lamp, looking like a child who has made a beautiful thing out of something nobody wanted.

Milly crowed. 'Bring that thing around here, Emma. I want Mrs Manson to see it. Glory be, and they sent the other one to the White Elephant Sale! If ever I saw a white elephant in the beaded flesh –'

'It's my own property,' Emma said indignantly. 'I've had it for years, and I take good care of it. I like beads.'

'Where did you get it?'

'At the White – never you mind. It gives me a nice, soft light, easy on the eyes. How are we coming on?'

'Fine.'

'You going out again this evening? Doctor Babcock said you could. He said you should take things easy.'

'What's behind the unselfish build-up?'

'Well, I thought if you were going to be in, I might slip out for a while myself. My sister's daughter just had her first – only five pounds for all her trouble. Still and all, I thought I'd like to hear my sister brag.'

'Go ahead. I don't want to go out again. And five pounds is okay, so let her brag.'

'You, and not even married yet. You never did tell me where you went this morning and what you did.'

'I didn't do anything, just walked. Bounced a ball with a cute kid. Oh, sure, and I got picked up, too.'

'If you did, then you invited it.'

'Not me, not this one. This was a woman, and she said she knew – now, now, Mrs Manson, please.'

'Maybe that spoon's too full. It looks too full to me.'

'Don't rile me, Emma. She picked me up at the bus stop. She said she knew you, Emma. She asked how you were.'

MISS SILLS! Emma! Emma, listen. This is what I prayed for. Listen, Emma, it's Miss Byrd, I know it's Miss Byrd. Emma, ask questions, ask –

Emma said, 'I know everybody in this town, and everybody knows me and how I am.' She smoothed her apron and looked at the clock. 'I promised Hattie – What was the woman like?'

'Ordinary, except for her face. Too much make-up.'

'Don't know her.'

'Green coat and hat.'

'I know seven, eight women with green coats and hats. All my friends know how I am. You might as well give up that jelly, Miss Sills. Can't you see she don't want it? I'll give it to Hattie. Well, I promised Hattie I'd take the front door and the phone while she has a rest. If you want me, ring. I'll come back later, anyway.' Emma took the lunch tray when she left.

Milly tucked in the edges of the steamer rug and moved her chair beside Mrs Manson's. Mrs Manson closed her eyes again; it was the same as closing a door. There was nothing to do about that.

Behind Milly, the door to the hall was open and the house was as quiet as the room. The roses on the table were dropping their petals; they weren't lasting. Not the way they should. Only one day old, and they were dying.

The chair was low. From where she sat she could see the yellow trees against the sky. Now and then a leaf fell, drifting slowly as if it knew the first, lone journey downward from the sun led to the end.

It was silly to shiver in a warm room. The fire was ready for lighting if she wanted it. All she had to do was walk across the room. But it was too much trouble, too much effort. I'm tired, she thought, and why shouldn't I be? Maybe

I can sleep. At least I can try. Her head dropped forward, and she sighed.

They sat side by side with closed eyes, but only one of them slept. The clock ticked on, the minutes passed, but only one of them counted.

IT was after four when Doctor Babcock came in. Milly woke and saw him standing before her. She got to her feet, stumbling, only half-awake. 'Doctor Babcock, I'm sorry! But Mrs Manson seemed to be resting, and I –'

He waved her apologies aside. 'A charming picture, Miss Sills, charming; and no harm done, no harm at all.' His hand took one of Mrs Manson's. 'Any change? I'm afraid we're in a state of depression.'

She stood behind Mrs Manson's chair and nodded. He was a fool to talk like that where she could hear.

He went on: 'But that's to be expected – yes, we expected that. And Emma says there's an aversion to food.'

'I wouldn't call it that. I think she does very well, considering. Doctor Babcock, if it's warm to-morrow, can I wheel her out on the porch?'

He thought it over. 'Not yet, Miss Sills. This lovely room, the sanctuary of four walls – I think we'll be happier here. The outdoors is sometimes – frightening.'

Since when? Milly answered silently. Put them out in the sun and air as soon as they can sit up, that's the way I heard it. 'Yes, Doctor Babcock,' she said.

Doctor Babcock left Mrs Manson and made a slow tour of the room, examining everything small enough to handle. Even Emma's work-basket was looked into. Milly adjusted the rug again and whispered to Mrs Manson. 'The way he's looking at things, you'd think he was going to put us up at auction.'

Doctor Babcock made another turn around the room and came to a stop behind Mrs Manson's chair. 'Miss Sills,' he said, 'I'm distressed. About you. I'm not happy about you, not at all happy. You're beginning to show the strain. Now,

101

I want you to understand that this is no reflexion on your capabilities, but I truly believe you need assistance, or even better than that, a little rest.'

'No, I don't,' Milly said. 'I mean, thank you, but I'm not tired and we don't want another nurse. Mrs Manson and I get along fine, we're used to each other, we can practically talk. You don't want anybody else, do you, Mrs Manson? See, she says no. That look means no. She says you're very kind, Doctor Babcock, but Miss Sills is my one and only dream girl and she's all I need.' A fine line to give the boss, she mourned; every word a step home to mother, and sitting by the phone all day waiting for a call to take care of more tonsils. 'But whatever you say, Doctor Babcock. I only mean –'

He smiled broadly. 'No explanations, my dear, I understand. We'll wait and see how things develop. Now, about Emma. I've suggested to Emma that she sleep in her own bed to-night. I don't want Mrs Manson relying too much on Emma. Someone unconnected with the past, a stranger like yourself, a – dream girl, did you say? Ah, yes, a dream girl is what we need!' His laughter filled the room.

No tonsils to-day, she decided. 'Any instructions, Doctor Babcock?'

'No. Everything as usual.'

When he left, she returned to her chair beside Mrs Manson. She studied the pale face and closed her eyes until Emma came. It was four-thirty then.

Emma lighted the fire, and they both sat before it. Mrs Manson had shown no interest in the fire; she'd looked at it once and closed her eyes again.

'We'll leave her where she is,' Milly said softly to Emma. 'It's the only privacy she has, sitting off by herself like that. It's all right for a little while.'

Emma held her hands to the blaze. 'I've got the blues,' she whispered. 'I can't get Robbie out of my mind. He's been walking behind me all day.'

'Is to-day anything special?' Her own voice was low.

'No, just a Sunday. He was always around all day Sunday, running up- and downstairs, slamming doors. Hattie says she heard him last night.'

'Hattie's crazy. You said so yourself.'

'I know I did. And so she is. But –'.

Milly looked over at the chair. 'Are you awake, Mrs Manson?' She turned back to Emma. 'No, this time she's really asleep. She never tries to fool me, she knows she can't. We can talk if we're careful, you know ... Robbie. I don't know much about Robbie. George keeps changing the subject, and the papers were careful not to say more than they had to.'

'They always do that when it's money and banks and prominent people. But she paid up, every cent. There's no reason you shouldn't know about it. Nobody lost a penny through us. We paid.'

She could hardly bring herself to believe it even now, Emma said. 'Robbie was spoiled, we know that. But why would he steal a lot of money that he didn't need or even spend? Nobody could ever prove that he spent a penny more than his regular income. Why would he steal money, then, and where did it go? Not so much as a nickel ever showed up.'

What's more, she said, they'd never been able to find a single person who'd ever seen him in the wrong kind of company. No gambling, no horse racing, no bad women. There was no sense to it, none at all, and as for what he did afterwards –

EMMA described what she knew of Robbie's last day. 'He came home while I was at the stores,' she said. 'I'd have spotted something wrong if I'd been home and seen him. But I was at the stores, and Hattie had the kitchen door shut and didn't hear him come in. And when I came back, I started to work right away. I was busy phoning for the extra things Miss Nora wanted for a special dinner. She was counting on Mr Brucie to come. I was planning a wonderful dinner, like she wanted, and then they told me.'

Her tremulous whisper led Milly step by step. They stared into the fire as Emma filled the hall with running feet, crouched before the attic door, and emptied the dusty tool chest on the floor. They heard the doorbell ring above the sound of tools.

'Mrs Perry was calling,' Emma said, 'and the man with the pheasant, because Hattie was afraid to open the back door. That pheasant was in the icebox for over a week – we had to give it away ... He'd written her a little note. It was in his typewriter. He said, "I never was any good, but you wouldn't believe it." No love or nothing. She saw it before we did – we couldn't help that. We were trying to – you know, you – you have to cut the rope ... I gave that boy the first bath he ever had.'

Milly's hands went out to Emma. 'Don't talk any more,' she whispered. 'That's enough. I know how you feel.'

'You know? In a million years you wouldn't know. And it wasn't enough that I saw him as I did. I had to be the one to find her, too. Lying at my feet, the same as dead, and Mr Ralph and Mr Brucie out of their minds. She'd be dead this minute if it hadn't been that Doctor Babcock had come to call ... I don't know what we've done, it's like a punishment.'

'Hush.'

The coal crackled, the firelight was on their faces. They drew together, the bent black figure and the straight white one. On the other side of the room a shaft of setting sun came in at the window and found the chair.

HATTIE came in at five-fifteen with her plate of meat, an uncooked lamb chop and a slice of turkey breast. Her mouth was set in an obstinate line. She had clearly been told to keep it shut, and just as clearly she was going to make somebody suffer.

'That's a poor-looking chop,' Emma said. She took the plate and crossed to the chair. 'Open your eyes, Miss Nora, time to wake up. Hattie's here with your dinner meat, and if you want my advice, you'll take the turkey. The lamb that gave that chop could ill afford to spare it.'

Mrs Manson looked at the plate. For the first time, she seemed unwilling to play their little game.

'Serve them both, Hattie,' Milly said. 'Two dinner trays, one for me, too. We'll decide which we want then. It's all right, isn't it, if I eat up here to-night?'

'No reason why you can't,' Emma said. She bustled to the door. 'Come along, chatterbox. I'll bring up that sherry, too, Miss Sills. A nip of sherry, a nice fire – Hattie!'

The sun was low in the sky; long shadows came into the room. Milly moved aimlessly from window to porch door, from door to bed to fireplace. Once she returned to the bed, for no reason that she knew. She smoothed the covers as if she were removing the outline of a body, not preparing to receive one.

The room slowly filled with dusk, but she ignored the lamps. She sat by the fire, wondering if the radio would bother Mrs Manson if she played it softly. There was a radio within reach of her hand; she stretched out her hand, but let it fall almost at once. Nothing she could think of was worth doing ... I used to like the autumn, she thought, but this year it's different. It used to be full of – I don't know, promise or something – but this time I feel old, and I'm not old. To-night I'm so old that I can't look forward. I can't think of anything I want, and I've always wanted something. Now that I don't want anything, what's the use?

She looked at the still figure, shrouded in dusk. Sleep, she said to herself, sleep, Mrs Manson. You think too much when you're awake, I know. Those attic stairs – Emma says they're dreadful. How could she do it? ...

Miss Sills, Miss Sills, go home, Miss Sills. It's growing dark. Your mother has a house; go there. All day I've seen the night getting ready. The things that could have held it back – Hattie, the lamp, Miss Byrd – are gone. Go home, Miss Sills. Miss Sills, so young and so wise, leaning forward to look into my face, telling me how frightful life can be. Little Miss Sills, my friend, go home. You don't know what comes and goes in this house . . .

One by one the others drifted in, Mr Manson, Bruce Cory, George. There were no highballs this time; they seemed to know that talk and laughter were out of place this time. This time.

Milly offered chairs, but they were declined. Someone turned the radio on, and the soft, invoking voices of a Negro choir filled the dusky room. *Abide with me: fast falls the eventide.* The voices and the dark together were insupportable.

'Turn that off,' Milly heard herself say. 'I don't like it.' She was startled by the sound of her voice. It cracked like a whip. 'It's gloomy,' she said defensively. Some tactless fool, she thought. If I knew which one, I'd give him what for.

The music stopped. George walked around the room, turning on lights. Bruce Cory said, 'I'm sorry, Miss Sills.'

Why did I do that? she wondered. *Miss Sills, this is no reflexion on your capabilities, but you're beginning to show the strain.*

Mr Manson said: 'I'm afraid we came at a bad time. Is anything wrong?'

'No, Mr Manson. I guess we're tired, that's all. It's been a tiring day.'

'We'll go. Babcock was here, wasn't he?'

'Yes, he was. But he didn't say anything in particular. He stayed only a little while.'

'Cory and I went into town for an hour or so. I wish I'd – well, we'll get along and let you rest. Anything you want, Miss Sills? You don't make many demands. I wish you did.'

'No, sir, I don't want anything.'

They left, Manson and Cory, but George stayed.

'Come out on the porch,' George whispered. 'You can, can't you? I want to talk.'

THE garden ,was dark; across the autumn grass, patched with fallen leaves, the Perrys' lights gleamed through the trees. Mr Perry was working on his side of the hedge, a stooped, black figure in the stream of yellow lamplight, curiously alone. 'His flowers,' George said vaguely. 'Come along this way.' He led her to the far end of the porch. She knew Hattie's room was directly beneath them.

'I've got the wind up,' George said.

'Same old wind you're always talking about? I didn't come out here for that.'

'Milly, listen. I'm not kidding. There wasn't any wind last night. That lamp didn't blow over; it couldn't. It was knocked over, by you or Emma or somebody else. And I don't mean Mrs Manson, either. Do you think Emma did it?'

'No. She'd tell everybody right away and start paying off, week by week. And it wasn't me. You make me feel funny, and I was bad enough before.'

'Listen. I prowled around here at the crack of dawn, also before I came in just now. I was looking for prints. I wasn't sure that what I saw last night was a dog. It ran on all fours, but it was too big. If it was a cat burglar making a fancy getaway, then we ought to tell the cops. And if it was a dog, we ought to tell them just the same. A dog that walks into second-floor bedrooms and knocks over fifteen-pound lamps ought to be tied up – or shot.'

Milly rested her arms on the railing and looked down into the dark tangle of ivy. There was a light in Hattie's window. The ivy was broken; she could see the loose, limp rope of leaves and stem.

'I know that poem, too,' she said slowly. 'I can even quote a different line.'

'You're catching on,' he said. 'But let me. I do it prettier. "Are you a beast of field and tree, or just a stronger child than me?"'

They drew together; his hand was on her shoulder, her face was close to his.

'George,' she whispered, 'where were you at ten-thirty last night?'

'Bed. Why?'

'I called you up from home, but nobody answered.'

'I heard the phone, but I didn't do anything about it ... I've got you close, Milly. Don't shiver.'

'Who's shivering? You haven't said anything about finding prints.'

'I found some, all right. Of shoes, men's shoes. Manson and Cory were out there this morning with Babcock. Their prints are all over the place now.'

'But you didn't see anything the first time – I mean, at the crack of dawn? You didn't, George, did you?'

HE was a long time answering. His hand left her shoulder and pressed her cheek. 'I'm going down to the barracks and talk to Ferd Pross. There was something funny going on around here last night. Ferdie will know what to do.'

'George, you did see something! What was it?'

'Something stood in the flower bed under Hattie's window, either before or after climbing the ivy. The same thing that got into Mrs Manson's room. It was frightened off – my guess is the lamp – and I don't know where it went. But at one time during the night it stood in soft, wet earth, ran along the porch, swung over the railing, and tore the ivy. That's one of the things I'm going to tell Pross.'

'What – what's the other?'

'It left the wrong kind of tracks. Wrong for an animal, wrong for a man. They were spaced as an animal's would be, four nice clear prints, front and back. And big. Maybe I ought to laugh, but I don't feel like it. Because they weren't feet, and they weren't paws. They were hands.'

She heard herself say, 'Hands?'

'Yeah.' He went on, softly. 'So: "Are you beast of field and tree, or just a stronger child than me?" If that's some guy's idea of a practical joke, Ferdie and I can act funny, too. Of course they aren't there now; they got stepped on this morning. Ferdie may try to tell me I'm crazy, but I'm not.'

'George, what did they look like? Were they – like a starfish?'

He said, 'How did you know that?'

She quoted Hattie. 'But she said only *one*.'

'That can be all right, that can still make sense. It could have been reaching down to get a grip or a foothold. When she yelled, it swung back to the porch, out of sight. Then when she left, it dropped to the flower bed and vanished. Don't ask me where or how. One set of prints was all I could find. Maybe it floated.'

'I'm not afraid,' she said.

'No reason to be. A dirty trick by some heel whose mind didn't grow as fast as his body. Just keep the door locked. I'm pretty sure that was a one-night stand.' He kissed her briefly. 'This is no time for prolonging pleasure. I've got to get down to see Ferdie. Maybe somebody else saw the thing and reported it. Maybe Ferdie will hang around here tonight.' He kissed her again. 'Maybe I'll drop in myself.'

He had reached his side of the hedge when a sudden recollection made him stop and look back at the house he had just left. *You need two pairs of hands around here.* Who said that? When? Hattie? No, Emma. This morning. Emma. That was right, but it wasn't enough. It was older than that, it went farther back. Two pairs of hands. Now, what does that –

His mother was in the living room, knitting. 'Well?' she asked.

'No dinner for me,' he said. 'I've got to see a man about a dog.'

'Knowing you, dear,' she said thoughtfully, 'I suspect that's vulgar.'

It was six-thirty when Emma brought two dinners on a large tray. Emma and Hattie had surpassed themselves, but Mrs Manson wouldn't eat. Milly cajoled, begged, and threatened, but Mrs Manson refused to open her mouth.

109

Even the sherry, which she ordinarily liked, brought no response. When they saw it was useless, they put her to bed. She fought that, too, if it could be called fighting. The mutiny was in her eyes. It was the same look Milly had seen the night before when she'd refused the hot milk and the sleeping pills.

'You run along, Emma,' Milly said. 'Maybe she'll change her mind when she sees me eating.'

After several half-hearted offers to stay, Emma agreed to go. 'If you want anything, ring for Hattie; but don't expect any conversation – she's still not talking. And she knows my sister's telephone number, in case, which I hope not.'

Milly ate her dinner with elaborate and false enjoyment, and drank a glass of sherry. Mrs Manson watched without expression. When the tray had been placed in the hall and the fire built up, there was nothing else to do. Emma's lamp shed a dim light on the bed and the inevitable steamer rug. The porch door was closed, and so was the door to the hall. The room was too hot, but Mrs Manson liked it that way; at least, they thought she did. They thought, they thought, they thought. Would there ever come a time when anyone knew what she wanted?

Milly went to the window seat and huddled on the cushions like a child, with her arms around her knees. The lights across the park looked far away.

EMMA has gone, and Miss Sills is asleep. Curled like a kitten, her head in her arms. How long will it be before she wakes? How long before Emma comes home? One hour? Two?

Emma. Does it mean anything that Emma is out? Each time, Emma was out. Each time the house was empty except for Hattie, in the kitchen with the door closed. Except for Hattie and me and –

Why does my body ache? Perhaps because it is fighting or because I'm thinking of the last time it was alive.

Why did I go up there the last time? If I hadn't gone, I'd

110

be living to-morrow. I'd be walking to-morrow, riding, driving, going to the theatre. My heart would be empty, but I'd be living, and perhaps in time someone else would have learned what I learned. In time to do something. Someone else, even a curious stranger; it couldn't have stayed hidden forever.

Why did I go up there? You know why. You went because you always turned the knob; every time you passed, you turned the knob slowly and quietly, knowing the door would be locked, but turning the knob because you had to. And that time the door opened.

And you told yourself you were alone in the house!

It's all right, it's all right. This is preparation of a kind, too.

Climb again . . .

THE knob turned soundlessly, and the door swung open. She stood at the foot of the winding stairs, looking up, listening to the soft footfalls above. Someone else had found the un-locked door.

Hattie? No, Hattie was in the kitchen or in her own room. Emma? Emma had gone to market; she'd seen her less than ten minutes ago, haggling over fish. Ralph? Brucie? Brucie had promised to come out. No, too early for them. They were in town, at the bank.

Someone who knew their daily plans and schedules had broken in. She was supposed to be at the Civic League meeting, but the pity in the other women's faces had driven her home.

She started up the stairs, shaking with fury, not fear. Robbie's attic, his own place, his last place on earth. She moved without sound, hugging the wall, hesitating only once, asking herself what she would do or say when she reached the top. She told herself she ought to call the police. I ought to call the police but I don't want – I don't want the story in the papers. They'll reprint the pictures, they'll –

Why don't I go to my room first and see if he's taken anything? If he has, I'll tell him he can keep it. I won't prosecute. I'll reason with him. I'll tell him to go, go quickly. I'll explain how we feel about the attic.

But if he has my jewellery, why did he go to the attic?

Hattie. It must be Hattie, looking for extra blankets. It has to be Hattie.

Then she heard the laughter, low, almost bubbling, happy, victorious, and familiar. She covered her mouth with her hand and crept forward.

At the top of the stairs she crouched behind the partition. There was sun on the floor again. Robbie's old toy trunk, filled with broken treasures, had been brought from its corner, and it was open. Herself unseen, she watched the hands as they lifted the packages one after the other, lovingly. There was no look of surprised discovery on the face. It was the face of one who had returned to gloat.

She stood erect. 'Thief,' she said quietly.

The answering voice was as quiet as hers. 'This is unfortunate.'

Neither moved. They looked at each other over the open trunk. A golden bar of sunlight slanted through the western window and fell between them, a metaphoric pale that placed the other one beyond the limit of civilized mercy and protection.

When she could force herself to look down again, she saw that the money in the trunk was incredibly green. The building blocks were drab and dull beside it, the once-bright trains and trucks, the painted wagons, and the battered wooden animals were ghosts. The money was real.

She said: 'I misjudged you. I didn't know you had the mind for a thing like this. I thought you were reliable and capable. I even thought that you lacked imagination. I didn't know you could plan and execute a thing like this. Did you do it alone, or did someone help you? I can't understand how you did it alone.'

'No imagination? Yes, everyone thinks that. Dull and

pompous. Yes, I did it alone. I've always been underestimated.'

'Why did you do it?'

'Because I like money, and I don't like rich women who inherit theirs. Because my own efforts never got me quite enough of my own. I thought a secret nest egg would be very pleasant, doubly pleasant when I found I could arrange it with complete safety to myself. I still think so.'

She told herself to wake up. She spoke aloud, but didn't know it. 'Why don't you wake up?' she said. 'Why doesn't somebody wake me up?' She looked from the face to the trunk again. There were splashes of brilliant yellow among the clean greens and faded blues and reds.

SHE said, 'He made those – for Christmas, I think. He made them for a joke, like a stocking toy. They were supposed to be funny. You think they're funny now, don't you? I don't. I –' She put her hands to her head. 'I'm the dull one,' she said, 'but then, I never had to be anything else. I never had to worry about anything, or work to live. There was always someone to take care of me and do my thinking for me. But now I want to think for myself.'

'Don't.'

'But I want to know how you did it. I used to hear people talk about the way we managed the bank. They used to laugh and say it looked wide open, that the Board of Directors and even the watchmen thought they could go anywhere and carry off anything – until they tried.'

'It wasn't difficult. I'm capable and reliable. You said so yourself.'

'You are also – You killed him.'

'I did.'

'Why? Wasn't there anyone else you could use?'

'There may have been. I didn't look very far. He was there; he was made to order. That's how it started. Then he had the effrontery to spot me, *me*, the last person in the world they'd have thought of! So I had no choice. He had

Cory blood – the inquisitive, shrewd, banker blood. He'd taken me in completely. I didn't know he could even add. Fortunately, he couldn't hide his feelings, and I saw the end in time. So I did a little talking in the right places.'

'That's what was wrong with him at lunch. He wouldn't tell me then.' She could have been standing before a counter of merchandise, accepting and rejecting. One finger lay along her cheek. I will not scream, she thought, I will not scream, not yet, not for days and days. I will not scream now.

'That's why he came home early,' she went on. 'To tell me the truth. He had been openly accused, and he knew –'

'Don't burden yourself with details. They don't matter.'

She thought that over. They don't matter. The details don't matter. Why don't they? I know, I know why. Because I won't have any use for them. I'm to kill myself like Robbie; disgrace and shame will make me follow my son. Mrs Ralph Manson, of Larchville, whose son – 'You don't know me,' she said.

'No?' The low laugh bubbled up again.

She pretended not to hear it. She took a step backward – a small, unnoticeable step. 'Tell me one thing more,' she said. 'Didn't he – defend himself?'

'Oh, yes. That surprised me. I'd always thought of him as a spoiled brat, without stamina. But he was no coward.'

'Thank you. You see, some of the details do matter, after all. And the open window? I wonder now why you didn't close it. Wasn't that – dangerous for you? He might have cried out.'

'You're underestimating me again. I opened the window afterwards. You know, you're taking this almost too well, so I'll give you the rest of it. Bodies stay warm. In a place like this, he would have been warm for an uncomfortable length of time – for me. So I opened the window to – you understand?'

'Yes, I understand. Haven't we all been stupid? You came in the front door?'

'Certainly. You've also been stupid about that, leaving it unlocked to save your servants. I made sure, of course, that there was no one in sight.'

'It's only unlocked in the afternoons,' she explained carefully. 'I always thought that afternoons, in a place like this – I'm glad it was you who typed that note.'

'I thought it was a good note, under the circumstances. I'm not much of a writer. He could have done a better job himself, but we didn't have time for that. And speaking of time, there isn't much of it left now.'

'No,' she agreed. 'Emma will be coming soon. I saw her in the market, and she knows I'm home.'

There was tolerant curiosity behind the soft voice. It was more human than the fresh peal of bubbling laughter. 'I'm glad she knows you're in the house alone. But how, exactly, do you think that can help you?'

'Help me? Emma? I don't need Emma for what I'm going to do. I'd rather she didn't come. This is all mine.'

'Wait. What do you think you're going to do?'

'I'm going to the police. I'm going to hang you higher than that rafter.'

The air churned. Between her and the sun a human, black projectile rose and catapulted forward. She closed her eyes when it struck.

When her body rolled against the wall at the turn in the stairs, like a log jammed in midstream, she knew she hadn't long to wait. Strong hands turned her over and sent her the rest of the way. A thin scream came from nowhere.

SHE opened her eyes to nothing. After an endless search she saw a lighted lamp in another world. Soon it became familiar; it was her lamp, her room. Her bed.

Living, she told herself. Why?

Voices drifted through the gloom, like recorded voices on an old record. Thin, without bodies. But when she tried, she could see bodies standing in a row at the foot of the bed.

'At my feet, on the floor, at my feet. I came in, and I

heard a sound, and I ran. I knew where it came from. Unconscious, I said to myself, or dead.'

'Lucky for us that we happened to be –'

'She should be dead. She should be dead. I don't understand it.'

'I've been afraid –'

She was lying at the foot of the attic stairs again, hearing Emma scream in the lower hall, looking up at the figure bending above her, reading the eyes that looked down into hers, watching the quick retreat to the top of the stairs so that whoever came – Forget that now, she told herself. Listen to the voices, listen to every word. One of them will tell you what you must do.

'Shock and paralysis. I beg your pardon, you were saying?'

'She telephoned, she told me to come as soon as I could. I thought she was ill. When I came, she asked me to wait while she went upstairs. After a while I followed. I was uneasy, disturbed –'

Who said that? Who? Listen.

'And the attic door was open. Obviously she'd found the key. She was preparing to take her life in the same way. I struggled with her, she was demoralized, raving. She fell. When I heard Emma and the rest of you, I –'

Liar, her mind said. Thief, murderer, liar. You flung me like a sack of meal, but the others came and you couldn't finish. Wait until I tell them that.

'At my feet. Lying there on the floor. Oh, Mr Ralph, Mr Brucie!'

'Quiet, please. Miss Byrd?'

'Yes, Doctor Babcock?'

'A close watch for the next five hours. At the slightest change, call me.'

'All of us will watch. Babcock, it was Providence that you were –'

'Providence? Not at all. The dear lady had been on my mind, I felt that a little call – But I must warn you, this will be a hopeless vigil. She will live from hour to hour – perhaps.'

'Will she talk to us before she –'

'There will be no speech, no movement.'

'No speech?'

'We'll get another opinion, we must. You understand how we –'

'Naturally another opinion. I was about to suggest it myself. Mr Cory, not too close, please. When and if consciousness returns, she must see no one – strange.'

'Strange? I? But she'll expect to see me, she knows I'm here, she asked me –'

The voices faded, the figures melted away.

So that's the story! ... She could feel the bitter laughter in her throat. Wait until I tell mine. Not now, in a little while. When I'm alone with someone who will believe me.

Why aren't my bones broken? Perhaps because I didn't fight. Why don't I feel pain? They said I should be dead. Yes, I should be. I would be if the others hadn't come when they did. I will be, unless I tell. They said no speech, no movement. That's not true, either. I can talk and I can move. I –

It's true.

THE light from Emma's lamp was a dim pool on the bed table. In it were the bottle with its four pills, the vacuum jug, a clean, folded handkerchief, the jar of talcum powder. Undisturbed, still in the same positions ... No one has come while I've been away, she thought. It's too early. Is the door locked?

Miss Sills' cap is white against the dark window. Her stiff white skirt, her square-toed white shoes. Small, square white shoes like a summer Sunday morning. Sunday School. Clean them with the shoe white; you can do that yourself. Now wipe the edges of the soles – no, no, not with the sponge, there's too much whitener on the sponge. Use the cloth, that's what it's for. Stand them on the window sill,

117

one behind the other; they'll dry in no time at all . . . I never spoiled a child in my life.

The door to the hall is closed, the door to the porch is closed. Miss Sills and I are closed in. The doors may be locked from the outside, we may be locked in. The door to the hall –

The door to the hall opened.

She watched the white figure emerge from the shadows on silent feet. It had no face. It was covered with white. Two arms reached down to her.

Miss Sills.

Miss Sills said: 'Hey! Sorry. But what's the big idea? Why the pussyfoot, why the disguise?'

He said something through the mask.

'Sure,' Miss Sills said. 'That's sensible. I didn't mean to yell at you, but I was only half-awake. I don't mind admitting you scared the – you scared me for a minute. I thought we had Martians.' Miss Sills went to the bed and turned back the covers. She bent down. 'He frightened you, too, didn't he? That's a shame. I should have stayed over here. But it's all right, it's all right now. You really did frighten her. Take that thing off, and come out in the open for a second. See, Mrs Manson? It's only Breitman.'

Only Breitman.

'He has a cold, Mrs Manson. He caught it last night when he left here. He's only taking precautions for your sake. He'd just as soon scare you to death, but he draws the line at a sneeze.'

Only Breitman.

HE talked to Miss Sills while he worked; she couldn't hear all he said. Miss Sills stood at the foot of the bed, her cap awry, her stiff skirt wrinkled where her arms had hugged her knees. She watched him and laughed with him. He wore a wrist watch. It said eight-thirty.

When he was through, he went to the fire, and Miss Sills gave him a glass of sherry from the bottle that was still on

118

the mantel. He slipped the mask under his chin when he drank. Miss Sills laughed again. She knew Breitman; they had worked together before. Breitman was the best masseur in the business, she said.

When Breitman left, Miss Sills followed him to the door. She sounded as if she were sorry to see him go. Miss Sills was lonely, she liked people, she liked life around her.

After Breitman left, Milly went to the end of the hall and looked down the main stairs. The lower hall was dim. She crossed to the head of the kitchen stairs. No light or sound there, either. Hattie had gone to bed. Or slipped out. Usually on Sunday nights Hattie moaned hymns with the door open.

They're getting mighty casual around here, she complained to herself. You'd think they'd tell me when they go out; you'd think they'd ask me if I wanted anything. She returned to the room, rinsed Breitman's glass, and looked for something to do.

There was nothing in Emma's work-basket, no mending or darning, only the tatting, which looked so effortless in Emma's hands and turned into a cat's cradle in her own. Even Mrs Manson was all right. Mrs Manson was taking one of her little jaunts into another world; she was seeing something far away, far away and high up. Maybe a mountain-top; she'd travelled a lot in Europe. Well, whatever it was, there was peace in her eyes. Peace, or something just as good. There was no fright.

She went to the porch door and rested her forehead on the cool glass. No lights over at the Perrys'. Half-past nine. They couldn't be in bed. Gone to the movies. Mr Perry liked movies. George said he liked the tough ones. George said that sometimes when the old man thought he was alone with his flower beds, he flattened his back against the hedge and made like standing against a warehouse wall. Fist in pocket, making like a gun. A lookout. The old man was cute, poor thing. Acting tough all by himself and saying, 'Yes, dear,' the rest of the time.

119

Maybe George was with Ferd Pross, the State Trooper. He and Ferdie had gone to Boys' High together. He could tell Ferdie anything and know he wouldn't be laughed at. George was up in the air, all right; he couldn't fool her. And so am I, she admitted, and I'm not fooling myself either . . . Why doesn't George talk to Manson and Cory? Maybe he has; maybe they're doing something about it this minute.

She was suddenly relieved. That's why they're out, she decided. That's why they didn't say anything to me. They didn't want me to know they were worried.

She went to the fire. It was burning itself out. Nearly ten o'clock. It would last until bedtime, until Emma came back.

She sat in Emma's chair, and planned a spring offensive against George's mother, the whole thing to take place in the Sills' back garden, which was big enough and had two dogwood trees. Let's say the first of May, and no veil – I'd feel like a fool in a veil after this cap. No bouquet; let the dogwood handle that. A white prayer-book and high heels, even if I do fall flat on my face. And Mrs Manson in her chair, under the trees. With me. Beside me. Mrs Manson will give me away. Oh, oh, trouble ahead. Now listen, Mother, I've been everything a daughter should be. I hate to talk like this, but you force me. And I do think that, on this day of all days, you might at least try to understand and have a little consideration. Who am I fighting with? What's all the rush? . . . Maybe I'd better tell George.

SHE was almost sorry when Emma came in at eleven. By that time everything had been settled but the chicken salad : veal or no veal.

'Hello,' she said. 'Have a nice time?'

Emma said: 'It's blowing up outside, a nasty, damp fog all over. I hate it. But you're cosy enough in here. You sound real happy, too.'

'That's the voice that breathed o'er Eden.'

'Whatever that may be. Well, I just looked in for a minute. I'm going down to my bed. I'm beginning to feel

120

my neuralgia. That fog. Will you be going down yourself, for hot milk?'

'I don't know.' They looked at the bed. Mrs Manson's eyes were closed. 'If she stays like that, I won't. Better not to start anything.'

'Well, if you do, don't lock up. They're still out. No trouble?'

'Breitman got himself up in a mask, because he's playing with the idea of influenza. Frightened her at first, the big gorilla. But aside from that, everything's fine.'

'George come over?'

'No. Haven't seen a soul.'

'Well –' Emma opened her handbag. 'Your mother sent you a note.' She drew out an envelope and gave it to Milly.

'My mother? But how did she know –'

'Sent it to my sister's. My sister's boy took it. Don't be so fussy. You've got it, haven't you? Well, I'm for bed. Be sure you ring if you want me.' Emma was still talking when she closed the door.

Milly stared at the envelope in her hand. The address was lettered in pencil: 'THE NURSE. KINDNESS OF EMMA. PERSONAL.' She took it to the lamp by the bed. Mrs Manson was watching her.

'So you're curious, too?' Milly said. 'You don't miss much, do you?' She held the envelope before Mrs Manson's eyes. 'That's not from my mother, and you know it as well as I do. Emma's out of her mind. Well, there's only one way to find out. May I sit on the edge of your bed, madam, if I promise not to bounce?... Well, what do you know, there's something in it. Feels like money, like a quarter or something.' She opened the envelope and took out a key. 'Look!' she marvelled. She held the key to the light before she put it on the bed table. 'Wait till I read it, then I'll tell you.'

The note also was in pencil. Across the top of the first page a sentence in capital letters said: 'DO NOT READ THIS UNLESS YOU ARE ALONE.' She winked at Mrs Manson. 'This is going to be good. Wait.'

She read to herself, frowning, engrossed; she forgot Mrs Manson. She was alone with the crackling paper in her hand.

'I WON'T sign my name to this, but you will know who I am. I said you had a good heart. There is something wrong in that house. I know it. It isn't a thing I can take to the police, because I haven't proof of anything, only what you might call my convictions. Too many things have happened in that house, and those people are not the kind that have such things happen to them. Also, I cannot go to the police because they would have to take my name, and then if they investigated and found nothing, my name would leak out, and that would be the end of me. Even now I think somebody watches my apartment at night.

'Once I knew a lady who feared for her life, I don't mean myself, and people thought she was imagining things, even the police thought she was. But it was proved that she wasn't. Your patient has the same look this other lady had. That's what I mean.

'It is not my wish to get you into trouble or danger, but I've no one else to tell this to. I couldn't find out your name, because I was afraid my interest would become known to the wrong person. I'm sure who the wrong person is.

'This key fits the attic door. It was made from an impression. Never mind how I came by it. Now, this is why I'm sending it to you. Every time there is no one in the house but the patient and her nurse, and maybe the cook in the kitchen, somebody walks in the attic. I've heard them, because my hearing is very acute, even when they walked softly. Sometimes in daylight, sometimes at night. The patient has heard it, too. She knows what it is, but she can't tell you. That's when she has the same look as the other lady I told you about.'

Milly turned the page with a shaking hand. It was ridiculous, it was crazy. It could be true. She read on.

'I couldn't use the key myself. I never had a chance.

122

Never mind why I never had a chance – just let us say I came into possession too late. But if you know someone you are sure of, give the key to them. And tell them to be careful. Tell them to watch everybody, to trust nobody. But go to the attic.

'Maybe some day I will see you again. You didn't think much of me, I could see that; but I don't blame you. I've been half out of my mind and very nervous and not myself. But you'll understand that later.

'I remain, Your Friend.'

She folded the letter and put it in her pocket. 'Mrs Manson,' she said, turning slowly, 'do you mind if I – *Mrs Manson!*'

Mrs Manson didn't hear.

One of Mrs Manson's arms was uncovered. One hand was inching forward through space, the fingers opening and closing, taking handfuls of air, curling around the air, holding it, letting it go. The hand crept on until it reached the bed table and dropped. It struck the lid of the powder jar; the lid spun on the rim of the table and fell soundlessly to the carpet. The jar overturned.

'*Mrs Manson.*' Milly's voice was a whisper.

MRS MANSON'S hand covered the key. Her mouth twisted and stiffened and relaxed. Her eyes met Milly's. I can't talk, her eyes said, but this is the smile you've been waiting for. Her eyes blazed and talked.

'Don't,' Milly said. 'Don't try. Let me. Mrs Manson, do you know who sent that key? It's the other nurse, isn't it?'

It was.

'Do you know what she means? She says it's a key to the attic. I know it is – you've proved that. But do you know what she wants? She wants someone to go up there, she says you –'

There was no need for more. Mrs Manson's eyes blazed their verification.

'Shall I go? Shall I go now? There's no one home.'

Mrs Manson tried to say yes, but fear and pity struggled with frenzied hope; the fear and pity and hope were as clear as printed words, clearer than speech.

'There's no one home,' Milly whispered. 'This is a safe time. It's better for me to go myself, now. If we wait until I call George – Mrs Manson, we'll never sleep if I don't go now. If we wait, we might not have another chance ... But I don't know what I'm supposed to find, or see. I don't know what's there. I –'

Mrs Manson's eyes led her to the hand covering the key. Covering the key, lying in the spilled powder.

'Mrs Manson! Can you move one finger, can you write in that powder? Can you write even one word?'

Their breathing was like thunder in their ears. One finger. One. It moved, slowly. One word, one. The word grew, letter by letter. It was 'trunk'.

Milly took the key. There was a flashlight in the table drawer. She took that, too. She went to the hall door and looked at the outside lock.

'There's no key here. I can't lock you in, but I promise to hurry.' She returned to the table and blotted out the word with her palm. She was smiling. 'I'm going to put that hand back where it used to be, too,' she said. 'Just for fun. And here's my watch, right here, under the light. So you can see how quick I am, so you won't stew.'

She didn't look back.

The house was still silent. The attic key was stiff in the lock, like all new keys, but the door opened without sound. She closed it behind her and climbed the stairs, following the flashlight beam.

Trunk. Trunk. What trunk? Attics are full of trunks. How will I know which one? What will I find? How will I know it's what I want, even when I see it?

She came to the top and turned her light around the room. There was a table holding a covered typewriter. There was a leather sofa with broken springs. There were cardboard boxes, hampers, discarded luggage, a dusty rocking-horse, three bicycles that told how fast a boy grows. There was a round-topped trunk with something painted on the side in large, red, crooked letters. Robbie . . .

The hand crept from under the rug and found its laborious way to the table again . . . Don't let anything happen, she prayed. I am on my knees. Heaven, I am on my knees. Don't make her pay for me . . . The fingers curled once more. Her face was dark with pain. It would be a longer word this time.

SHE looked down into the trunk. The flashlight beam dug into the corners, picked out the colours and shapes. She saw bundles of paper money, play money for keeping store. Building blocks, trucks and trains, battered little wagons. When she took one of the bundles in her hand, she saw the money was real. She knew what it was then.

She looked from the money to the four gloves. Big cotton gloves, covered with thick bright-yellow paint, with bleeding hearts and arrows on the cuffs. She made herself take one of them in her hand. The paint was soiled and cracking, but it had been fresh and new not too long ago. At one time they had been what her mother called furnace gloves. You bought them at the five-and-ten and wore them when you did things like carrying out ashes. They were padded on the inside; two of them had room enough for hands. They were stiff and firm; the fingers were spread, but you could wear them on your hands. The other two were fastened to shoes, pulled over a pair of old shoes, filled out as if they held hands, but fastened to a pair of shoes. Like starfish.

She crept down the stairs in the dark. When she reached the hall, she heard the front door open and close softly.

Mrs Manson watched her as she closed the room door behind her and moved a chair against the knob. Her hands left wet prints on the chair, but she didn't know that.

When she went to the bed, she said: 'Don't worry about that chair. It's just a – well, it's a precaution.'

125

Mrs Manson's eyes questioned her steadily.

'Yes,' she answered, 'I saw it. Mrs Manson, I can't use the phone. The one in here is disconnected – you know that, don't you? It was done before I came. And the others aren't safe. I won't kid you, Mrs Manson, but don't be frightened. I'll think of something. I saw everything you wanted me to see. You saw it, too, didn't you? You went up there and saw it, too, and that was when you fell. I know you didn't fall, not like they say. But don't be frightened. It'll be all right. I'll think of something.'

She left the bed and went to the porch door. She didn't open it. She dropped the latch into its slot, a flimsy latch that wouldn't keep a child out. A latch that a hairpin –

The Perry cottage was still dark. They could have come home while I was up there. It doesn't mean they're still out, just because it's dark. They could be home, in bed.

The street lamp shed a faint light along the edge of the garden, contesting the fog. There were no figures out there; no one moved along the hedges or under the trees. If Ferd Pross had agreed to watch, he hadn't come. But it wasn't much after twelve. He might think it was too early. Too early for a prowler, that's what Ferd might think.

She went back to the bed and sat down. 'I have an idea,' she whispered. 'I'm going to turn out the lamp. You won't mind the dark, will you, if I hold your hand? This is what I mean about the dark. Last night George saw the lamp go out. Maybe he'll see it now, maybe he's watching. If he is, then maybe –'

She reached for the lamp and saw the new word cut into the film of powder. It gleamed up from the polished wood. *Murderer*.

'I know,' she said. 'Mrs Manson, *can you write the name?*'

HIS father and mother had gone to bed; their doors were closed. George closed his own quietly and went to the window without turning on the light. Mrs Manson's lamp was still on. So far, okay. He went to his desk and groped for a cigarette. He smoked it, sitting on the edge of his bed.

Ferd Pross hadn't laughed. He'd looked as if he'd wanted to, but not for long. They'd gone for coffee at the dog wagon, and Ferdie had listened and asked questions. He'd promised to watch the house. He'd said, 'I'll do it myself, part of the time anyway, and I'll put a man on when I leave.' He'd added, 'If anybody but you gave me a line like this, he'd get the alcohol routine.'

George had answered, 'Not me, Ferd, not this time.'

'What do you think it is, George?'

'I don't think. Not now. Not yet.'

He went to the window again, raised it and leaned out. There was no one in sight. The fog was low on the ground; the lights along the distant street were dim; but he knew he would see Ferdie when he came.

'Give me half an hour or so,' Ferdie had said. 'I'll be around, front or back.'

Maybe I'm sticking my neck out, George told himself. Maybe they gave all his things away. Maybe she wanted all his stuff out of the house, and they gave it to some playground outfit. Maybe some kid just happened to get hold of –

No. Not a kid, not a trick like that. An overgrown lout? ... Stop thinking with your mind closed, walk right into forbidden territory and see if you can find a way out. Now, then, suppose Robbie –

No, no, no. Wait a minute. Don't say no so quick; you've been saying no all day. To yourself. Who are you fooling? Say yes for a change, and see what you get. Suppose Robbie –

He shivered and went back for another cigarette. The first one had burned down to his fingers. When he returned to the window, the street was still empty. The garden was empty. Mrs Manson's light –

Mrs Manson's light went out while he watched. Out and on, out and on. Out.

By that time he almost knew the answer was yes.

He dialled the barracks on the hall phone. Pross? Pross, a calm voice said, had left. Had he said where he was going? No, he hadn't said anything, but he'd made a couple of phone calls and sounded excited.

He thought of the phone calls he would like to make, but he was afraid to use the time. But when he saw his mother standing in her doorway, he gambled with a handful of minutes.

'Listen,' he said, 'this is more important than it sounds. That afternoon when Robbie came home early, did you see anyone else? Anyone, *anyone*.'

'Did you wake me up for that? Is that all you can say, after staying out all night and leaving me alone with your father?'

'Please, Mother,' he begged. 'Quick, did you? Anyone, anyone at all.'

She told him, divided between curiosity and anger. 'And what's wrong with that? George, you're hurting my shoulder!'

'Sorry, sorry. Was it before or after Robbie came home?'

'A few minutes after. But why *I* should be half-killed because – *George*!'

'Stay where you are,' he said. 'I mean it.'

THE fire was nearly dead. It was the only light; it was almost no light at all. Milly reached for Mrs Manson's hand in the dark. 'The business with the lamp was a signal,' she lied softly. 'I told George that if I ever wanted him, for anything, I'd do that. I wish I could see your face, Mrs Manson. I'd like to look you straight in the eye and tell you what I think of you. I'll tell you to-morrow.'

She knew they both were listening. If the porch door opens, I'll hear it, she thought. She'll hear it, too. If the hall door opens, there'll be a light along the edge, from the hall. Unless the light –

'Do you want to hear about my wedding?' she whispered.

'It's going to be in the spring, and you're in it. If you want to be. I've got it all planned in my head. We'll be the talk of the town. We'll –'

She heard the latch on the porch door. Something was pressing against the glass, a dark shape.

'Mrs Manson?' She put her lips to Mrs Manson's ear. 'I'm going to carry you. I'm going to carry you to the window seat. You'll be all right there. George will be here in a minute. No, Mrs Manson, don't cry now. No, Mrs Manson, not now.'

The porch door opened. She stood with her back to the window seat, making a wall of her body and outstretched arms.

It swayed across the floor on all fours; she knew how it would look if the lights were on. She could hear the soft padding of the four starfish hands as they moved over the thick carpet to the bed.

She tried to kill it with her mind. She willed it to die. Beast, beast, I'm killing you.

She heard the bed shake as the body lunged.

Light burst. From the ceiling, from the hall, from the porch, it flooded the room. She was blind with light. Sound crashed and reverberated. George's voice rose above a hideous clamour. George shouted, 'Ferd!' From somewhere, Ferd answered.

She began to see, then. The grappling, rolling figures on the floor began to take shape. She reached behind her and covered Mrs Manson's eyes with her hand.

George, Ferd Pross, battered and bleeding. Babcock? Babcock and young Doctor Pleydell. How did Pleydell –

They rose and fell in a heaving mass, separating, coming together, a swollen sea of speechless men, young and old, with one objective.

Cory. Cory had a gun. George flung himself at Cory's arm. Milly gathered her strength and screamed. 'No, George, no!'

The end of time had been reached when they dragged the

129

black shape from the floor. They took away its masquerading cape. They made it stand alone and let its face be seen.

She turned and hid her own face on Mrs Manson's breast.

She knew it was George who came to stand beside them. She knew his hand with the high-school class ring that he wore because she always made fun of it. There was powder on his hand; he saw it when she did, and he rubbed it off on his coat. She knew then that Ralph Manson's name and story were no longer written on the table.

Someone said her name softly. A new voice. 'Miss Sills.' She raised her head, afraid to believe. Then she cried as she had never cried before ...

SHE was in her chair, in the window, waiting for morning. Morning was almost there. They had left her again, but not all of them. The ones she loved had stayed.

They said it was all right to think now. They said she could think all she wanted to. They said she could sit up all day and night, for ever, if she wanted to. And think herself black in the face because she was a good, good – Stop that, she told herself. You don't have to do that any more.

That young man, the State Trooper. He was the one who'd called Babcock and Pleydell. He'd told them what he thought and asked them if his theory were possible. Medically possible, emotionally. And Babcock said he had been thinking the same way, had almost come to the same conclusion ... The Trooper said he didn't want a car for Christmas. Would a big red bow look too silly on a windshield? Ask Bruce. No, not now, later.

Bruce. Bruce had thought like Babcock. The first night had been too full of individual anachronisms. Miss Sills had been too hard to wake; not compatible with Miss Sills. The other one – she still couldn't say his name, even to herself – the other one had given too much attention to the porch door, the lamp, the litter of twigs and leaves on the floor. Bruce, trying desperately to prove himself wrong, had mapped out and timed a possible route, using the porch

130

door as entrance and exit, starting from the rose room, allowing for the flight to the garden, the return. Then, at dinner, he'd told them all he was going into town. But he'd gone to Robbie's room and waited in the dark ... Robbie's room was the right place. Thank you, Bruce.

'Want anything?' Bruce asked now.

She shook her head. Her eyes told him she had everything. It was still hard to talk.

George Perry came in from the porch with Milly Sills. His look of confusion was not improved by his temporarily vertical hair. He bent over her chair. 'What does a woman mean,' he asked, 'when she says "no veal"?'

THE HOUSE

Part One

TO-NIGHT I walked in the garden again, and the dog followed me. He follows me whenever I leave the house. Sometimes I tell myself I have escaped him; I wait until he is asleep on his rug in the kitchen passage, or until he has disappeared on what I think is an expedition of his own. But in a little while I hear that measured tread behind me, padding through the thick, wet leaves or over the old stone walks. He never looks at me, never touches me, but he takes his place at my side as if he belonged there. I try to understand it, but there is no explanation. Not yet. Father was the only creature in his world. I say, 'Go home, Tray.' He feigns deafness and waits for me to move on.

To-night I could see his black coat shining in the half-dark. We stood at the hedge between our grounds and the Barnabys', away from the stream of light that poured from their windows, and watched the Barnabys' party. I had been invited, but Mother said the invitation was in bad taste, because they know too well that I am in mourning.

They were dancing in the living room, and in spite of the cold and the damp, the windows were raised. I could see the blazing logs in the fireplace, the long, white-covered table holding drinks and sandwiches. Mike was playing the piano. Even their grandmother was there, dancing and singing with the others. Once Mike turned his head, and I thought he saw me, and drew back; but no one came to close the windows and draw the shades. I saw young Joe, in his first dinner coat, his fair hair plastered to his head. He danced by the windows as if he were showing himself to an unseen audience. Both Mike and Joe know that I walk at night, but

135

they never ask me why. I'm glad they don't, because I wouldn't know how to answer.

I looked at their big white house, lighted from top to bottom, and turned to look at my own. There were no lights showing in mine. Tench, Mrs Tench, and Anna were in their cottage down by the old stable, and Mother was asleep, or pretending to be, for my sake. We say good night to each other at nine o'clock, and neither knows what the other does until morning.

My house is dark, inside and out, and the rough grey stone looks wet. The four turrets rise above the trees, and their windows are covered with grime. The trees are thick and too many; we have no flowers, because no sun comes though the interlacing branches. Now, in November, the oaks are bare, but the evergreens still hide the pale autumn sun. I say that I walked in the garden. It is not a garden but a wilderness of trees, carpeted with moss and leaves. I call it my house, but it isn't mine yet. In December, on my twenty-first birthday, it will be legally mine. Father left it to me. I think Mother was deeply hurt when he told her what he had done, but I have a plan that will make her happy again. If Mike and I –

No, I mustn't think about Mike. Not now. But I will give Mother the house if I ever marry anyone. She loves it.

In these past weeks she has talked of Father constantly, remembering and reliving, helping me to understand their lives. They were devoted to each other and needed no one else. I was sent to school in Canada when I was six, and my long holidays were spent with hospitable schoolmates. So, although I went home for birthdays and Christmas, I saw too little of my parents. Mother thinks of that now and tells the story of their life together, giving it colour and movement, so that I feel as if I had been there.

She was poor when she was young, 'a very respectable poverty' she says; she laughs when she describes her clothes and the tragedy of a stocking run. She lived with her older cousins in the cottage they still own. Father was a catch; she cannot understand how she got him. Her little face is full of wonder as she tells me. 'The women who threw themselves at that man's head!' She takes me through their courtship day by day, spicing it with flowers, sweetening it with ribboned boxes of candy. 'I wore the ribbons in my hair, and he never guessed.' And then she comes to the day when they were driving and she saw the house and fell in love with it.

The turrets rose above the trees as they do now. There were no other houses near by; the Barnabys came later. Except for the Barnabys, there has been no change. The house stood then, as it does to-day, in the centre of a small forest, surrounded by fields.

'There is my castle,' Mother said that day.

My father smiled. 'I've heard it called other things.'

'Château, perhaps,' Mother guessed. 'Or manor house.'

'Prison,' Father said. 'And madhouse.' He flicked his whip at the gloomy turrets. 'I almost agree, too. It lacks only bars.'

Mother tells me: 'I cried then; I was heartbroken. That beautiful house, empty, desolate. To say such things about it!' She cried throughout the drive and refused to be comforted.

He told her she was a child in spite of her grown-up airs. 'What would you do with such a place if you had it?' he asked.

'Live in it and be happy the rest of my life.'

In three months they were married, and for a year they travelled abroad. I know the clothes she wore, the deep garnets, the turquoise blues, the gloves and the hats that matched. I know how she looked; she was twenty-five then, and she is sixty-five now, as he would be, but she is not the kind of woman who ages. When they returned, he told her they would live in a hotel until he could find a suitable house. Her trunks of clothes, her hat and shoe boxes, filled the hotel suite.

One evening when she was waiting for him at the hotel, he

137

sent a closed carriage and a note asking her to meet him at the house of a friend. It was a dark night, and the drive seemed endless; the coachman refused to raise the blinds. She tells me now that she was frightened, but I think she knew her destination before she started. She exaggerates, but the picture she paints is a romantic one. The wind howled, the trees moaned, the carriage rocked from side to side. She was young, she wore silk, she was loved.

The destination was the house, of course. Father was on the stone veranda, the cousins beside him, the servants in the background. She spent most of the night running from room to room – there are twenty – and opening closets and wardrobes and chests. It was perfect, it was complete, and nothing has been changed.

As time went on, the top floor was closed; there was too much work for a staff of three, and they wanted no more than that. The same silver is still polished each Friday, and the same china stands in orderly rows behind glass doors. The cousins, Carrie, Jane, and Bess, still come to tea two afternoons a week. They were here this afternoon, and Tench took their wraps and served their tea as he has always done. Nothing is changed except that I am home, my father is dead, and my thoughts will not let me sleep.

It was wet in the garden to-night, the fallen leaves were wet. Tray stood near me at the hedge, listening to the music and watching the Barnabys. I grew up with the Barnabys as much as I grew up with anyone. Until I was six, we played together, and Mike said I was as good as another boy would have been. After that, I saw them only at Christmas. But the holidays were too short, and they made other friends, too. There were parties every night, people drove out from town; but I was lost, out of place. My clothes were not right, even when I was eighteen, I was dressed like a child. Mother called it 'keeping me young.' Old Mrs Barnaby, Mike's grandmother, would pin up my hair and help me braid it again before I went home, but there was nothing she could do about the clothes I wore. I used to see her watching me thoughtfully.

Then, last spring, when I went home to stay, things changed; Mike said it was like the old days again. I was Issy once more, not Isobel. Every morning I waited for the shout across the hedge. 'Issy!' The days were never long enough. Mike and I rode and walked and played tennis and contrived to avoid Joe. Joe is seventeen and in love with growing up. Mike is twenty-two.

Mike said I was learning to be human. He said I was almost presentable. Father gave me an allowance for my clothes, and Mrs Barnaby told me what to buy. Mother was preoccupied and thoughtful, and Father spent much time in his own room. I told myself they were old and tired, and I forgot them. I'm paying for that now.

'There's nothing wrong with your face,' Mike said, 'but your manners are too good. They're practically deportment. And do you have to talk like an Empire Builder?'

'What do you want me to do?'

'Be your age. Comb your hair in public, scream across tables, swipe food from other people's plates. Occasionally.'

That was how we were when I went home in April.

Last week when they planned their party, it was old Mrs Barnaby who invited me. She talked to Mother on the phone. She told Mother I was young and required pleasure, and mourning was unsuitable and old-fashioned. I know what she said, because their cook met Anna in the village and repeated the conversation. She'd listened in on the kitchen extension. Mother told Mrs Barnaby that I was not well, but she didn't tell me that.

IT is late, and I am sitting in the dark. I do not want a light. Someone else may walk at night as I do, and look at my windows and wonder. My bed is ready for me, and after a while I shall lie down. Then Mrs Tench or Anna will find the print of my head on the pillow and be satisfied. I am cleaning house in my mind.

This afternoon I had tea with Mother and the cousins. They talked about Father, and after I had my tea, they sent me from the room. Cousin Jane said I had a long face and that four grieving old women were bad company.

'Go up to your pretty room,' Cousin Jane said, 'and read a nice book. Or work at your embroidery. Surely they taught you that at the convent.'

They thought I went to my room, but I sat on the stairs and listened. I always listen to everyone, even to Tench and Mrs Tench and Anna. I didn't see Father after he died, no one did, but I know too little about the people who found him and what they said. So when Mother and the cousins sent me from the room, I went no farther than the stairs. The cousins have carrying voices, and the hall and stairs are stone sounding boards.

I heard Cousin Jane say, 'Will she sell the house?'

She meant me. Mother must have shrugged her answer, because I heard no reply.

But Cousin Jane's voice was high and sharp. 'Find out,' Cousin Jane said. 'Find out at once, and don't let her do it. You belong here; it suits you, it always has. Not one woman in a thousand could carry off a house like this. Close as many rooms as you like, but don't let her sell it. She doesn't need the money, lucky girl. Marsh must have been out of his mind. What am I saying? Of course he was out of his mind. He proved it.'

'This is my home,' Mother said quietly. 'It will be my last on earth, and until my time comes –'

The teacups rattled, and silver rang against china. The cousins are always hungry, and Mother gives them a knife-and-fork tea.

'What are you going to do with his clothes?' Cousin Bess asked. 'If I were you, I'd sell them. Everyone does that now, even the nicest people; you'd be surprised if you knew. And you're not the type to brood over moth balls. Sell everything he owned; don't give a stitch away, not even to Tench. I've never seen so many clothes, all in perfect condition, too. I made it my business to investigate. Don't look at me like that, dear, I was only trying to help. And it isn't as if he'd had a disease.'

I held my breath. No disease? Out of his mind? That was what I wanted to hear.

No disease? He kept to his room for days at a time. I saw him; I went to his bedroom door and looked in whenever the door was open. He was too white. I would say, 'Father, are you sick?' And he always said, 'No. Go away like a good girl.' There was never a doctor, there was no medicine, and he ate almost nothing. Some days he'd get up and dress and drive into town. I'd see him leave his room and walk slowly through the hall and down the stairs, his hand on the balustrade; but if he saw one of us, the servants or Mother or me, he'd walk briskly and speak crisply, perhaps even whistle in his tuneless way. He wouldn't let Tench drive him. Tench would bring the car to the door, and the dog would be waiting on the front seat. Father was a good driver; that's one of the things I think of now.

Out of his mind? Is that the answer?

SITTING on the stairs this afternoon, I heard the cousins talk about his generosity; they sounded like crows on a fence, counting hills of corn. They are in their early seventies, and to-day they looked like crows, too. Tall and thin, perched on red damask chairs, their veils and scarves streaming to the floor like long black feathers, their long teeth snapping over words and food. They wear mourning, too, because he gave them an allowance and remembered them in his will. We are all in mourning; even Mrs Tench and Anna have put away their bright lilac prints, and Anna wears a black uniform when she serves.

I heard Cousin Carrie say, 'I see you still have that dog.'

Mother said, 'He was devoted to the animal.'

'Well, the animal wasn't devoted to him,' Cousin Carrie said. I could imagine her tossing her head. The cousins talk with their heads and hands.

Mother said, 'Why do you say that? They were inseparable.'

Cousin Carrie's teeth clicked. 'My dear Maude, are you blind? If you used your eyes, you might see a few things. That dog is sleek and well content, and it isn't natural. He was a gaunt and nasty brute when his master was alive, and now he smirks.'

'Carrie?'

'He was so devoted to Marsh that he's glad he's dead. He's laughing about it.'

'Bessy, Janie, make her stop. She's hurting me.' Mother was close to tears.

I heard the mediatory rustles and gasps, but Cousin Carrie went on.

'I'd get rid of him if I were you,' she said. 'I'd lose him or arrange for an accident. I can't bear to look at the brute. Have you noticed how he follows the girl around?'

'Isobel?'

'I see you haven't. Well, I have. Jane and Bess know what I mean; we've spoken of it. When Marsh Ford was alive, that dog didn't look at Isobel, or at any of us, except to snarl. And now he grins.'

'Carrie, I beg you –'

'Use your eyes and listen to me. When Marsh went driving alone, didn't that dog always sit beside him? Always?'

'Yes.' Mother's voice was soft and faraway, and I knew what she was thinking and seeing: Father and Tray walking in the garden together, Father and Tray beside the library fire, Father and Tray on the front seat of the car, Tray asleep on the rug at the foot of Father's bed ... On the front seat of the car.

Mother began to cry. 'Oh, please, Carrie, don't!'

'Very well,' Cousin Carrie said. 'But you know what I mean. I think that dog had something to do with it, that's all. I wouldn't put it past him, but I'll say no more. Except that he's probably behind the *portières* this minute, listening to every word we're saying.'

142

I heard the rustles and gasps again, and someone pushed back a chair. If Cousin Carrie went to the door, she found no one. I went upstairs and locked myself in my room until Anna came to tell me they were leaving.

MOTHER was quiet at dinner to-night, but she smiled at me when our eyes met. There was no conversation until we had our coffee in the library. Then –

'You're too pale, Isobel. Did you love your father so much?'

I couldn't answer.

'An only child is sometimes a tragedy.' she went on. 'For the parents as well as the child, and it's no one's fault. Your father and I were already growing old when you came; we could hardly believe it. I nearly died when you were born, Isobel. Did I ever tell you that?'

'Yes, Mother.'

'Don't look so woebegone, dear, as if you were wondering if you ought to apologize. I'm afraid the cousins are right – you're developing a long face.'

'I'm all right, Mother.'

'Of course you are. We all have our ups and downs. Isobel, this past month hasn't been easy for me, either, and the weeks that led to it should have prepared me, but they didn't. I know how you feel; in my own way I share that feeling. But if we cling together, help each other –'

'Yes, Mother.'

'You understand why I declined the Barnabys' invitation, don't you?'

'Because I am in mourning.'

'Yes. Old Mrs Barnaby is thoughtless and inclined to overrate pleasure. Death imposes conventions on old and young alike, Isobel; it locks doors, and a tragic death double-locks. But you must be patient. Your beloved Mike – dreadful name, but I know such corruptions are fashionable now – your beloved Mike will not run away. In another year, perhaps, or even in six months – But there, it's bad luck to plan ahead. Your poor father is a sad example. He planned for your coming of age, and now –'

'It's all right, Mother. But I'd rather not talk about it.'

She refused her usual game of solitaire, and we sat by the fire until she went to bed. I walked with her as far as her door. She kissed my cheek and told me to sleep well, and I know she watched until I turned into the hall that leads to my room.

When I left the house much later, no one knew it. I was careful. But Tray knew. He had vanished after dinner; he was not on his rug when I went through the kitchen passage. But wherever he was, he knew, and followed me.

To-night I stayed in the garden until the Barnabys' lights went out. I watched the guests leaving. I knew all by name, and some of them I had met. I saw old Mrs Barnaby – they call her Lucy – emptying ashtrays, collecting bottles and glasses, ruffling Joe's plastered hair and laughing at him. I saw Mike and wanted to call him. I willed him to think of me. I begged him silently to know I was there.

Tray watched, too, standing motionless beside me. He reminded me of something I thought I'd forgotten. Once, when I was a child, I saw a stone dog crouched at the foot of a grave. There was a story about it. A living dog had grieved for his master and died there, and the stone dog was a memorial. I thought then that it was ugly and pretentious. I wonder what Tray would do if I took him to Father's grave. I wonder if he goes there alone when he disappears for hours each day. I have never seen him leave the grounds or return, but Anna says he does. He frightens Anna. One night she locked him in the kitchen because it was warmer than the passage, and in the morning he was still locked in, but his coat was damp and his paws were full of sand and gravel. He had not been with me that night – I had stayed in my room. But I told her I had let him out.

IT was raining before we left the garden. Tray followed me to my room and waited until I had locked my door.

There is no sound in this part of the house. There are two things I can do until morning. I can sit here by the window and watch the rain, or I can lie in bed and remember. I can sit by the window and remember, too.

Mother wants me to take Father's room, adjoining hers. After all the years of close companionship she cannot bear to have it empty. I've seen her standing at the door, looking at the canopied bed with its deep-blue cover, the deep-blue chairs, and the dark, glowing furniture. They keep it in perfect order, as if he were there, never forgetting the bowl of red carnations that he loved. This morning there were red carnations on the mantel above the fireplace, and they doubled themselves in the mirror. The room is exactly as he left it; it has an air of waiting, its emptiness seems temporary ... His face was whiter than the linen on his pillowcase.

No disease? Why do they say that? He was ill for months; he took months for his dying; he fought it secretly, as if it were disgraceful. There were good days and bad days. On the bad days, when he stayed in bed, I wanted to be with him, but he sent me away. I would stand in the doorway and speak to him. I never entered without permission. Tray was always there, defensive and protective.

Father would quiet Tray and smile at me. 'Run along,' he'd say. 'Amuse yourself. I'm an old man, and I'm resting.'

He was sixty-five, not old enough for death, and he wasn't resting. He was shrunken and drawn, and his mouth curled with pain. I know it was pain. He wouldn't eat. Mrs Tench made custards and broth and took them to him herself, but she was unlucky, too. Only once did he ever ask me for anything, and that was when he wanted milk. A full bottle. When I brought it, he took my hand, and Tray got up from the floor and put his front paws on the bed.

'What do you do with yourself all day?' Father asked me.

I told him I walked and read and saw the Barnabys.

He smiled stiffly. 'Do you like that? Is it sufficient? Does it keep you happy?'

'It's what I always do when I'm home, Father.'

He dropped my hand and rested his own on Tray's head. 'It seems little enough. I had other plans for you this year. I had enormous plans for the twenty-fourth of December. When a man has an only child and that child comes of age –'

'There is plenty of time, Father. Summer is still here.'

'So it is. We don't know each other very well, do we?'

I had no answer for that. I couldn't tell him that he was, or had been, no more than a well-dressed stranger, courteous when we met in the halls and on the stairs, considerate at the table, a counterpart of the fathers of girls at my school who invited me to their homes for holidays. Those fathers, too, asked if I were amused and happy, and they saw to it that I was well served.

HE seemed to know where my thoughts were, for he said, 'Do you want to go away again, Isobel?'

'No, Father. I'll stay with you. I want to.'

'Why?' His eyes flamed.

'I think we should live together now. Mother thinks so, too. I may be – I may be able to help you.'

'Help?' He laughed out loud, but his hand returned to mine instantly. 'My dear girl, that laugh was for myself, not you. So! Not quite twenty-one, and ready to help.' His eyes closed for an instant, and Tray whined. 'You are much on my mind these days,' he went on. 'I plan for you constantly; I am as watchful as Tray. I want you to know that and remember it. My style –' he smiled again – 'my style is unconventional, perhaps, but I can't help that. Not now.' There was nothing I could say. His hand gripped mine; it was hot and dry. 'Do you like this house, Isobel?'

'I've not spent much time here, Father. Sometimes I think I hardly know it.'

146

'That means you don't like it. But I hope you will stay on if anything should happen to me. Do you think you can promise? Will you stay for at least a year?' He made his voice casual, he could have been asking for the morning paper; but the gripping hand betrayed him. He could have been asking for his life.

'Father, let me send for a doctor!' Then, because my voice had suddenly become shrill, I tried to be casual, too. 'You worry Mother and all of us, and Mike Barnaby asks about you, and I don't know what to tell him.'

'Tell Mike Barnaby I'm old and tired and my skin is over-adequate for my poor bones. But I can still make my own decisions, thank you, and no doctor is one of them. I asked you about the house, Isobel. You weren't changing the subject, were you? I'm waiting for your promise.'

'Of course I'll stay.'

'Thank you, my dear. You may not know it – I'm not always certain of how much or how little you do know – but I used to visit this house when I was a child. When I bought it for your mother and myself, I found I could remember every inch of it, I could find my way blindfold. Well, perhaps not blindfold, but without thinking. That interested me. I'm giving the house to you on your birthday. I've told your mother. Can you see yourself as a house-holder?'

I could see myself living forever in the dark rooms.

He read my mind again. 'Only for a year, Isobel. Then you may do as you like. And don't misinterpret my use of the word "blindfold". There's nothing wrong with my eyes. Isn't this the cousins' day?'

'Yes, Father.'

'Then I trust you to paint a convincing picture of my condition. Say whatever you like, but keep them out of this room.'

He sent me away then. Tray followed me to the door and stood watching as I went down the hall. The door closed, and I heard the bolt plunge into its socket. That was beyond

147

even Tray. I knew then that Father had more strength than I thought.

That was in August.

THE cousins never saw Father when he was ill, but they talked about him and speculated. In late summer and early fall, when the afternoons were mild, they took their tea on the veranda. And they always asked about him. On those afternoons they dressed alike in long white linen suits, white canvas shoes, and small, high Panama hats. I can see them now, turning their large pale eyes from Mother to the laden tea table, from their chatelaine watches to the rented car that waited extravagantly under the *porte-cochère*.

'Maude, are we going to see dear Marsh to-day? He's well, isn't he?'

'Very well,' Mother would answer. 'And very busy. He's resting now and begs you to excuse him.'

'Busy! Marsh?' They would laugh then, Cousin Carrie leading the others. 'Marsh Ford never did a stroke of work in his born days, unless it was clipping coupons.'

Mother would smile gently. 'How unjust. He does a great deal that you and I know nothing about. Money doesn't take care of itself, dear Carrie; it needs coddling.'

'Is he coddling money when he goes off on those long drives? With a dog for company? Down back lanes and muddy roads, parking for hours in disreputable places? Saloons, squatters' shacks – don't tell me I don't know what I'm talking about! I've seen his car in the village, and my cleaning woman knows him by sight.'

'Marsh is democratic, dear Carrie. Come, your plate is empty. Another ice?'

'Yes, I will. They won't keep. Jane and Bess, another ice. Not pistachio, Bess, you know what it does to you. Cake, too, Bess. It will dry out otherwise. The pink kind. Fresh-strawberry filling, isn't it, Maude? The last of the season, I dare say. You know I didn't mean a thing about Marsh,

148

Maude. Give him our dear love, and tell him we hope to see him soon.'

Each time they came, they talked of the same thing: Father. They still do. When he was alive, they wanted to know how he spent his days; now that he is dead, they will not let him rest. Their large pale eyes still probe and devour; they think the same thoughts and use the same words. Only their clothing varies with the seasons.

I have never known the reason for the long drives; I have never known why he died as he did. He didn't have a disease. He was out of his mind. Get rid of that dog.

I must do something, talk to someone. Mike rarely comes to the house these days. Is it because I am in mourning? Or does he know more than I do? Is there anything to know?

This afternoon, when the cousins left, I walked with them to the car. They always send for me when they are ready to leave. They kiss me good-bye as if we would never see one another again. Mother says that is because they are starved for affection and like to pretend I am theirs.

'Do you miss your father, child? Of course you do, it's only natural; you'd be a very strange girl if you didn't. Still, after all, you didn't know him very well, did you?'

I watched the car move under the arching trees and turn into the distant road. Their cottage is five miles away, in the small village at the crossroads. Between us and the village there are fields and woods and the cemetery.

The house will soon be mine. I want to sell it now, but Mother will not even let me speak of that. She walks through the house at night. I hear her footsteps in the hall, but I never open my door. I am afraid I will see her climbing the stairs, moving along the hall in her long black dress, opening and closing the doors of rooms we never use, holding a candle in one hand and shading it with the other. I know she carries a candle, because I have seen the drops of tallow on the floor. I am afraid to see her face. I think she is remembering her first night here.

To-morrow I will go to Father's room and see what he has left behind him. There are wardrobes full of clothing, but one suit will be missing. There is a desk full of papers. Among these things I may find something that will tell me what was in his mind that morning a month ago when he left the house for the last time.

That morning I had been walking along the main road and was turning in at the gate when his car came down the drive. Only an hour before, he had returned his breakfast tray untouched and told Mother he was not to be disturbed. And there he was, hatless, driving like a man possessed, the dog on the seat beside him. I raised my arm as he went by, and I will never forget his sudden gesture of dismay.

If there are letters in his desk, and if I read them, what will I find? He never spoke of friends; if he had them, he kept them to himself. Did he have a special friend, one whose name was too dear for speech? The only names he used were those of his broker and lawyer, and the only guests we had were the cousins and the Barnabys. Perhaps when you are sixty-five, you have weeded and culled until only your first choice remains. Mother was his. I used to see his eyes meet hers with a look of acceptance that told me there was nothing in her heart and mind he did not know. I used to see her meet that look with a smile.

I did nothing that last day. Mother kept to her room, and the Barnabys drove to town for Joe's new dinner coat. The day dragged. I remember nothing of consequence. I knew that Mother would be strained and silent at dinner, and I dreaded it. She suffered on Father's bad days, and at lunch, which I ate alone, I knew what Anna meant when she said her back ached with the burdens other people were carrying. The day grew older, heavy with foreboding.

At seven that evening, when Father had not returned, Mother and I dined together, and later we both played solitaire in the small, circular room that overlooks the driveway. Mother sat facing the windows. She played her cards quietly; there was a decanter of port on the table at her side, and a box of Turkish cigarettes was within reach of her hand. She plays the same way now, quietly, and the setting is the same. The decanter of port is still brought in, the cigarettes are within reach, and she still faces the windows. But her dress is black instead of turquoise.

That night was clear and cold; Tench, putting fresh logs on the fire, was elaborately cheerful. He said it was a fine night for a drive or a brisk walk and declared his intention to try one or the other. I thought he was making tactful conversation, but he was making a prophecy. At ten o'clock one of his friends in the village called him on the phone, and he took his small car from the stable and drove off. We didn't know about the call until later, or that he stopped at the Barnabys' to pick up Mike. We saw him drive by the windows and thought nothing of it. Hadn't he said it was a fine night for a drive?

IT was Mrs Tench who gave the first alarm. At eleven o'clock she brought us a pot of coffee, unasked, and her hands shook as she set it on the table.

'We don't want that, Mrs Tench,' Mother said absently. 'Go to bed.' Then: 'What's wrong with your hands? Have you a chill?'

'Drink it,' Mrs Tench said. 'There's nothing wrong with me.'

Mother said, 'Ring for Anna, Isobel. Mrs Tench isn't well.'

That was when Mrs Tench told us. 'Don't ring for Anna,' she cried. 'Anna's no good at a time like this. She's all broken up, and I'm not much better. Heaven help me, I was told to tell you properly, and I don't know how! They think something has happened to poor Mr Ford.'

Mother poured a cup of coffee with a steady hand. 'Where is he?' she asked.

Mrs Tench averted her eyes. 'I don't rightly know. Tench got a phone call asking him to come to the old quarry on

151

the other side of the cemetery, and he went. Then a few minutes ago some man called me. I don't know who he was; he said he was talking for Mr Tench. He said Mr Ford was –'

'Dead?'

'That's what he said, Mrs Ford.'

'How?'

'How?' Mrs Tench bit her lips. 'Maybe they'd better tell you, Tench and Mr Mike and the rest. They'll be coming later.' She poured coffee for me. 'Drink this,' she said.

Mother left the room as if she were leaving a stage. She walked, with a majestic kind of lightness, straight to the hall and up the stairs. I didn't see her again for two days. I saw Mike that night, and Tench, and Father's lawyer. They came long after midnight, bringing the cousins, and told me what had happened. The lawyer talked to Mother in her room.

This is what they told me: Earlier in the evening a man from the village, checking his rabbit traps a quarter of a mile from the old quarry, saw what he thought was the reflected light of a bonfire. At first he ignored it. The village boys often build fires in the quarry at night. They roast potatoes and stolen chickens. But after a while he decided the fire was too large and too hot, and he walked over that way.

It was Father's car. It had turned over, and when the man reached it, there was nothing he could do. He ran to the village and phoned Tench. The licence plate lying some yards from the twisted smouldering mass had told him enough.

I've never known more than that. Mike said, later, there was nothing more to know. He and the lawyer and Tench made the final identification; there were shreds of clothing, a scrap of Harris tweed –

I asked them about Tray. Loyal, fanatic Tray. I had seen Tray beside him, his ears laid back, his mouth open, his body braced. They shrugged. Mike said, 'No dog.'

152

The coroner said suicide while of unsound mind, but I will never understand why Father chose such a difficult and painful way. I tried to tell myself it was an accident.

'Why don't they call it an accident?' I asked Mike. 'The car was overturned, the lane is narrow, he could have lost –'

'You know in your heart that it wasn't an accident, Issy. He knew every foot of that ground; he knew where the lane turned at the quarry and how far it was to the edge. There was no skid; his tyre marks were clear and clean. And the night was clear, too. Lots of stars; he could see even without car lights. Chin up. He knew what he was doing, and it must have been what he wanted.'

Unsound mind?

Anna found Tray the next day. Her cat had hidden a litter of kittens in a corner of the old stable, and Anna paid them regular visits. That morning she slipped out before breakfast, and no one knew she had gone. Mrs Tench was in the kitchen when Anna came back. She was crying. She said Tray was in the stable, chained to a post. He had a bowl of water and a half-eaten steak.

'He wasn't there last night when I took out the milk for the cat,' Anna screamed. 'He was dead then, burned up in that car!'

I went to the stable and untied Tray. I saw the bowl and the chain and the meat. The bowl and the chain had not come from the house; they were new and strange.

'Someone found him on the road and brought him home,' I told Anna. 'Someone who knew about our trouble and didn't want to disturb us. That was kind.'

Anna backed away. 'There's not a mark on him,' she whispered. 'He saved himself. The devil!'

EVERY night for a month I have locked my door and talked to myself until morning; I've told myself a story as wakeful children do. But my story is real.

Night has come again, and I am telling myself the story of the day I have just lived through. This time it has grown

153

beyond me; in twenty-four hours it has changed its mood and shape; it is more than mine; it is too much for me alone. But I have Mike now.

This morning I was wakened by a pounding on my door. I knew it wasn't Tench – he never comes to my room. And not Anna or Mother. Anna's fingers nibble at doors, and Mother is almost soundless in everything she does. I watched the knob turn uselessly and waited until I heard a voice. I always wait before opening doors until I hear a voice.

It was only Mrs Tench. 'Are you all right, Miss Isobel?' she called. 'Do you know it's after ten?'

I knew she wouldn't leave until I let her in, but I remembered to hide the muddy slippers I had worn in the garden. 'I'm sorry, Mrs Tench. I overslept.'

'Maybe you needed it,' she answered. She had brought me fruit and coffee; it was the first time she had ever done that. She closed my windows and smoothed my bed. Her eyes flicked about the room. 'You didn't need all that air, Miss Isobel. Night air's unhealthy. Did the dog sleep in here with you? I was just wondering.'

'He's never in here, Mrs Tench.'

'Maybe you fed him, then? I'm only asking.'

'I never do. What's wrong, Mrs Tench? Is he sick?'

'Sick? Not a bit of it. He was outside your door when I came upstairs, that's all. Looking like he wanted you to let him in, or feed him, or some such thing. Anna says he –' I saw the break in her speech before I heard it; it showed first in her eyes. It said she hadn't meant to speak of Anna and was angry with herself. She went on rapidly. 'I've got something nice to tell you. Mr Mike telephoned, he wants you to go for a drive, and your mother has no objection. I asked her. Eleven o'clock, he says. There's a sharp wind, so you'll need a heavy coat. A nice drive, you ought to enjoy that; it's like the old days coming back. It'll put some honest colour in your face, so you can stop pinching your cheeks before you come into a room.'

154

'WHAT were you going to say about Anna, Mrs Tench?'

'Anna? Oh, that. That's nothing. You know Anna. She carried on because the dog refused his breakfast. She's foolish about animals. One of these days I'm going to smack her. Now you drink what I brought, and I'll help you get dressed.'

That was something else she had never done. I must have looked surprised, for she said, 'I always favoured humans. Animals can do for themselves.'

She drew my bath and fussed about the room, using her handkerchief to rub non-existent dust from furniture and staring out of windows that could show her nothing she hadn't always seen. Ordinarily, Mrs Tench is calm, she is like Mother; but this morning she was noisy in a small, unordered way. I have never known her very well, although she has always lived here. Sometimes, when I was a child, I used to think I saw her face bending over me at night; but when she spoke to me in the morning, the face was not the same, and I told myself I had been dreaming. This morning, when she handed me my clothes and stooped and rose and helped me, I thought I saw that old, bending face again, and I wanted to touch it.

I said, 'Mrs Tench, did you ever take care of me before?'

'Did I – what are you talking about? Before what?'

'Before to-day. A long time ago. Did you ever bend over my bed at night?'

'Pure imagination. You always had too much.'

'Mrs Tench –' I didn't know how to say what I wanted to say – 'Mrs Tench, are you taking care of me now?'

'I do what I can, if that's what you mean, and there's no need to look at me like that. Taking care! Nobody takes care of anybody when they're grown up; grown-up people take care of themselves. Now, if you're ready to go down, I might as well go along with you. Wait a minute.' She made scolding sounds. 'Your hair's a living sight! You made a fine mess of your hair when you pulled that sweater on.'

Mrs Tench's hands smoothed my hair for me. That

almost furtive touch was like a twice-told tale when the first telling has been forgotten. It was as old as the bending face, as dim and warm, and it stirred the sleeping years in the bottom of my heart. I waited for the words that should have followed or preceded the smoothing hands. I couldn't remember the words, but I knew they had been foolish and kind. If she could help me to remember anything, anything –

'What are you mooning about?' she asked.

'I'm trying to remember something. You used to say something, I can't remember – yes, I can! Mrs Tench, what does "skin the rabbit" mean?'

'You're addled.' She picked up the breakfast tray and set it down again, almost angrily. 'Well, all right. It's nothing but nonsense, a kind of game you play with children when you help them with their clothes. It means this, and this is how it goes. Skin the rabbit!' She jerked the sweater over my head, wrong side out. 'That's what you say, and that's what you do. Black! I never cared for mourning, not even for myself.' She unfastened my skirt, black like the sweater, and hung both in my closet. When she returned, she had a yellow wool dress I had bought in September. 'You'll look all right in this,' she said. 'I can't wait for you. I've already lost too much time as it is.'

She was gone before I could answer, but I could follow her in my mind. Down the broad stairs, her dumpy little figure held erect, the breakfast tray firm in her hands. Mrs Tench never fumbles.

I SAW no one when I went down. My mother, I thought, is behind one of the windows, watching the driveway as she always does, and I will wave to the windows when I leave, even though I cannot see her. She will think I am opposing her wishes about mourning, but I am only trying to please Mrs Tench. When you are taking your life apart, looking for something, people like Mrs Tench are useful. Even a phrase is useful. To-morrow, even a phrase may help.

I waited on the veranda steps for Mike. The stone was cold and damp. The drive-way was a dark-green tunnel ending in a pale-blue arch. The sky beyond the open gates; the road. No one travelled on the road while I waited; the blue arch was empty until Mike came. His car is red, and he loves it; even the leather seats are red. When he turned into the drive, I ran to meet him, not forgetting the windows behind me. Before I reached the car, I heard the soft, familiar pad of following feet. I had been waiting for that, too.

'Ho,' Mike said. 'Send your pal back to wherever he hangs out, and get in.'

'I want him to come. Please, Mike.'

'What about my leather? Look at those ugly feet. Oh, all right, all right, but don't expect me to sit next to him.'

We drove into the road, with Tray beside me. That was my first victory. We went toward the village slowly and in silence. The woods lining the road cast shadows before us, thin shadows because the sun was thin. Tray was a stone dog, erect and motionless, his eyes closed.

'Why have you stayed away, Mike?' I asked carefully. 'Why haven't you called me before?'

'I've been giving you a chance to get straightened out,' he said. 'You've been fighting a cockeyed battle in your mind, and it seemed like a good idea to let you win it alone. That's the only kind of victory that sticks. And by the way, what's behind this hedge-prowling when you ought to be in bed?'

'Who saw me?'

'Lucy. Last night. And Joe says it's a regular thing. That's crazy, baby.'

That was the way I wanted him to talk. That was the kind of talk I needed. 'I live in a crazy sort of house,' I said. 'Even my father said it would make a good madhouse.'

'Your father –' The car jumped forward.

'Watch your driving, Mike. We don't want another accident.'

'I don't have them,' he said. 'Tell me where you want to

go. We'll go anywhere you say. We can even take that yellow dress to town for lunch.'

'The dress was Mrs Tench's idea,' I said.

'Taking orders from Mrs Tench now? I should live to see the day when you take orders from yourself. Where do you want to go?'

'Can we go to the squatters' settlement?' I thought his answer would never come.

'Why?'

'Because my father had friends there. I'd like to see the kind of friends he preferred to my mother and me. I want to know what my father was like.'

THE car slowed to a crawl. 'I can tell you. He was okay. I can tell you what he found at those shacks. Broken old men, disappointed old men. People he could help. He wasn't a cheque writer, he was a doer. If he saw a mess, he straightened it out himself. If he didn't like a thing, he fixed it, his own way. He was a medieval kind of guy, like the old Patrons. I sound like somebody who just read a book. Where to, baby?'

'The shacks, Mike.'

'Issy, that's no good. The shacks haven't anything to do with your father's death. That was his own idea. He's not the first man in the world who decided he had the right of exit. Got that one out of a book, too. Anyway, it was what he wanted, right or wrong, and you can't do anything about it.'

I said, 'I want to talk to someone who knew him. If you'll let me do that, Mike, I won't trouble you again. After today, I'll be satisfied.'

'Satisfied, for heaven's sake. What does that mean?'

'It means I'll let him rest.'

'Rest!'

'He didn't say good-bye to me. I think about that too much. He raised his hand when he drove by; he knew he wasn't coming back, but all he did was raise his hand. I

158

think about it; I see it, an unfinished gesture. Everything about him is unfinished, even though he's dead and buried.'

'Issy –'

'He must have counted his last days; he knew which one would be the last, and he chose to spend it with strangers. I want to see those strangers. If I can follow him through the last day, up to the end, then I won't think about him any more. I can get rid of him.'

After a pause, Mike said, ' "Rid" is a cockeyed word.'

'It's a haunting word.' I felt him turn to look at me, and I closed my eyes for safety. Like Tray. I sat like Tray. I was Tray. We were replicas of the old stone dog in the cemetery. I put my hand on Tray's head and let it rest there. It was the first time in my life I had ever touched him and he didn't flinch. I wondered if he could read my mind.

I heard Mike laugh, too easily. 'That's a sweet friendship between you and the dog, all of a sudden. Where'd I get the idea you hated him?'

I laughed easily, too, and opened my eyes. 'Hush. He reads and understands English. The cousins say so.'

We turned from the main road into a narrow lane.

'Where are we going, Mike?'

'Where do you think, crackpot? The shacks.'

THE lane went up, then down, between small, barren hills. I heard the wind follow. At the end we came to an open field, ringed with leafless trees. There was no grass, only sand and rubble; the colour had faded from the sky. The trees were supplicating dwarfs, raising bare and knotted arms to heaven. The world might look like that a thousand years after it was gone and forgotten. A band of swallows came from nowhere, swooped and cried, turned and fled.

'What is this place?' I asked.

'The one you wanted. Or almost. We get out here and walk a bit.'

'Walk where?'

'See that line of rocks? That's the edge of a small ravine.

159

The shacks are down there. How about me going on down there alone?'

'No. What time is it?'

'Eleven-thirty.'

'Only that?'

We walked to the rocks.

'Look,' Mike said. But I had already seen – Tray was leading the way. As we drew near, we saw a break between the rocks and a flight of rough-hewn steps leading down. Tray waited at the top of the steps, watching us. I knew I was right to come.

'Have you been here before, Mike?'

'No. Never had a reason before.'

There were perhaps a dozen shacks scattered along the ravine. Some of them were falling into ruin, some boarded up like houses whose tenants have gone away. Only one showed signs of habitation; its sagging door was propped open, and a wisp of smoke curled from a make-shift chimney. There was no filth, no litter; there was no sound but the wind, our footsteps on the stone, and Tray's padding feet.

An old man came to the door of the open shack. He stood in the shadow of his doorway, an old, old man, bent like the dwarf trees. The hand he raised to halt us was brown and thin like the twigs.

'Are we trespassing, sir?' Mike asked.

There was no answer. The brown hand reached for the door, to close it.

I spoke quickly. 'Please let me talk to you. I'm looking for someone who knew my father. His name was Ford. Did you know him?'

'No, I did not.'

'Do you know the dog?'

'I have seen the dog before. What do you want?'

'My father is dead. I know he used to come here; he had a friend or friends here. I only want to talk to someone who knew him.'

'There is no one here now. Since a month or more they

are all gone.' He spoke in a soft, tired voice, with a trace of accent.

'Who were they?'

'Only men like myself.'

Mike talked then, persuasively jingling the coins in his pocket. 'We'll be grateful for anything you can tell us. If you've ever lost anyone, you know how the young lady feels. There's no trouble behind this; it's all on the up and up.'

I said, 'Please.'

We were inspected from the shadows. We were measured, labelled, and accepted. He said he knew nothing, had seen little, that we were welcome to that little. 'I have nothing to sell,' he said. He said an 'outsider' had come to the shacks one night in early spring. That was the first visit, but later he had come often, sometimes twice a week. He had never seen the man's face, but he had seen the dog and heard the car as it entered the field above.

'Which shack?' Mike asked.

'The last one, at the far end. That is where the two men lived.'

THE two men had lived there for several months. He didn't know their names. They kept to themselves and spoke little. Sometimes at night when he went out to gather firewood, he walked to the far end of the ravine. If the dog was there, he knew he would hear three voices in the last shack. Sometimes the lamp burned late. They had hot food in there; he could smell it. Sometimes there was wine; he saw the empty bottles in the morning. Sometimes there were laughing and singing. The dog guarded the door and paced the ravine. Sometimes the dog barked; sometimes he prowled among the rocks. Sometimes he bayed the moon.

'Now they are all gone,' he said. 'All.'

Mike said, 'Thank you. Did you see them go? I mean the two who lived there?'

No, he hadn't seen them go. They must have gone at night, when he was asleep. Perhaps to the south, where it was warm. One of them was sick; he sat in the sun when the days were fine, shivering.

When we asked if we could visit the shack, he nodded. It was clean, he said. He had gone there himself, to forage, when the others went away. It was clean and ready for the next men who needed it, whoever they might be. 'When the snow comes,' he said, 'the men come. One, two, or three. Sometimes more. No names, no questions. Then in the spring they try the world again.'

He wouldn't take money.

Tray followed us to the last shack, but he refused to enter it. It was unlocked. The single room was damp and cold. It held two chairs, a table, a stove, and a bed. A fire was laid in the stove, ready for the snow and the next men. Twigs and scraps of paper, bits of coal and dried moss. Nothing spoke of Father.

I thought of his bedroom with its shining grate and deep, soft chairs. I saw our dining-room, the round table covered with lace, the silver that was too heavy for my hands when I was a child, the covered dishes holding rich food, presented by Tench. Tench, in his fine black coat. I saw the trays that went to Father's room and were returned untouched.

I tried to see him as he must have looked when he sat at that stained table with a bottle before him, talking to people whose names I didn't know. Laughing. Singing. Out of his mind?

'Well, have you got the picture?' Mike asked.

'I have a picture,' I said.

'I know I don't have to warn you, but keep this little jaunt under your hat. What your mother doesn't know won't hurt her.' His arm went around my shoulder. 'It's old stuff, Issy, as old as life. Look it in the eye and forget it. He was sick – think of it that way. He was disappointed in himself; that's a disease from which nobody's immune. I don't know how he got that way or why, but that's the answer. The poor devils who lived here had nothing; that's why he liked them

- he could give them things. Nobody could give him anything, he had it all, he was born with it. He – I don't know –
he had it all and he was fed up. When the others went away,
he simply decided to go, too – *his* way. That's not so crazy
as it sounds. He knew you and your mother would be all
right. He figured you didn't need him. Don't blame him;
you don't know how your own mind will behave when
you're his age.'

I KNEW how my mind was behaving then. 'He never gave
me a chance to know him. He sent me away when I was six;
he kept me away until I was grown. Then he brought me
back, to a house that was strange and parents I hardly knew.
Why?'

'I don't know. Stop thinking about it.'

'He wanted me to think about it; he knew what he was
doing. He brought me back and pretended he had plans
for me. He gave me the house and made me promise to live
in it. He knew what he was going to do. He knew he was
going to kill himself and haunt me the rest of my days. He
wanted me to think, and wonder, and reason it out, and
find no answer. No reason, no answer, that's what he
wanted. He wanted me to be Marsh Ford's daughter, walking alone as he drove alone. Marsh Ford's daughter, his
counterpart, for all the world to see and recognize and
wonder about. But I'm the one who's doing the wondering.
Mike, did he hurt me because he hated me?'

'He didn't hate you. Nobody does. Nobody can.'

'Somebody does. Every day since I've been home, every
hour, I feel two minds like two pairs of hands, pulling me in
opposite directions. Two pairs of eyes, watching me from
different places. One is *for* me, the other *against*. Is one of
them *myself*? I listen at doors. I take sentences apart and
look for hidden meanings. I try to question Mrs Tench
about my childhood. Could I have hurt my father when I
was a child? Is that why he, why I –' I stopped because of

163

his miserable face. 'Never mind, Mike. I was only talking. That was hurt talk, it doesn't mean anything. I was only –'

'Blowing your top?'

'That's it. Can't we go now? I've seen all I wanted to see. And I do thank you, Mike.'

'Sure we can go. Where to? Lunch? The club has music on Thursdays.'

Thursday. Until that minute I had forgotten it was Thursday. Thursday, the one day in the week when I could be alone in the house, the only day, and I had never taken advantage of it. Standing with Mike in that miserable shack, I began to make my plans.

They had no definite form, not then. They were plans for an afternoon of freedom; for thinking, for wandering, for being alone. I told myself I would do the things I had always wanted to do, I would look for my childhood in the house where I was born. I found it. And I found two other children hiding behind the years; two little girls like me, a child named Katy and another one whose name I have forgotten. I found them in the convent garden, whispering a story. They brought the garden to my father's room this afternoon and whispered as they used to. They told me the same story they had told me years ago, a story about a house. I think they came because they knew I would need that story, soon. I needed it to-night; I will need it again to-morrow.

Standing in the shack, I answered Mike. 'I can't lunch to-day, Mike. You've just reminded me of something. Thursday is the servants' half-day and we lunch early. Mother and I have dinner with the cousins. Tench drives us all in. The old ritual, remember?'

He was satisfied.

When I turned at the door for a last look, I saw the gold pencil. It was lying in a corner, waiting to be found. I knew what it was before I picked it up; I knew what the engraving said: *Love to Father from Isobel*. I had saved for it when I was twelve and given it to him for Christmas. I put it in my dress pocket, and Mike looked away. But Tray watched me through the open door, grinning.

'The cousins are right,' I said to Mike. 'He does grin.'

Mike left me at the entrance to our drive, and I walked to the house with Tray beside me. I knew what I was going to do and say ... Was that only this morning?

It was nearly one o'clock when I entered the house, and Anna met me at the door. I know now she wanted to talk, but Mother called to me from the dining-room, and I went in.

Mother was reading letters and jotting notes on the backs of envelopes. She looked up with a frown that changed at once into a smile. 'Oh dear, that yellow frock! Really, Isobel, I do think –'

'I'm not in mourning,' I said. 'Not any more. Please, Mother.'

'You mean it depresses you?'

'Yes, Mother.'

'So that has been your trouble. I wish you had told me before. How was your drive? Was it fun? Did you see anyone we know?'

'No, Mother. We kept to the country lanes because we had Tray with us.'

Anna, handing me salad, knocked the wooden spoon to the floor.

'Anna,' Mother said, 'we'll serve ourselves. You needn't wait. And tell Tench I want the car at three. Also, I expect you to be ready to leave when I am, all of you. No more of that silly quarrelling, or sulking, or whatever it was that I heard this morning. I've a thousand small errands to-day and too little ·time for them. Three o'clock, Anna.' She returned to her envelopes and pencilled notes.

I watched a column of small, neat figures grow and mentally rehearsed the first lie I had ever told her. Mother, Mrs Barnaby wants me for dinner to-night. She sent word by Mike. I'd love to go. The cousins won't miss me. Please say yes.

Mother added, frowned, and added again. She jabbed and dug, crossed out and rewrote, until the pencil broke between her firm little fingers and she flung it aside. 'Let it go,' she said. 'I don't like summing up.' She was laughing at herself, quietly. I couldn't laugh then.

'Will this help?' I slid the gold pencil across the table.

At first she didn't recognize it. 'No, but thank you, dear. I'm afraid nothing can help me. I'd hoped to find a new fur coat at the bottom of that column, but it looks as though I must wait a month or two.' Then: 'My dear child, wasn't that your father's?'

'Yes. It was a present from me. He lost it and I found it.'

'Then by all means use the pretty thing if it gives you pleasure. Isobel, you'll change your frock before we leave, won't you? I understand, but the poor cousins, you know, might not.'

I told my lie. 'Mother, Mrs Barnaby wants me for dinner to-night. She sent word by Mike.' I told it easily and elaborately. 'The cousins won't miss me. It's you they really want.'

'It's you Lucy Barnaby wants!' She sat with her chin cupped in her hands. 'Lucy Barnaby thinks I'm a selfish mother; she's as transparent as a child. And she knows quite well this is our evening at the cousins'. Isobel, shall we give a little dinner ourselves and show old Lucy Barnaby I'm not a jailer?'

'I don't know, Mother. But she asked me there for to-night. I'd love to go.'

'Oh, that! Yes, of course you may go. My poor little girl, does a small thing like that please you so much?'

I had reached out and taken her hand. 'I've been lonely,' I said. That was all I dared to say, and it was true.

'I know. I've watched you and grieved for you.' She said nothing of her own grief and her sleepless nights. 'And I know you miss your little friends at school. We brought you home to a strange house, my dear, but your father wanted it so.'

'I'd like to give the house to you, Mother.'

'Give it? This house? To me? My dear child, you are very generous and sweet, but it isn't yours to give, not yet. Not until your birthday. We'll wait and see how we feel about it then. Now!' She reached for the gold pencil. 'For the present, a little party, *en famille*. Why didn't I think of that before? It's high time we gave some thought to you, conventions to the contrary. I never did believe in outward mourning, but the poor cousins – However, I can talk them over to my way of thinking. The prospect of an unexpected dinner –' She was both laughing and sober. 'I think I need this little party, too. It will give me something to do.'

'Yes, Mother.'

'A pretty table, cards later, perhaps a little music. To-morrow? Yes, to-morrow. Why wait? I can see the cousins' faces!' She rolled the pencil between her fingers. Her eyes clouded. 'I haven't seen this for weeks,' she said softly. 'It hurts. He always carried it. I thought he had it with him when –'

'No. I found it.'

'So you told me.' The new mood left as the old one returned. She moved envelopes about the table as if they were cards. She drank her coffee in sips, as if it were the evening port. She was back in the circular room, on that night, waiting and watching the windows. I wanted to cry for the pain she was hiding from me.

'The dinner, Mother,' I said. 'If it will tire you, don't do it just for me.'

She stood up slowly, gathering her envelopes, not returning the pencil. 'I'm doing it for myself, too,' she said. 'Don't forget that.' She touched my cheek as she passed my chair. 'Give Lucy Barnaby my love. I'll send her a note in the morning.' She walked firmly from the room.

The rest of the day and the early evening would be mine in an empty house. I was planning, alone, when Anna came into the dining-room.

Anna came to clear the table, too quickly. I knew she

167

had been listening at the service door. She was wearing her holiday hat, to prove that she was early and everyone else was late. Her eyes were red. 'You didn't eat anything,' she said. 'You messed your food around the plate. That fools your mother, but it don't fool me. There's people in this world that would give their lives for what you waste. You're the same as somebody else I could mention but won't. Well, I'm ready to start, but I don't see anybody else. No names, of course.'

'Is anything wrong in the kitchen, Anna?'

'Wrong? What did she say to you about me after she sent me out of the room?'

'If you mean my mother, she said only what you heard yourself. Have you and Mrs Tench had a quarrel?'

'Quarrel? Me? I never quarrel. Ada Tench is a second cousin on my father's side, and I never let myself forget it. But I have rights like anybody else. I have my own work, and I do it. I don't ask anybody to do it for me. Ada may be my senior and twenty dollars a month more, but I don't need her help.'

'What help, Anna?'

'Who brings your breakfast when you sleep late? I do. Did I bring it this morning? I didn't. Why? You ask me that one. Why? I don't want to say anything unless I'm asked outright.'

'But I know why. Mrs Tench said you were worried about Tray.'

'Worried! That's like her. I was having hysterics, if you call that worried. I was out of my mind, and she threatened to slap me in the face. Ada. She said if I so much as opened my big mouth again, I'd get fired. But I won't get fired, because I'm not talking. You didn't happen to hear me having hysterics?'

'No. Anna, will you give me some coffee, please?'

She filled my cup, her hand shaking, and leaned against the table. Anna is a tall, thin woman with hungry, craving

168

eyes, unlike Mrs Tench in every way. She should have married and had children to spoil. Sick children. She collects young animals. Her kittens and lame squirrels overrun the stable. She has a cage of fallen birds in her room at the cottage. I don't know how she finds so many.

'Anna, Mrs Tench said you were upset because Tray wouldn't eat his breakfast. Is that your trouble? Is that what you want me to ask you?'

'There, you did it! You asked! You wanted to know about your own breakfast, and I had to tell you!' She sat in my mother's chair, forgetting herself. 'Miss Isobel, when did you ever see hamburger in this house?' The words were absurd, but the look on her face wasn't. She was frightened. 'If you make fun of me –'

'No, Anna, no. Don't look like that. I missed you this morning, and I'm glad you're talking to me now. What do you mean?'

'If you laugh –'

'I won't laugh, I promise. I never laugh at odd things. Something odd happened this morning, didn't it, and Mrs Tench doesn't want you to tell me?'

She leaned forward, her elbows on the table, and whispered. 'Listen. You listen. I've been watching you this past month. You can't fool me, I've known you too long. I've been watching you for longer than a month, and I know you've been asking yourself questions in your mind the same as I have. You don't talk to anybody; you keep to yourself; but you do your thinking just the same. Now that's all I'm going to say about that. I'm not supposed to have good sense, according to some people, but I can see things, can't I? Now you listen. You remember that morning?'

'Which morning?' But I knew.

'You know. After your father. That one. You remember about the bowl and the chain and the fresh meat?'

'I remember.'

'Did you ever think to do anything about that bowl and chain?'

'No. Why should I?'

'Did you think that dog walked into the five-and-ten with his money in his mouth and said to the girl, "Please give me a water bowl and a nice chain, I got to tie myself up in the stable to-night because they think I'm burned alive"? Do you think that?'

'I told you what happened, Anna. Someone found the dog on the road and brought him back. And took care of him.'

'Who did?'

'I don't know. Perhaps one of the poor men down in the shacks. My father used to visit them. Did you know that?'

'I heard it.'

'He was sorry for them. He gave them food and talked to them. Maybe one of them took care of Tray.'

'Did one of them ever come forward and tell you so? That kind always comes forward; they want credit for a good deed. Credit and the hand stretched out to take it in cash.'

'I'm only guessing, Anna. Anyone could have done it. Tray's name and address are on his licence plate.'

'HAVE it your own way. You could be right and you couldn't. I won't argue that. But let's hear you guess this one. You remember the night I locked that dog in the kitchen because the passage was cold? I did it out of pure kindness. I locked that door myself. Tench himself locked the windows earlier, like he always does. Everything was locked, locked, locked. And then what? Then in the morning himself is still locked in, but his coat is soaking wet and he's got sand and gravel on his feet. Remember that?'

I drew back as far as I dared, pushed my chair away from the table. It was an old story but a new terror.

Her lips were dry, and she drank the water from my mother's glass. 'Don't go,' she whispered. 'I haven't finished. You can't go yet.'

'I won't.'

'Listen. Now I'm coming to it. I give him a bowl of milk

every morning. He always had it before; your father said he was to have it. I used to send it up to your father's room and he had it there. So now I give it to him myself, in the kitchen. He comes for it; he knows it's there. Well, this morning he didn't come. I called him, and he didn't come. Then I went to look for him. I thought he was dead or something. I thought somebody's poisoned him at last. But he wasn't dead. He was sleeping in the furnace room, and he'd already had his breakfast. Some of it was still there, on the stone floor. Hamburger, raw, fresh. Good chopped round, good enough to cook and eat yourself. What's your guess about that, Miss Isobel? We haven't had any chopped meat in this house for weeks. Where did he get it? Did he walk out of the house again, it being locked, and go to the chain butcher with his money in his mouth and say, "I want some chopped round, please"? Five miles there and five miles back?'

'He – he found it?'

'Where is there any place to find it?'

'The Barnabys' cook –'

'No, I asked. I went over there myself and put it to that woman. I made her swear. They don't have any hamburger either. Fresh meat that you could eat yourself.'

'It dropped out of a car, Anna. Anna, you've got to clear the table, it's getting late.'

'Late? I'm ready. Listen. You know what I think?' Her face was as white as paper. 'You remember how your father was, Miss Isobel? He wouldn't eat what we brought him half the time. Like the dog. But he didn't starve either. Like the dog. He got his food from somewhere else, too, only he didn't leave it around for people to find. You know what I think? *I think your father's soul entered that dog.*' She covered her face with her hands.

I leaned forward and watched the tears trickle through her fingers. I didn't know my own voice when I heard it. I was whispering as she had. 'I dare you tell that to your priest, Anna.'

171

She uncovered her face, and we looked deep into each other's eyes.

'I dare you. I dare you tell that to your priest.'

'Do you want me to burn? I can't tell, I can't tell.'

'I dare you.'

'I'll lose my own soul. I'll lose my faith. I've lost it.'

'Tell him and see what he says. Then tell me. I want to know what he says.'

'He'll say I'm lost.'

'Ask him. Tell him. He may only say you're crazy.'

We drowned in each other's eyes.

She said, 'Are we?'

AFTER lunch I sat in the circular room and waited for three o'clock. I sat in the circular room and held a piece of embroidery in my hands, an old-fashioned piece, clamped between wooden hoops. My convent work, disarming work, suitable to a loved and sheltered child. The bright silk skeins were on the table, my little stork scissors were beside the silk. I wore my gold thimble. I knew how I would look to anyone who passed the open door.

I knew what would happen at three. I knew the routine of the Thursday holiday. At three, Tench and Mrs Tench and Anna would drive Mother to the village. They would call for her when they returned from town, late. The servants would shop, but this time Anna would slip away from the others. She would have a suitable excuse, and she would shop, too, for the sake of appearances. Anna would buy another kind of face cream, and Tench and Mrs Tench would buy another savings bond. They believe in the future; they talk about it when they sit in their cottage at night. I've heard them, when I've stood under their window on the nights when I couldn't sleep.

Mother would gossip all afternoon with the cousins. They believe in the past. They like to talk about the days when they all lived together in the little house in the village.

The cousins would entertain at the piano, one of them

172

playing, another singing, another keeping time and turning the music. I've seen and heard them, too, sitting on the hassock that is called *my* hassock because it once was Mother's.

'Our dear old piano! Have you ever heard a better tone?'

'Here comes your favourite, Maude! Do you remember? *Robin Adair*. "What's this dull town to me – Robin's not near."'

Mother would listen, shading her eyes with her hand, crying a little, thanking them when it was over.

At dusk Mother would say, 'Something smells good, dears. I hope you haven't gone to any trouble.'

'We've put the big pot in the little one for you, Maude dear. We found you a plump squab. A little chop for the rest of us, but we found you a plump squab.'

They would find her a hothouse peach, or a pear – 'Such luck, we found it quite by accident' – and serve it on a Dresden plate. 'That old plate, it takes you back, doesn't it, Maude? Dear Marsh – do you remember, Maude? We gave him a tea cake on that very plate the first afternoon he called!' Do you remember, do you remember? The Thursday routine.

THE car arrived at three, and I turned in my chair to watch. Tench and Anna on the front seat; Mrs Tench in the back, already making herself properly small in one corner. Anna sat with bowed head and clasped hands. I speculated about Anna.

When Mother came down the stairs, I didn't hear her. When she called my name, I jumped. She stood in the doorway, wearing a long seal cape and smiling. 'That's nice,' she said. 'There's nothing more becoming to a woman's hands than needlework. My love to Mike, and don't stay too late.'

I followed her to the front door. Mrs Tench became smaller in her allotted corner, Tench touched his cap, Anna sat upright and stared ahead. They drove away.

I closed the door and leaned against it. The house was empty. For the first time in a month, I was alone in the house. I was surrounded by open doors, I was facing a stairway that led to other doors, both open and closed. I was free to trace my life from room to room, to read the record of my years in the pictures on the old playroom wall, in the white nursery furniture that was stored in one of the closed rooms. I told myself I would look for what I had lost, or never had. But I didn't know where to begin.

I remembered the Christmas morning before I went away to school. I was six. I didn't know I was going away. Father led me to the playroom door. It had been closed for two days, but I knew my tree and presents were inside, waiting. I could hear a music box. I told him I had heard it once before, when he had gone into the room with a package under his arm and closed the door behind him. When I said that, he looked at me for a long time without speaking. His eyes were grave; I thought I had offended him. I remember what he said, stooping to look into my face: 'Always open doors when you hear music.'

Remember, remember.

The house was empty. I could go up or down. I could sleep or read or sew. I could go down to the cottage by the stable and look at Mrs Tench's flowers. I could go to Mother's room and handle the jars and bottles on her dressing table, open her wardrobe, touch the soft, light dresses she never wore now. I could go to Father's room and change the water in the bowl of red carnations. I could look through his desk and remember to leave it as I found it, the right things in the right pigeon-holes, the ivory paper knife on the left-hand corner of the blotter, the writing case in the centre, the top letter on top.

I went up the stairs.

Mother had left her door open. I told myself to remember that when I was ready to leave. She had dressed hurriedly; I could follow her progress from bath to wardrobe, to chest and table. Black-bordered handkerchiefs had been unfolded

174

and discarded; hats, slippers, and veils. The dress she had worn at lunch was lying on a chair, one sleeve torn from the shoulder. I touched nothing. She values privacy; no one is allowed to touch her things; she is always present when Anna cleans. Anna.

When I frightened Anna at lunch, I knew what I was doing. I wanted to frighten her. I wanted her to talk, I led her carefully; she said what I wanted her to say. I'd been waiting for someone to say that.

THERE was a heap of torn paper in the bottom of Mother's wastebasket, letters and envelopes from lunch-time reduced to shreds. I stirred them, turning up figures and words. Bills, and a draft of her shopping list; food for the party dinner. Lobster, wine, an item I couldn't read; my name, torn across, old Mrs Barnaby's name followed by a question mark. Five thousand dollars with a line drawn through it. A heavy line. The words and figures told me why she had dressed in a hurry. Calculating and planning, she had forgotten the time.

I thought: Five thousand dollars for a new fur coat? I can give her that.

I went to the wardrobe and stroked the garnet and turquoise dresses on their scented hangers. They were separated from the dead, dull black by a transparent curtain. When she reached for the black, she could see the pretty colours waiting.

I went to Father's room.

I sat in the chair beside his bed and counted the days I had known him. I began with the year I was six. *Always open doors when you hear music.* Now I am nearly twenty-one. I counted. In all that time I had known him for less than a year. I had been with him and talked to him less than a year.

He gave me this house and said he had plans for me, but he sent me from the room and locked the door. He said I was much on his mind, but he spent his last hours with strangers.

I went to his desk. I forgot to watch the clock that kept time for no one.

He left very little behind him when he went away. A few photographs of boys at school, grown boys with oddly wistful faces, posed against stone steps and ivied walls. They wore lettered jerseys and small caps and held their tennis rackets stiffly. He could have been one of them. A handful of yellowing letters from people I had never heard of, asking him to look them up when he went to Boston or New York. A small bundle of notes from Mother, written on violet paper. A letter from me. I could remember writing it. That was my first summer at the convent, when I was still six.

I wrote it secretly, without help, late at night by candle-light, and another child crouched at the foot of my cot and watched me with round, hopeful eyes. The other child was an orphan, a charity pupil; we were not supposed to know that, but I knew. She and I were the only children who stayed at the convent that summer, and I was boasting. *I* was not an orphan, *I* lived in a big house, almost as big as the convent. I spent my holidays at school because I *wanted* to. I could go home to my big house and never come back to the convent if I *wanted* to.

I boasted about my mother, who was beautiful, and my father, who gave me presents at Christmas. The music box, singing behind a closed door on Christmas morning. She refused to believe me. She believed in the house and my father and mother, but she said Christmas was an orange.

That was when I wrote my letter, triumphantly, while the soft summer night filled our little room with fragrance and the candle flickered. 'My dear father, Please send me a Christmas for Katy. Your loving daughter Isobel.'

He had kept it. Well, I had kept his answer too. It was in my own desk, locked away. 'My dear daughter, I cannot send you a Christmas for Katy; they are not in season. But when the proper time comes, I will not fail you. Father.'

OLD letters, not new ones. Mother's notes, written before they were married and progressing from 'My dear Mr Ford' to 'My darling Marsh.'.

'My dear Mr Ford, Your roses have made my room a garden ...'

'My dear Mr Ford, The cousins ask me to thank you for the opera tickets. A rare treat for them and one that will give boundless pleasure. And the carriage! They had worried, a tiny bit, about the long trip to town and back, but I told them you would think of that, too. You see, I am beginning to know you! ...'

'Darling Marsh, When I said I liked candied violets, I meant a very little box! What will I do with five whole pounds? Eat them, every one, and think of you! ...'

'Darling, darling, I cannot let you give me those sapphires. Not yet. They are much too grand for my present position, and I will be talked about. But, oh, how I want them. Darling, if I wear them under my pillow until the engagement is announced, do you suppose – Please don't tell the cousins! ...'

'My darling Marsh, You misunderstood me. I was reticent because I have been taught that a woman does not discuss such things before marriage. If I gave a wrong impression, dear Marsh, it was because I spoke from convention, not from my heart. I want children. Why do you think I love that great enormous house? Do you understand?'

In the last envelope there was an old photograph of the great enormous house. Some of the pines were not fully grown, the turrets were clear against the sky, the creeper had not reached the narrow windows. The shrubbery along the drive was low and clipped; sun lay in patches on smooth, trim grass. Grass, not moss and leaves. But even then it prophesied. There were no figures on the veranda, no signs of life or work or play. No chairs to lounge in, no garden hat beneath a tree, no open book face down, no sprawling doll, waiting.

I do not believe in ghosts.

Even now, this minute, in my own room, in the dark, I would say those words out loud if I dared. But this afternoon, in Father's room, little Katy came back to me for a second time and brought another child with her. I stood before Father's desk, looking at the photograph, and Katy walked across my mind, hand in hand with another child. Their heads were close together, and they were whispering. I knew they were telling stories; I knew they were coming to find me as they found me long ago.

They were not ghosts, only children I used to know, come to talk to me again. They were a summer afternoon in a convent garden, restored and resurrected by Katy's Christmas letter. Their little footsteps echoed in the room; their whispers rustled.

They were telling a story about a house. I looked at my house in the photograph and remembered. A shadow moved across the room. It was only a branch that bent to the window. I told myself the story was childish nonsense. I told myself it was a nursery legend. I put it out of my mind.

I OPENED the window and watched the November wind rush in and lift the valance on the bed. The red carnations swung like pendulums, the door slammed. I hardly heard it. I circled the room and talked. 'This is goodbye,' I said clearly. 'If you hear me, this is good-bye. To-morrow we're opening the house to other people; and you'll have to go. I'm warning you. I'm going to live without you from now on. I'll give your things away, all of them; I won't come here again until you have gone for good. I'm sorry.'

I went to the wardrobe and turned the handles with both hands. The double doors swung open.

The smell of her Turkish cigarette was heavy and fresh. I could have been facing her, talking to her. Not talking to him, to her. I saw his limp clothes hanging from the rods and two empty hangers in a gaping space. I thought I saw the heavy blue smoke curl to meet me. That was imagination; there was nothing to be afraid of, nothing.

She had gone there, as she often did, to brood and wonder. I have seen her at night with a candle in her hand, moving along the halls. This time she had gone in daylight, drawn by conscience. She'd told him we were cutting ourselves free. So we both had told him.

When I turned to leave, I saw the candle wax on the wardrobe floor. Not one drop, but an accumulation, one on top of another, old and new. I stooped. The old drops were white and dusty, and the new were yellow and clean.

I have never seen a yellow candle in this house; but there is nothing to be afraid of, nothing. Not yet.

I closed the window, bruising my hands, and left the room. In Mother's bathroom I looked for a lotion to rub on my hands, but she never labels anything and I don't like unlabelled bottles.

There was nothing to be afraid of, nothing. I told myself I was acting and thinking like a child, caught in the net of a child's story. Legend, folklore, nursery dramatics. A Scotch nanny, whiling away a rainy afternoon, making up a story as she went along, not knowing it would travel as it did, across the ocean to a convent garden. I put the story out of my mind again.

The day was growing dark. I ran downstairs and out of the house. I called Tray, but he didn't come. The sky was fading at the end of the driveway. I went to the old stable, looking for Tray. He wasn't there. It was warm and dusky in the stable. Anna's cat came to meet me, arching her back like a witch's cat. She had a pan of milk, half full. Anna never forgets.

Anna must have thrown away the chain and bowl.

MRS TENCH has a flower garden in the summer. Tench dug rows and beds and cut away the trees. Even in November, at dusk, the cottage stands in light. It looks as if it stands in another country. I walked along the flower beds; the rose-bushes were wrapped in straw. Close to the cottage, under the casement windows, a few chrysanthemums were blooming. Hardy pink. Mrs Tench cuts them for her sitting-room. I walked closer to the cottage. Mrs Tench says I am always welcome there. She says I am welcome to the flowers when there are any.

There were too few. I thought it would be like robbing her. I walked under the windows, counting the blooms. Mrs Tench never locks the windows, she says there is nothing in her house to tempt a thief. She thinks Tray is a good watch-dog.

I called Tray again. To-day was the first day since – the first day I have had to call him. To-day, this afternoon, there were no pattering feet behind me.

I unlatched one of the sitting-room windows. Mrs Tench is a good housekeeper. In the dusk I could see the white antimacassars on the big plush chairs. Mrs Tench likes big furniture, dark and solid. Her table lamp is hung with prisms and has a hand-painted shade. She painted the shade herself, when she was a young girl.

I moved on, around the cottage, counting the chrysanthemums. There were still too few. On the western side I came to Anna's room. On that side the sky was streaked with green and orange, but her room was dark because the windows were filmed with dust. Last night's rain had beat against the windows and set the dust.

Anna, I thought, is not a good housekeeper. I rubbed the dust away with my handkerchief, making a small, clean circle. I made another and another, and soon the pane was clear. After that, I opened the window and dusted the inside.

Anna's birds were quiet; too quiet. I hoped they were asleep. But if she had forgotten to feed them, if they were lying on the bottom of the cage, surrounded by empty little cups –

I leaned over the sill. The cage was on a table less than a yard away, and the birds were asleep on their perches. I could almost reach them. The little cups were full. I should have known they would be. Anna never forgets a thing like that.

180

The black pool on the floor by the door was only Anna's sweater. Anna had dressed in a hurry, too. It was the old sweater, the one she wears over her head when she runs between the cottage and the house.

If Anna could read my mind this minute, she would cover her head with the sweater and scream. She is superstitious; she believes in the supernatural. If a picture falls, or a cup breaks, Anna remembers that she dreamed it would. After a thing has happened, she shakes her head and says she saw it coming. This afternoon, in Father's room, when little Katy returned with the other child and I remembered the old story, I foresaw nothing. But if I were Anna instead of myself, if my mind worked like Anna's –

Am I like Anna?

It was only an old sweater on the floor. And the birds were sleeping in their cage.

I was lying when I told myself I was worried about the birds. I was acting a lie when I cleaned the window and opened it. The trip to the stable and the cottage was a lie. I went because I wanted to see Anna's pictures.

Her walls are covered with holy pictures, madonnas and saints. She talks to them and says they give her comfort. I leaned on the sill and tried to see the patient faces through the dusk.

THE sky was dark when I left the cottage. There were lights in the Barnabys' living room, one window was raised. Not much, not more than an inch or two, but it was enough. I know the pattern of their lives: tea at four-thirty, talk until dinner. Talk. I moved along the hedge to the place where I had made a little window for myself long ago. Long? A month ago.

Every evening they talked before dinner, old Mrs Barnaby, young Joe, and Mike. 'What did you do to-day? What will you do to-morrow?' I saw the birchwood fire, the ragged sheets of music, on the open piano, the uncleared tea table, the light that flashed from Mrs Barnaby's diamonds.

181

'Unwholesome,' Mrs Barnaby said. 'But what do you think you can do about it?'

'Plenty.' That was Mike. 'And I'm doing it from now on. What do you know about psychiatry, Lucy?'

'Nothing, thank the Lord. I've had a fine, rowdy life.'

'It shows, too.' Young Joe.

'You had one allowance cut last week, my boy. Don't let your tongue make you a pauper. As I say, I've had a fine life and all the money a decent woman needs. I brought up my own children, and I'm bringing up theirs. I try to see the bright side; when I can't see it, I look for it. I look and look and look and look.'

'What does she want, Mike?' Joe asked.

Mike didn't answer.

'I'm boiling mad,' Mrs Barnaby said.

'About Isobel?' Mike asked.

'Raining cats and dogs last night. Why wasn't she in bed? What are those people thinking about? What have they ever thought about? Hiding under hedges like an animal!'

Mike said, 'So you're boiling. Well, come to the point. Isobel or "those people"?'

'I don't know. I can't make up my mind. That infuriates me. Joe, you've been wetting your hair again. Where did you get the water? Out of the jug? Well, stop it. Do you want to be bald?'

'Did old man Ford really hang around those shacks?' Joe asked.

'Everybody knows that.' Mike. 'It started last spring when Issy came back from school. After he died, I talked to his lawyer about it. He thinks Ford was looking for companionship.'

'Marsh Ford was born to companionship,' Mrs Barnaby said. 'In the old days he had hundreds of friends, he belonged to all the clubs. Every woman in town made eyes at him. He wore the first cape I ever saw. No, Marsh Ford simply went out of his mind. In a nice way, of course.'

182

'He must have been out of his mind, in a nice way, of course, when he sent a kid like Issy to a boarding school at six and kept her there. I never did get that.'

'Some marriages are like love affairs,' Mrs Barnaby said slowly. 'People don't want anyone else, not even a little child. Isobel was a nice little thing, too. Affectionate and happy. Now I don't know what she is.'

'She's what they made her.' Mike. 'Look at the facts. They're her own flesh and blood, and they practically threw her out when she was a baby. They brought her home when she was grown, ostensibly to sweeten their declining years, and ignored her. No friends, no life, except us. And too little of us. Mama played cards alone, drank port alone, and entertained her buzzard relatives. Papa took to his bed in the daytime and drank God knows what in Shantytown at night. Accompanied by man's best friend, his dog – and I'll take a werewolf. Daughter begins to wonder if she's a leper, and why not? Then, to make it stick, to round it out, the old man pats her on the head, tells her the house is hers, waves good-bye, and bumps himself off. She says he haunts her, she says he won't go away. How do you cure that?'

'Time will do it if anything can. I think she's sound.'

'I know she is.'

'Do you want to marry her, Mike?'

'Yes, Lucy.'

'I'll reset your mother's ring ... Mike, there's something in this room! I feel eyes, Mike. There's something in this room, I tell you!'

'There's nothing here, Lucy. And if you're thinking about Issy, she went to the cousins'.'

I went back to my dark house and entered by the kitchen. I wasn't hungry. That was fortunate, because Mrs Tench and Anna watch the food. I sat in the kitchen and watched the Barnabys' lights. After dinner they would go their separate ways, Joe to his room in the attic, Mike to his room on the second floor. Joe would study, and Mike

183

would do accounts. He looks after the estate. Old Mrs Barnaby would read for an hour, then go to bed. Her bedroom light would be my signal. When I saw it, I would telephone Mike. I'd say, 'I want to see you, Mike, I want to tell you something.' When he came, I'd tell him Mother thought I had been dining with them.

'I had odds and ends of things to do,' I'd say. I'd make him believe me. 'Personal things. But Mother doesn't like me to be alone, so do explain to your grandmother, will you? Oh, yes, you're going to have a surprise to-morrow. Mother and I are giving a dinner! Only the cousins and you people, but it means she's feeling better, doesn't it? I can hardly believe it! We had a wonderful lunch to-day, Mother and I. We talked, and she actually laughed. I think my yellow dress was responsible. I think it made her realize that I've been – that I – but you understand, Mike. I think we're going to have a wonderful winter after all. This little dinner to start with, and then there's Thanksgiving. Perhaps you can come then, too. And my birthday. I'll have a birthday party; I'll insist on it. I can, because I'll be of age. You'll have to lend me your party list. I've forgotten most of the people, and I'm sure they've forgotten me. Forgotten! That reminds me, there's something else. Such a small thing, Mike, too small to speak of seriously, but it's about Anna. You know Anna, too silly for words. But she has some fantastic notion about our dog's food. He brings food home, and she doesn't like it. Do you suppose your cook feeds him? Can you find out without offending her? I mean the hamburger or chopped meat or whatever it is. He found some and brought it home. Your cook said it didn't come from your house, but I suspect Anna was rude and made her angry. Do straighten it out, will you, Mike? It really does upset Anna. She made quite a mystery of the chopped meat to-day. Of course he may have stolen it, but where? Isn't it silly? But you know how Anna is. And by the way, have you seen Tray since this morning?'

That's what I planned to tell him, and I did, almost word

for word. I rehearsed it, over and over, sitting at the kitchen table and watching the Barnabys' windows. Around and above and behind me the house held its breath.

I T was nine o'clock when Mrs Barnaby went to bed and I called Mike on the phone in the kitchen passage. Tray's pan and his rug were there, both empty.

'Mike? This is Isobel.'

'Where are you, Issy? What's up?'

I told him I was home. 'Mike, I want to see you.'

'What's wrong? You sound funny. Why aren't you at the cousins'?'

'Nothing's wrong. Mike, can you slip out for a few minutes?'

'Sure. Right away. Where?'

'That old cedar tree with the bench around it.'

'On my way.'

I went back to the kitchen and turned out the single light. When the others came home, they would find everything in order. Mike and I, in the double darkness of the night and the old cedar, would see the car when it turned in at the drive. We would meet them on the veranda, properly, saying the right things. 'Good night, Issy, it was nice having you come to dinner.' 'Good night, Mike, and thanks for everything.'

That was how I planned, standing in the dark kitchen at nine o'clock, before I went to meet him. That was what we said, too, when he brought me home at eleven, and we stood in the empty, lighted hall and challenged the house with words. Good night. Good night. We warned the house that I had returned. We tried to let it know what we had seen. We raised our voices and made them strong and sent them up the stairs like hostages.

It was a few minutes after nine when I locked the kitchen door and went out to the tree.

'I'm crazy about this,' Mike said, 'even if I can't see my hand before my face. I don't know what's on your mind,

185

but we ought to be burying a body. Are you convulsed with laughter or shivering?'

'Neither. Mike, will you watch for the car and walk back with me when they come? I want Mother to see us.'

'Do you mean to say we aren't getting away with anything?'

'Oh, we are! Mother thinks I had dinner with you!' I began the carefully rehearsed story, filling in the weak spots when his silence told me they were there. 'The cousins,' I went on. 'Not to-day, I simply couldn't face it. So if your grandmother –'

'Okay, she'll lie for you this time. She'll overdo it, of course, the same way you're overdoing it now. On the level, why did you want to stay home?'

'I told you, Mike. I had odds and ends of things to do, and I didn't want a lot of fuss made about my dinner. Mother was perfectly agreeable. She understood; I don't see why you can't. Now here's the really important thing. Mother wants you all for dinner to-morrow. The cousins, too – not much fun for you and Joe, but much, much better than nothing at all. It was her own idea, too. I still can't believe it.'

'I'm having a little trouble that way myself. Is that all you had to tell me, Issy?'

'That's all. You see, everything's going to be all right from now on. Mother even laughed at lunch.'

'I hope she did a better job than you're doing.'

'Mike! Oh, yes, I nearly forgot, there *is* something else. Talking about lunch made me remember. It's Tray again, Tray and Anna. You know how she is about animals. Now she has some fantastic notion –' The planned speech, casual, carelessly spaced, better than the first one, much better.

His face was a pale blur, close to mine in the dark. He let me finish without an interruption. Then he said, 'Chopped meat? How exciting! Sure, I'll fix it. Maybe it was Joe. But aren't you a little tense about the whole thing? You know Anna is bats.'

'She is, isn't she? She doesn't like Tray, she's afraid of him. By the way, have you seen him around? He seems to be missing.'

'Again? Don't worry, he'll show up. Is that what you were doing down at the stable? Looking for Tray?'

'Yes, that's what I was doing.'

'Well, don't worry, he – oops, sorry.' He was looking over my shoulder, toward the house. 'We're going to be a little late, but I can fix that too.'

'Late? Who? Late for what?'

'I forgot to watch for the car. They're home.'

'Car? I don't see it.'

'Neither do I, but look.' He turned me around to face the house.

THERE was a light in one of the windows, a small, yellow light behind the trees, high in the house, high in the trees. One light.

We turned to look at the stable; it was dark. The cottage was dark. The distant road, the driveway, the house, all dark. Except –

We raised our eyes to the one small light.

'Issy, whose room is that?'

'The house is empty.'

'Someone came home alone, before the others.'

'How?'

'Cab. We must have missed it.'

'You know we didn't miss it.' The small light moved, from the left to the right, high in the trees, as if a hand had hung it there.

'Whose room is that, Issy?'

'The house is empty and locked. I have my keys.'

'I say whose room is that? What is that window?'

'I don't know. It's too high. I can't see. It's hidden in the trees.' When people whisper slowly, their words sound like pebbles dropping into deep water.

'Somebody didn't go, that's it. Somebody put one over

on you. Somebody didn't go, or else came back while you were down at the stable. That's it.'

'I saw them go, Mike. All four. No wonder I heard the house hold its breath.'

'You heard the house *what*? Easy does it, baby, easy. Here comes the car. Now you'll see, now you'll know I'm right. Somebody came home early.'

The car turned in at the drive. We watched it crawl beneath the trees and stop at the veranda steps. Someone left the driver's seat and crossed the path of the headlights. Tench. One of them. One. Tench. He opened the door, and the ceiling light finished the count. Anna on the front seat. Anna. Two. Mrs Tench and Mother, three and four. All four, all of them.

We lifted our eyes to the hidden window high in the trees. The light went out.

'Whose room is that?'

'I don't know, I don't know.'

'Your wiring's off, that's the answer. Joe said he saw –'

'What did he see?'

'He said he saw that light last week, and I called him a liar.'

I told him then.

The car crawled down to the stable, and the night was black again. The cottage came to life and sank into darkness.

'When I was about seven, I think it was seven, a child at school told me a story. It was about a house and a room –'

I told him about the monster.

Part Two

WHEN we left the garden last night, we knew what we must do the next day.

It is afternoon of that day. I am waiting again, but this time I am not afraid, because Mike and Joe will be here in a little while. Mike, Joe, Mrs Barnaby, the cousins.

Breakfast and lunch are behind me. In two hours, more or less, the party will begin. I know every move we will make afterwards. Mike and Joe and I will go to the old playroom to see my music box. They will make it convincing.

I talked to everyone in the house this morning, a few words to each. I went where they were and watched what they were doing. That was my idea, not Mike's.

When I went to the kitchen, Tray was leaving, and I met him face to face. He stood aside to let me pass. 'Good-morning, Tray, I've missed you.'

Mrs Tench was washing vegetables at the sink, and Anna was drinking coffee at the worktable.

'Did you have a pleasant time yesterday, Anna?' I asked. I wanted to know whether she had talked to her priest.

She coloured. 'I did all right. The dog ate his breakfast this morning, Miss Isobel, a nice bowl of milk.' She looked into her cup, not at me.

'He's an old fraud, Anna, don't worry about him. What did you people do in town?'

They had been together all the time, Mrs Tench said. She emphasized together. They had shopped together, gone to the movies together, to buy a nice bond, to the tea-room for the special blue-plate dinner. 'Only it was chipped white. A dollar fifty and not worth the fifty. They can't fool me with their wilted lettuce, warm vinegar on other people's leavings, and I told the woman so.'

I said, 'I had a good time, too. I came home late. Everybody was in bed when I came home. Where's Tench?'

'Out back.' Mrs Tench frowned. 'What's on your mind, Miss Isobel? You're a hen on a hot griddle. "Where's Tench?" Out back washing the car, which is what he always does on Friday morning, as you know. You'll do well to go out yourself and have a nice walk.'

'I'd like to help you. Is there anything I can do? I can get the candles ready if you tell me the colour you want.'

'All done, Miss Isobel, but thank you.'

'I hope we're using yellow. It's a warm colour.' Where did the yellow wax on the floor of Father's closet come from?

'Your mother wants white,' Mrs Tench said.

I LEFT them talking for my benefit. I know how people sound when they want to be overheard.

'Those lobsters look very nice and lively, don't they?' Anna.

'The – oh, yes, to be sure they do. But you might give them a poke. I like company; I like visitors and getting out the best cloth and doing things pretty. We're going to enjoy this, Anna. And Miss Isobel! It's a treat to see her, taking an interest. And the madam! Well, they can't grieve for ever – he wouldn't want it so.' Mrs Tench lowered her voice. 'Psst! Gone?'

'Wait. Sure, not a sound out there. Listen, you ought to feel my heart, like a jumping jack. I was afraid you were going to give me away. Did you get a good look at those eyes, Ada? Looking over the place, all over you and me. In another minute I'd have hollered. And all that talk, as if I didn't know what she was getting at. It was me she came out here to see, on account of what I said to her yesterday and she said to me. She was trying to find out what I done. I certainly thank you for not giving me away.'

190

'You ought to know I wouldn't. I'm dying to know what happened, myself. But what with Tench hanging around, I couldn't ask. What did the priest say?'

'Read me the riot act. Skinned me alive. I got to go back next week for more. Pray for the poor man's soul, he says, and stop making a fool of yourself. He talked terrible. Pray for the poor girl and her mother, he says, and stop reading trashy books. You can't beat an educated priest for talk. Why didn't you tell her she left her handkerchief in here last night? All over dirt from my own windows. Anybody could see that.'

'What's the good? She thinks we don't know. What do you suppose she was doing?'

'What does she do when she stays up all night? I know what a bed looks like when you don't sleep in it. And what does the madam do when *she* walks all night? I see that candle going past the windows at all hours, and I clean up the grease and stubs, and she sees me doing it too, and don't say a word. One day it's a sin to laugh and go to a little party next door, and the next day it's a party in your own house.'

'There's all kinds of grief, Anna; it comes to everybody in a different way. Sometimes people can't sleep for thinking of the things they didn't do or say, and wish they had. But it passes.'

'Grief! Look back, Ada, I ask you, look back. They never acted like other people. Sitting in the same room together, eating at the same table, you'd think they were strangers. And the girl was always odd; you know it. Grief!'

'Things might have been different if they'd had more children. She was a nice little thing. Always smiling, always saying "please" ... Hush, did I hear something?'

'Only the dog sniffing in the passage. You see, you're getting the same as me. You're hearing things and don't know what they are.'

I FOUND Tench outside the stable.

'Good morning, Miss Isobel.'

'Good morning, Tench. Did you have a pleasant time yesterday?'

'The old routine, Miss Isobel, the same as usual. And yourself? Did the neighbours give you a fine dinner?'

'Oh, yes. We're being very gay, aren't we, Tench? A dinner to-night, too. How long has it been since we gave a dinner, Tench?'

'Now, I'd have to think about that. I doubt if I could answer that right off. Were you wanting some of my wife's flowers, Miss Isobel? You don't have to ask, you know. I came across the footprints in the beds this morning, so I figured it was flowers you were after. That ground's soft, shows up everything. You wait here, I'll get you some. You should have helped yourself.'

I let him cut a few sprays and thanked him.

Mother was telephoning when I reached the library door.

'I knew you'd agree, my dear Mrs Barnaby – in fact, it was you who opened my eyes. When I saw that pale little face across the luncheon table, I was shocked. My own child was a stranger to me, a pathetic stranger! ... But you think she looks well otherwise? ... No, nothing; nothing that she will admit to. That frightens me a little when I think of it; he was the same, you know. But not a word of this to the cousins, Mrs Barnaby. You and I together, and of course dear Mike, will work wonders ... Indeed we must ... Ah, here's my child now. Until this evening, then.'

'Good morning, Mother.'

'Good morning, dear. I missed you at breakfast. Nice that you could oversleep again. Lucy Barnaby says she is delighted; she sounded quite gay. And now I'm going to scold you, darling. What was all the shouting in the hall last night? High spirits?'

'I'm sorry, Mother. Did we wake you?'

'Of course you did. But I'm glad you had a happy evening; my own was a little dull. The cousins found me a large fowl with mushroom dressing. I persuaded them to share it with me, but I fear they are regretting the size.' She

192

was mischievous, twinkling. 'Their mouths were full of their own chicken when I told them about our party. How their poor faces fell! Two good dinners in succession, a smaller bird would have done just as well. Are you looking for something, Isobel?'

'No, Mother.'

'You seem – *coiled*. Tell me, what do you think of cards after dinner? Bridge?'

'Why don't we wait, Mother? Perhaps Mrs Barnaby would rather talk. She hasn't seen the cousins recently.'

'You may be right. Talk and a little music, but I'll put out cards in any case.'

She sent me away with a wave of her hand and returned to the telephone. That time she talked to the cousins. Tench would call for them at five. The black cut velvets would be charming. Black was always good. Additional chiffon at the hem? A flounce? Only if Jane did the sewing, not darling Bessy? Isobel? Isobel was not too well ... Why does she always say that?

THAT was hours ago, hours, hours, hours. I am still waiting, in my room, and my door is open. I can hear footsteps in the lower hall and accurately name them. Mother is the light, quick tread, Mrs Tench is the slow, heavy one, Anna is the shambling run. I know Anna's hands are red and wet and her face is blotched. Tench is not in the house, or, if he is, he is not moving about. Tray –

I haven't seen Tray since we met in the kitchen passage.

When Mike and Joe come, they will have paper parcels under their topcoats. Even Mrs Barnaby will not know the contents. Parcels packed tight with strips of towelling and sheeting, long white strips. 'Tell yourself it's a game we're playing, Issy,' Mike said. 'Tell yourself until you're black in the face, and make yourself believe it. It's a game.'

I can see and hear them all as if they are already here. The cousins, catering to Mrs Barnaby, storing up every word she says, for future quoting. 'As my friend Mrs

Barnaby said the other night – yes, *the* Mrs Barnaby – there's really only one! She lives in that rambling old white house that adjoins Maude Ford's, a delightful woman, so unpretentious, the fine old families always are. And her jewels are fit for a queen!'

Poor Carrie, Jane, and Bess, with too many gestures and too much animation, always afraid they will be overlooked and unappreciated, never quite sure they are properly valued, wondering, in their secret hearts, if they are as fine and clever as they tell themselves they are. I know what Carrie will say to the others when they drive up to the door. 'Bess, Jane, let's be airy!' They will come into the house laughing and tossing their heads.

Old Mrs Barnaby will be crisp, composed, and watchful. Mike will have told her only enough; she will ask no questions, but she will help. If Mother objects to the music box, Mrs Barnaby will smooth our way. I can guess what she will say. 'What's that? They want to play the old music box before dinner? I'd encourage them if I were you. Such an innocent pleasure –' Yes, Mrs Barnaby will help us, and with luck we will have almost an hour. Almost an hour in which to duplicate the first part of the story about the monster I told Mike.

Mike watched under my window all night. He doesn't know I saw him. So I know he is afraid, too, in spite of his talk of games and defective wiring. I remember what he said to me after I told him the story. He said, 'I don't feel my age, I feel six, and I want a woman's hand to hold. Give me yours.'

I told him the story another child had told me in a sunny convent garden. I told it in the dark, in my own garden, and I thought the wind stopped to listen and the dead leaves moved. The story that came back to me in my father's room and prepared me for the light I saw in the house when no one was home.

Once there was an old house in Scotland, a miniature castle, occupied by family servants while the owners lived

194

in London. One summer the owners returned after an absence of many years; they were young people, they had not visited the place since childhood. This time they brought guests.

One of the guests was a girl recovering from an illness. She told the owner of the castle that she could not sleep at night, that someone walked all night in the room next to hers. There was no bedroom next to hers, nothing but a winding passage and the apple room. They laughed at her, all of them; they said the apples rolled about at night.

Then one day when everyone had gone to the shooting, she went from window to window in the apple room and passage and hung a towel from each one. When she looked up at the windows from the ground below, there was one window without a towel. Next to hers.

The house party broke up that night. An old servant revealed the secret of the hidden room. Years before, the family had bred a monster. He was old, old, old. He wouldn't die. He lived there, walled up.

WHEN I finished telling Mike the story, we looked up at the house and trees. After a time Mike said, 'Whoever told that story to a kid ought to be boiled in oil. Anyway, that light still could have been the reflexion of a car on the road.'

'There was no car, and you know it.'

'All right, all right. But do you have to be macabre? It's the wiring, the wiring's off. Don't say anything to your mother, but have Tench call an electrician.'

'I was alone in the house from three until nine. I was alone.'

'Sure you were. Hammer that in. You didn't hear anything, did you?'

'I heard the house hold its breath.'

'Don't talk like that! Listen, you and your mother have been alone every night for weeks, so why get excited now? And Tray would have taken the place if —'

'You're frightened, Mike. Don't be ashamed of fear.'

That was when he said he felt like six and wanted a woman's hand to hold. 'But I'm not frightened,' he added. 'I'm trying to keep my balance. You're entertaining me too well. First that business at the shacks and now this. All your doing. Now I've got to apologize to Joe, too.'

'When did Joe see the light?'

'Last Thursday night. That's what I've been trying to remember, and now I've got it. He didn't come home from school in the afternoon and didn't phone, showed up at nine o'clock, and Lucy bawled him out. She sent him to bed without dinner. The next morning he told us about the light. I thought he was making what he calls conversation, handing Lucy a line. She loves to be scared to death, and he knows it. She'd threatened to cut his allowance the night before, and I thought he was taking her mind off money. She cut it anyway.'

'What did Joe say?'

'He built that light like Edison. He had Lucy on the ropes, but not for long. He gets a buck a week now. It used to be two.'

'*What did Joe say?*'

'All right. He said he was looking out of his window and saw a light in your house. High up, like the one we saw. But Joe told it good – he said it was a branched candlestick.'

'His room is in the attic, on our side. He could see. Did it move like the other?'

'All right, all right. He said it did. That could have been an illusion, the trees moving. The wind is high to-night.'

Yes, the wind was high.

'My mother walks at night,' I said, 'but she carries a single candle. And she wasn't home last Thursday, no one was home. I've been afraid for a long time, Mike, and I haven't known why. At first I thought it was my father's trouble, but now –'

He called me fantastic, medieval, loony; but he told me I could spend the night at their house. He said he could fix it. He said he could fix everything. I told him I had to go home because my mother was there, alone. I emphasized the word alone, but I didn't believe it. He laughed and said I was a ghoul. I didn't believe his laugh, either.

'Listen, baby,' he said, 'I'm a little too old for the Arabian Nights, but I don't mind playing a game with you. That's what we'll do, play a game. Get that into your head, a game. We'll dramatize your fairy tale, towels and all. Props, realism. To-morrow night, when the great hall rings with festive laughter. But how'll we work it, how'll we get away from the others? What excuse can we give?'

We decided to tell them we wanted to hear the music box. It is still in the old playroom, and the playroom is at the end of the second-floor hall, far from the library. A visit to the playroom had a reasonable sound. Three young people in a playroom.

'Leave everything to me,' Mike said.

He took me home, and we stood in the hall and sent our voices up the stairs.

I SAT by my window and waited for to-day, reliving the day that had passed. Mrs Tench bringing my breakfast, the drive to the shacks, my sudden decision about the cousins' dinner, the lie about Mrs Barnaby's invitation, my mother's smiling consent. Our own party, still in the future; Anna's behaviour at lunch – Anna had never talked or looked like that before. The letter I had written my father, the picture of the house that had no people in it, the children I'd forgotten, the story. The light.

A day of big and little things, all of them new, all happening for the first time. All building to an end. What end?

Now I am waiting . . .

Mother has come to my door twice, reminding me of the time. 'Come down at once when you hear the car, Isobel. This is an occasion for the cousins, and we must fill it to the brim for the poor lambs. A white frock? Quite bridal, dear. Am I going to lose my little girl too soon?'

The second time she came, she said, 'Tench has telephoned from the village that they are just leaving. You may be sure Carrie inspired the call. Do you think she expects a red carpet?'

It is five-thirty now. Dark. But not too dark for Mike and Joe and me. They will bring three flashlights, wrapped in the parcels with the long white strips. When I hear the car, I will go down and stand beside Mother in the hall.

Where will the cousins put their wraps? Not upstairs, not in any of the rooms upstairs! The cousins, running up and down the halls, washing their hands in different bathrooms, looking for safety pins. Jane, turning off lights because light costs money; Bess, opening doors because they are closed; Carrie, looking out of windows because she always does. 'Maude, what's the meaning of these dangling rags? What will the Barnabys think!'

But if they insist, if Mother insists, there is nothing I can do.

This may be the last time I will sit in my room and talk to myself.

That is the car now, coming up the drive. That is Mother calling to me, to Anna, hurrying to the door. The sharp click-click is the sound of her little spool-shaped heels.

The keys to every room in the house, every closet, are on a panel at the end of my hall. Labelled and numbered.

Am I ready? Yes. When the time is right, Mike will talk about the music box. He will flatter Mother and the cousins, and Mrs Barnaby will help him. Joe and I will say very little. Mike doesn't trust us. 'Leave everything to me. I'll fix it.'

IT is midnight. Everything is over. This is the last time I shall look back.

A few minutes ago Mike said, 'If you want to lie down before we leave, you have plenty of time. I've got some people to talk to. I'll come for you when I've finished. Keep your door closed, baby, but always remember that I'm outside somewhere and that I'm coming back to get you.'

198

But I heard the slow footsteps through the closed door . . .

Mother was waiting for me at the foot of the stairs when I went down to meet the cousins. It is all too easy to remember, the sounds, the smells, the wind that whistled through the hall when Anna opened the front door; the promise of broiled lobster that drifted through the service door because Anna forgot to close it, the pine needles that Tench had scattered on the library fire, the spray of freesia tucked in Mother's belt, the violet water Cousin Carrie was shaking into her bodice as she entered.

'Carrie,' Mother scolded, 'there's a time and place for everything. And here's Isobel. Come forward, dear. Anna, I think the south room for the wraps. If you'll follow Anna, darlings.'

'I'll take care of it, Anna,' I said.

I laughed and kissed the cousins one by one. 'The south room is a barn; you'll freeze. I know a much better place.'

'But we have our scarves,' Bess said. 'Our Liberty scarves, from Liberty's in London. On our heads now, but we plan to wear them on the shoulder in a careless, flowing drape. Where is that dear Mrs Barnaby?'

'She's on her way, she'll be here any minute. I'm sure she'll use the circular room, so wouldn't you like that, too?' I led the way. 'See the nice fire, as warm as toast and no stairs to climb.'

'Thoughtful of you, darling,' Mother said. 'This is Isobel's day of emancipation,' she told the cousins. 'Have you noticed her frock? Darlings, how sweet you look. You'll put poor Lucy Barnaby in the shade!'

The cousins had added chiffon flounces to their long black gowns and experimented with rouge.

'Maude, the chiffon came from that parasol you threw away when you married. Three wide ruffles, you remember. I knew they'd come in handy. Lined with pink silk. It cast a lovely glow. The lining will be a combing jacket for somebody's Christmas – we never waste a thing. Are there towels in that lavatory and everything needful? You know Bess.'

199

I want to remember everything that was said and done, everything. I want to remember who said this, said that. I want to know if coming events did cast their shadows before; I want to know if I was warned.

THEY told me I looked pale. Was my dress a new one? No? Well, white was not my colour, but perhaps a little rouge – White was half-mourning; some people called it whole; the Chinese? Nevertheless, a little rouge.

The rouge was kept in a purse that Jane had sewed into the lining of her muff. It was a round white box with a faded floral label, marked 'For the Nails'. I can see the little box as it passed from hand to hand and the cousins' cheeks progressed from pink to scarlet. Even when the night was over, the cheeks were still scarlet. Scarlet. Scarlet on deadly white ... The cousins laughed and tossed their heads and swung their beads proudly.

'Venetian,' Bess reminded me. 'Venetian from Venice. Your poor father's gift, years ago. We told him what we wanted.'

They dabbed at my face with a little wad of rouged cotton; they led Mother to the lavatory mirror and touched her cheeks lightly. She didn't protest.

'There, now,' Jane said, 'we'll have *you* wearing white next. Isn't everything lovely? I'm sure we've never had a better time, even though we haven't begun. I hope we're not unfashionably early.' She turned off the light while they were all still in the room. 'Nobody needs it.'

The violet toilet water was used once more, then hidden under the wraps. The flounces were shaken out and smoothed, the scarves were coaxed into the flowing careless drape and disciplined with pins.

'We have a little surprise for you, Maude,' Carrie said. 'Tench will bring it in, naturally; a parcel is out of place with formal clothes. A box of games, dear Maude, the nice old games we used to play. They're quite the thing again; they're very smart. I hear it everywhere, you'd be surprised.'

'There's bridge, Carrie, if you want it.'

'Don't you like Lotto? It's really Bingo, you know.'

I told myself the cousins were sound and good, that I had never understood them before because I'd never really known them. When Mrs Barnaby came, they would arch their brows and greet her with peals of high-pitched laughter. Even before she came, they were ready. When they walked from the circular room to the library, they tossed their heads to an unseen audience. 'Airy, let's be airy.' They were mine, I told myself, my own people, mine. They were ridiculous, they hadn't learned or grown as Mother had; but behind the posing and the postures, I thought I recognized and felt their soundness. I walked with Cousin Carrie's hand in mine, and I'm glad now that I did.

The Barnabys came a few minutes later. I took Mrs Barnaby's wrap while Mike and Joe went calmly to the hall closet with their topcoats.

Mike whistled when he saw Mother and the cousins, and Joe cried, 'Wolf, wolf!' Mike complained. 'I wish some-body'd tell my grandmother how to dress. She thinks a dinner invitation is an exhumation order for the old grey lace.'

Mother and the cousins laughed, the cousins tossed their heads and smoothed their scarves, and Mrs Barnaby's strong old face was wreathed with smiles. But Mrs Barnaby's eyes told me she had been coached. She was looking for something behind the other faces, behind the furniture, the *portières*, the curtains at the windows. I didn't know what she had been told, but she had clearly been convinced. 'I'll tell her to back us up in anything we do,' Mike had said. 'I'll tell her we're floating a private enterprise, that it's harmless and decent and the proceeds, if any, will go to a non-sectarian charity. And that's no lie. If I can wipe that look off your face, I'm going to lift somebody's mortgage.'

They were still laughing when Tench came in with the sherry. Mike and Joe, the cousins and Mother; I laughed, too. Tench with his tray of sherry, Anna with a tray of biscuits; they laughed. The room was full of foolish noise, and only Mrs Barnaby's quiet eyes questioned its source.

I REMEMBER too little of the early conversation, because I was waiting to hear one sentence, spoken in Mike's voice. The other voices meant nothing, the other sentences became gibberish. Bingo. Lotto. Do you remember Flinch?

I took the biscuits from Anna and handed them around. I know I talked. I watched Mike and Joe refilling the cousins' glasses and flirting with Mother. I thought my watchfulness was unobtrusive, but Mike's eyes met mine with a warning look. After that I sat beside Mother, and the only thing I watched was the clock. We still had time. I tried to look as a girl should look when she is rouged and dressed for a party in her own house. Her first party in her own house. Her own house.

Mike and Joe enslaved the cousins. Mother watched and listened, nodding her head and smiling faintly. If she wondered at their antics, she gave no sign of it. Under the dusting of rouge she was white and tired. Mrs Barnaby was tense in her chair, and I knew she was waiting, as I was, for one sentence. I thought we would never come to it; then, suddenly, the words that had been gibberish began to make sense. They were talking about games.

Games. The beginning of a perfect progression. Games. Toys. Playroom. A music box. Mike worked slowly, using the material the cousins gave him. Joe helped. Mike moved a mountain from our path, and Joe carried away the small stones.

'I don't like the gambling ones, either,' Carrie said. 'Our dear mother had a relative by marriage who was a clergyman, very devout. When he came to visit, he burned every card in the house. Playing cards, you understand, not Flinch. I haven't been able to enjoy playing cards since, not even a little game of Hearts for fun. Do you think he invoked a curse? I always lose.'

'Lose.' Bess turned to Joe. 'What tragedies that little

word implies! Do you mind if I make a personal comment? I can't help but notice your hair. You mustn't take offence, I naturally notice things. Stop using water; you'll rot the roots. You'll thank me for that one of these days. My sister referred to Flinch. A pleasant game, but do you remember Pit? Very lively. Janie dear, remember Pit?'

'Two, two, two! Corner on wheat!' Jane beamed. 'We brought them all. Tench has them. Everyone remembers Pit!'

MRS BARNABY looked straight into my eyes. 'Have you kept your old games, Isobel?'

Mother answered for me. 'I'm afraid she had nothing of that sort. Dolls, of course, and little beds, and a small stove. Childish things that she played with quietly. She was too young for games when she went away and too old for them when she returned.'

'People are never too old!' Joe. Young Joe. Almost shouting.

I began. 'I had a –'

'I'm a devotee of Fishpond myself,' Carrie declared. 'The cunning little hook, the anxious casting, the steady hand, the reeling in the fish! Properly played, it can be a very graceful game. The turn of a slender wrist, a pretty bracelet. There's nothing like a slender wrist and a pretty bracelet. I've been admiring yours, dear Mrs Barnaby. I had a friend who caught a fine husband with *The Melody of Love* on the piano. She couldn't *play*, it was the wrist and her grandmother's bracelet.'

'I packed the Fishpond in the box,' Jane.

'Isobel,' Mike said, 'didn't you have a music box once?'

'There!' Mrs Barnaby smiled at Carrie. 'That's what I meant by old games. I was sure I remembered a musical game or toy. And the little story about your friend made Mike remember, too.'

'Sure, you had a music box, Issy. Didn't you?' Joe. Too eager, too tense, too loud.

'Yes. It's in the old playroom.'

'Why don't we go up and look it over? Any reason why we can't?' Mike bent over Mother's hand. 'I'm crazy about your party. Now, if I can only play with Issy's music box –'

'Mike,' Mother said, 'is this the result of my poor, simple sherry?'

'I think these children are charming,' Mrs Barnaby said to the cousins. 'These modern children are really sweet. The old playroom, the old, shabby toys. Tell them to run along, Mrs Ford.'

'But dinner!' Mother looked doubtfully at the clock, at Mrs Barnaby, at the cousins.

For me, the clock was racing, but time in the room stood still. A log in the fireplace broke with a long, soft hiss. Mrs Barnaby's fingers tapped the arm of her chair. Mother's little foot swung back and forth as it does when she is thinking.

At last Carrie spoke. Her laughter was tolerant and chiding. 'My dear Maude, surely not dinner before seven. Even in the country.'

'These modern children are charming, as you say, Mrs Barnaby.' Bess.

'Isobel is coming out of herself, she's showing an interest. Quite emancipated.' Jane. 'And we can have a cosy talk while they romp. I've been admiring your brooch, Mrs Barnaby. Turn out the lights when you come down, Isobel. The dollars take care of themselves.'

Mother waved us from the room, and the *portières* swung together behind us. Out in the hall, Mike spoke distinctly. 'Got to get cigarettes from my coat pocket, Issy. Wait here while Joe and I rummage in the closet.'

They returned with the parcel, and we started up the stairs. Back in the library, Mrs Barnaby's laughter outrode the cousins'. I led the way. Mike was close behind me. He gripped my arm – to warn, or to reassure. Joe followed more slowly, as though to guard the rear.

Halfway up the stairs, Mike leaned over the balustrade. 'What is it, Tench?'

Tench was in the dining-room doorway, looking up. 'Can I get you anything, Mr Mike?'

'We're looking for our lost youth, Tench. Are you any good at that?'

'I think so, Mr Mike.'

'Fine. We'll yell if we need help. We're going to the playroom, Tench. Bang on the gong with all you've got when dinner's ready.'

We climbed, not looking back. I don't know how long Tench stood there, watching us.

'Always play it straight when you can,' Mike said. 'Keys, playroom, and hurry.'

ON each floor of the house there are two wide halls that form a cross. The stairs rise from the centre of the cross. There was light below us, there was darkness above. We came to the top of the stairs, to the second floor.

The keys hung from a panel at the end of my hall. My room is at the front of the house, facing north. The playroom is at the opposite end, on the side facing west. I found the keys; I had been afraid to take them earlier. Our footsteps echoed on the stone floor. I wanted to walk on the rug, but Mike said no.

'This is a noisy, childish frolic,' he said. 'Up to and including the next two minutes. After that, hush-hush.'

We unlocked the playroom door and found the light switch. Mike said, 'Show Joe where the box is and get it going. This is the wrong side of the house for us. We can forget all the west windows. We want east.' He unwrapped the parcels as he talked; the long white strips uncoiled and fell to the floor. They should have made a noise, they should have sounded like chains. They were as soft as snow. 'We'll keep together, always in sight of each other, no chance of duplication then.' He winked. 'Having fun?'

I said yes.

My rocking-horse had a braided tail tied with a red ribbon. I had forgotten that. My little stove had pots and pans, an oven and lids. It could hold a fire and cook, but I had never cooked on it. The little lifter for the lids was tied to the oven door. It was tiny and perfect. A shovel for the ashes.

Joe said, 'Issy, is this the box?'

He wound it. The box is round, covered with something that looks just like coloured beads, with a metal cup in the centre. My Christmas tree fitted into the cup, and when the music played, the tree turned. The tree turned round and round, and the music played *The Lorelei*.

'Not too tight, Joe, the tree won't turn,' I said.

Mike said, 'It's all right, baby, it's all right.' The music played, and the empty little cup went round and round. Mike took the keys from my hand. 'So much for the sound effects; the burning cigarette on the window sill, if you know your Baker Street. Now set me straight. Your own room is out, this one is out, everything on this side of the house is out. I'd say everything on this floor, but we don't want to take a chance. We'll do all the east windows, high and low. Come on, hush-hush now.'

FROM room to room, walking like thieves, opening locked doors, smelling dust, turning the flashlights on shrouded furniture. Opening unlocked doors, smelling clean rooms; opening closets with small windows. Windows. Opening windows with clean locks and rusted locks, dropping the long white strips and making them fast. Up another flight of stairs, the last but one. Up there, the air was thick and old. There was no carpeting. The flashlights found the rows of doors, all labelled. Trunks. Veranda Furniture. Nursery Furniture. Empty. Empty. Empty. Rolls of dust like weather stops against the doors marked Empty. Four doors, studded with nails, at the four corners of the house. The doors to the turrets.

I said, 'There's nothing in the turrets.'

206

'Ever been up?'

'Years ago. They're useless. Winding stairs and a tiny room at the top, like a platform. My father said the stairs weren't safe, the mortar is loose between the stones.'

'They have windows,' Mike said. 'This is where we don't skip. North, east, south, and west. This is no man's land.'

Rooms and closets crowded to the ceiling with things that had no shape. Two windows in each room, one in each closet.

'We're taking too much time!' Joe's face was streaked with dust. 'Can we hear that gong when it rings?'

'Listen,' Mike said. The music box was playing far away. A world away. 'We'll hear the gong.'

We climbed the turrets. Mike led and I followed. Joe was behind me. In one of them I saw a clean, dustless step – two, three, four clean steps – but when I bent to look, Joe whispered, 'Hurry.' One small window in each turret, a slit in the stone. We heard the wind.

Joe said, 'I bet nobody knows how thick these walls are. They're plenty thick. Say, you know what? This part up here was never wired! You'd *have* to use candles, see? This proves I saw what I said I saw. You, too, Issy. How soon can I tell Lucy?'

No one answered him.

His grubby hands caressed the walls, his eyes glistened. 'You know what, Issy? I could have had fun up here for years if I'd known what it was like. When I was a kid, I mean.'

North, east, south, and west, across the intersecting halls, up and down the winding stairs until we came to the last high window.

Mike whispered to the trees, 'Sister Ann, Sister Ann, do you see anybody coming?'

'I'm having fun,' Joe said.

Mike dusted his hands. 'That's that,' he said softly. 'Every window taken care of and two strips left over.' He crushed the white streamers into his pocket. 'Come along, we've got to wash.'

'Don't we reconnoitre first?' Joe. 'I mean outside. We ought to beat it outside while we have the chance.'

'We will if there's time. *Reconnoitre!* Soap and water in the playroom, General.' Mike turned to me as if he had forgotten I was there. He wasn't convincing. 'I could have had fun up here for years, too, Issy.'

Joe says, 'Say, you know what? I bet that light we saw was Anna looking for a bat's nest. She hasn't got a bat. But anyway, I've sure enjoyed it, Issy. That story you told Mike is strictly corn, but anyway, I've sure enjoyed it. Will I have things to talk about!'

We started down. The music box was silent; there was no sound from below.

'If we find any candle wax or anything, will she give me back that allowance cut?' Joe. 'A buck, it adds up.'

Mike was the first to hear the other footsteps. We had nearly reached the second floor. 'I'll fix it,' he said.

The steps were coming up.

We moved forward, laughing; we filled the halls with the same foolish sound that had begun the evening. An answering wave surged up the stairs and receded. The cousins, Mrs Barnaby, Mother. At the foot of the stairs we came face to face with Tench.

'Coming to get us, Tench?'

'Yes, Mr Mike.'

'Did you ring?'

'Yes, sir.' He stood aside.

'We'll wash up downstairs then. Dirty work, these little journeys into the past.'

Tench smilingly agreed.

The gong rang when we reached the first floor. We met the others leaving the library, clearly answering a first summons. Anna still held the small bronze hammer.

'Did we keep you waiting, Anna?' She shook her head.

Mother looked us over doubtfully.

208

THE tall white candles dripped. The warm white drops rolled slowly down. They fell on the wreathing smilax, and the small leaves trembled. Minute by minute the candles burned away.

The lobsters were red and empty on the pale-green plates, the yellow lemons were squeezed dry; but we had only begun. There were other knives and forks to lift, moulds of jelly to break, fruit to peel and nuts to crack, wine to swallow.

Carrie said, 'You set a pretty table, Maude.' She pursed her lips. She was telling herself she should have said, 'Anna does very well, Maude, but then, of course, you trained her.'

The candles ate the time. Each rolling drop of wax was time consumed.

It was a pretty table. We were black and white and grey, but the table was a palette. The table was a still-life painting, a canvas. We were figures on a canvas, hung in a waiting house. We were framed in light, waiting to be judged.

We were in the centre of darkness. The dark garden outside the windows, the dark curtains at the door, the halls and stairs beyond. The dark rooms overhead, locked and unlocked, empty or not empty. In one of them there was no one to see a bowl of red carnations; in another a music box had stopped playing. In all of them, along the eastern wall, the windows were flying flags of truce. Out in the garden, where the wind was high there was no one to see them.

I heard my name. 'This reminds me of Isobel.' Bess was talking to Mother. 'I hope you made the man give you the feathers, Maude. I'm thinking of a little toque on Isobel's fair hair. This is guinea, isn't it? Of course it is. There's the jelly. A little toque, using the breast and part of the tail.'

'Maude doesn't have to economize,' Carrie said. 'Isobel, your mother tells me you drove yesterday. Did you see anyone I know?'

'She was with me,' Mike said. 'And I don't know anybody you'd be caught dead with.'

'That reminds me, Maude.' Jane turned to Mother. 'I haven't seen that animal. Is he still, you know, well?'

'Isobel, dear, Cousin Jane is asking about Tray.'

'I saw him this morning,' I said. 'He's quite well, thank you.'

'Told you so, did he? "Good morning, mistress, I am well and hope you are the same." ' Jane was convulsed. 'I always said that dog could talk.'

Anna, arranging plates at the sideboard, dropped one. The small crash was followed by silence. Anna ran from the room.

'I hope that's open stock,' Bess said.

'Open or not,' Carrie answered, 'Maude doesn't have to economize.'

Mother shook with quiet laughter. 'You see why I love them,' she said to Mrs Barnaby. 'Janie, you frightened Anna, and I won't have it. Tray is her *bête noire*. I really think she believes he's devil-ridden. Sometimes I think Isobel is as bad as Anna.'

'Nonsense,' Mrs Barnaby said flatly.

'Look at Isobel's arms!' Jane cried. 'Gooseflesh. Would you like my scarf, dear? A Liberty scarf is very light and warm.'

'Nerves,' Bess said. 'From her poor father's side.'

EVEN before dinner ended, I think I knew we would never be together again, not all of us. Mike says I couldn't have known that, but he was not in tune with the house. I was; I had been born in tune, and the house played on me. I knew then that we would never be together again. Later the doctor told me that prescience is not uncommon. He thinks events can telegraph themselves like people asking to be met. I know they can.

When Tench and Anna served dessert, Mother complimented them. Carrie demanded Mrs Tench, and she came into the room wearing a white apron over her black uniform

210

and was complimented in turn. We were all together, sitting and standing about a lace-covered table wreathed in smilax and lighted by candles. We had come to the end of something, not only of the dinner itself but of a cycle. I thought of the waiting windows facing the east; they were in the future, they were ahead of me. But the present was growing dim, fading, sinking into the past.

Mother's cigarette smoke curled upward, blue and fragrant. The cousins' fingers stroked the lace cloth, furtively worshipping.

'Mrs Tench, you have surpassed yourself.' Carrie. 'The sweet was fit for a king!'

The sweet was ice cream, in a hollow block of ice, around which candles had been set. If the house has an emblem, it should be a candle.

The candles on the table had burned low. The bon-bon dishes held coloured crumbs, the grapes were sprawling stems, the wine was a sad remembrance in the bottom of a glass. The talk said nothing new; but the speechless things – empty walnut shells, the stems and cores of fruit, the dregs and ashes said, 'This is the end.'

MIKE and Joe were quiet. Mrs Barnaby said little. Mother encouraged the cousins and led them on to talk. It was the cousins' night.

'Our little girl lives in a dream world,' Carrie said. 'She lives a dream life, waiting for the prince. Twenty-one years old next month, a woman, and if I may say so, a rich one. Lucky, lucky Isobel!'

'Are you going to sell the house, Isobel?' Jane. 'Don't. It suits your mother. If I've said it once, I've said it a dozen times – not one woman in a thousand can get away with a house like this.'

'Isobel has hardly opened her mouth all evening.' Bess. 'Even these young men have hardly opened their mouths. Tell us about the music box, Isobel. What does it play?'

'*The Lorelei*, Cousin Bess.'

'Ta-*ta*, ta-ta-*ta* – how does it begin? I used to know the words, but I've forgotten.'

Mike said, '*Ich weiss nicht was soll es bedeuten*. That's how it begins.'

'Mercy, you're quite a linguist! What's the English?'

' "I wonder what it all does mean," ' Mike said. 'That's the English.'

Coffee in the library. The fire rebuilt. The cousins' box of games opened on a table. Mother's port and cards on another table in a far corner, waiting for the door to close on her last guest.

I was lost in the room, I was lost to myself, I drank coffee I couldn't taste. Over the clatter of cups the gibberish rose again. Pit. Flinch. Lotto.

'Please, Carrie,' Mother begged, 'not the noisy ones.'

Mike and Joe spoke to Mother and came to my side.

'We're going to take a brisk trot to the gate and back,' Mike said clearly. 'Your mother okays it, and so does Miss Carrie. After that, I'm going to court Miss Carrie with my facile wrist and Grandma's bracelet.'

Carrie's happy scream followed us to the front door. When the door closed behind us, Mike said, 'Never again. Never any of this again. This is strictly for crazy people.'

'Hurry, Mike. I want to get it over.'

'*You* want!'

'Personally, I go for this kind of thing,' Joe said. 'I could go for this any time.'

We were coatless. The wind fought back when we met it at the corner of the house.

Joe hummed *The Lorelei*. He said, 'That was a lousy translation of yours, Mike. I can do it more colloquially. But your way kind of went to my spine.'

'Mine, too. I was surprised.'

'Hurry,' I said.

The east wall hid behind the trees. The kitchen lights, at the far end, were dim. 'We can't see, we can't see!'

'Joe has a flash. Lucy never comments on the bulges in Joe's pockets. Come here, close to the wall. Look up.'

Joe trained the light. The white strips hung in even rows, protected from the wind by the trees. Mike counted with silent lips. I heard myself whispering, 'The blue room, the linen closet, the sewing-room –' We didn't need names, not even words; we needed what we had: dark windows in a high stone wall, each with its long white answer.

'Somebody's got to sneak up there and drag all that stuff in,' Joe said. 'I don't mind doing it for you.'

'Keep moving,' Mike said. 'The party isn't over. Isn't this the place where the halls cross?'

I said yes. The small room that was once my bedroom, the bath adjoining, the room with the flowered paper, the first eastern turret.

'You're thinking out loud,' Mike said. 'That's crazy. And you don't have to tell me what's what, I've been there.' His voice was sharp.

'It's getting you,' Joe said. 'Where's the old poise now, pal? Where's the ice water in the old veins? *Hey!*'

AHEAD of us a stream of light shot out across the path. The kitchen door had opened. We didn't stop, we walked on; Mike's hand, gripping my arm, told me to walk on. He whistled, Joe whistled, I walked between them. Anna came out into the light, wrapped in an old coat, pulling the old sweater over her head.

'Anna?' Mike called.

'Who's that?'

'The younger generation. Don't tell me you've washed up already!'

'I've got a headache, I'm going down to bed. Ada – Mrs Tench says I can. I'm sick.'

'Sorry to hear it. Want us to walk down with you? It's pretty dark.'

I thought: If she looks up, she will see the windows. If she looks up, she will see the windows and scream.

213

'The dark don't bother me,' Anna said. 'But thank you.' She covered her head with the sweater and ran. Once she had passed the dim kitchen windows, she was invisible. We heard the flying gravel under her feet, the crackle of dry leaves. The sounds grew fainter and died away.

'Got a baby bat in her pocket right now,' Joe said. 'Going home to play with it.'

We skirted the kitchen windows and came to the part of the wall that was in line with the old cedar tree. In line with Joe's attic window. Mike looked from the wall to the garden and back again. He was trying to get his bearings.

'Give us the light, Joe.'

Trunks. Veranda Furniture. Nursery Furniture. Storage. Words typed on small cards and tacked to doors. The light picked out the windows and the limp white strips. Trunks, Veranda Furniture. Nursery Furniture. Storage.

'You're thinking out loud again. I told you I knew –'

Joe said, 'Wait.'

The light wavered in his hand, slid down the wall, climbed and stopped at a narrow window. Empty.

The light slid down the wall again, moved up, travelled to the right and to the left and came back. An empty window, a slit in the wall, a window, blank, empty. Where the base of the south-east turret curved to meet the house wall, a narrow window, empty.

'How did we miss that one?' Mike asked softly.

'We didn't,' Joe said. 'The marker fell out.'

'See it anywhere?'

'No. Listen. We opened every door, we had a key for every door, and there weren't any keys left over. We saw everything there was to see. Two windows in each of those rooms, one in each closet, one in each turret. We opened every door. So what? So that's no window, that's a ventilator or something, they fixed it up to match the window in the turret.'

'Ventilator?'

They forgot me. They tried to break each other down, and they forgot me.

214

'Sure, a ventilator. Or something.'

'A ventilator with a windowpane?'

'Well, I don't know. Now that you mention it, I don't know. Maybe it belongs to the heating system or the plumbing. Could be important pipes and stuff behind it.'

'How would you reach the important pipes? Where's the door?'

'Now that you mention it – Well, maybe the guy who built the house –'

'What?'

'Maybe he wanted a window seat or something and changed his mind and walled it off.'

'Cheaper to wall up the window. You admit there's got to be a wall or a partition of some kind?'

'Mike, there's got to be. Or else it's an odd window in a corner of the trunk room with stuff piled against it.'

Mike said, 'Look at the trunk room in your mind, Joe.'

They forgot me. I stood between them and did my own thinking. I saw the trunk room in my own mind. The trunks were stacked in the middle of the room, the walls were bare and clear. The trunk room was a lie. The outside wall gave it away. I asked myself what was behind that small, empty room. A closet without a door? A little room without a door? A closet, a little room, without a door, a key? *Empty?*

How could a light shine in an empty room, a walled-up room without a door? How could a light move back and forth, be seen, turn itself on and off, without a hand? How could a hand, a body –

I HEARD Joe, answering nothing. 'Do we have to get permission to go up there this time? Do we have to tell those old girls what we're doing? That music-box stuff is going to sound crazy if we pull it again.'

Mike said, 'We don't tell anybody anything. Issy? I haven't forgotten you, baby. Easy does it. We've found the place where Anna raises glow-worms.'

The same wind that fought us back before urged us to

215

return. It lashed and whipped and drove us home. The same wind is outside my window now, not hindering or helping but hiding in the trees. Sometimes, now, a door slams far away, and I know it has slipped from someone's hand.

'We may be through in ten minutes,' Mike went on. 'If we aren't, they can think anything they like. We'll argue that one when we come to it.'

Behind the library *portières* the cousins were playing their games. They were shrill, absorbed, and happy. Mrs Barnaby played with them; her voice was low and patient. I could not hear Mother. She has begged off, I thought; she has gone to her own little table with the port, the cards, and the Turkish cigarettes.

When we climbed the stairs for the second time, and walked the halls, we kept to the rugs. Mike took the keys from his pocket. We climbed the last, bare flight. We did everything a second time, but we did not talk. There was no tinkling music behind us; we climbed and walked in silence. Mike separated the keys, chose the two he wanted and held them apart from the others. Trunk Room. South-east Turret.

The trunk room. He closed the door behind us.

Two windows, square and honest, anchoring the ends of the long white strips. We walked around the room, circling the centre stack of luggage; we walked slowly, like people pacing off a piece of land. Joe's flashlight moved from floor to wall to ceiling and came to rest on the wall against the turret.

'Somewhere about here,' Joe said, 'something ought to show.' The light played on the smooth, unbroken paint. 'Not a crack. Something ought to show. That window is about four feet from the right of this wall, but that puts it nowhere. I mean, it isn't in the turret. There's about four feet of space floating around in here somewhere, unless it's been filled in with stone and covered over, and that's dumb. Unless some screwball did the same thing with every corner of the house and we missed it before. We could go around and check, Mike.'

'Turret,' Mike said.

'Don't you think we ought to check the other rooms, on the other side, and see if –'

'Turret, Joe.'

'Okay, but we know that's only stairs and a kind of platform. The walls are plenty thick, but if there's anything behind them, it's got to be a very –'

Suddenly Joe remembered me and everything the search implied. He remembered and saw me, not as the girl next door who had told a story about a hidden room, tied it up with her own house, and let you run around tapping walls; he saw and remembered Isobel Ford. Isobel Ford, the girl his brother and grandmother talked about, the girl who hid behind hedges and watched other people's parties, the girl whose father had killed himself while of unsound mind. The girl whose empty house showed lights at night, lights that moved behind a window in a non-existent room. The girl who told a story.

POOR Joe, with his plastered hair and new dinner coat. 'Issy?' His voice rose and fell. 'Issy, I –'

I told him it was all right, that I wasn't afraid. I said there was nothing to be afraid of, nothing.

Mike said, 'Issy, it's cold up here. Go downstairs to the others. Tell them Joe and I went home for cigarettes.'

I answered carefully. 'How do I know I'll find the Hall there?'

'What?'

'How do I know who's in the library? We heard voices, that's all. One voice against another, overlapping, confused. We didn't see anyone. How do I know who's in the kitchen? How do I know Tench and Mrs Tench are in the kitchen, where they ought to be? How do I know Anna went to the cottage?'

'We saw Anna go.'

'I've seen too many things come and go. There's something hidden in this house, and we'll find it now, all three of us, or I'll –'

'We'll find it, Issy. All three of us, as you say. Now.'

I heard myself saying now, now, now.

That time, I looked for the clean steps in the turret. I moved my hands over each step, from side to side, from front to back, each step. I looked at my hands. When they were covered with dust, I rubbed the dust on my dress. There were four clean steps at the top, clean all over. The others were clean close to the trunk-room wall, as if something had walked down and up, close to the wall, hugging the wall. The wall between the turret and the trunk room.

'There'll be a door hère,' I said, 'hidden in the wall. It will look like stones and mortar, but it will be a door, an opening, a hole to crawl through. Here, in this place, up here, near the top. Didn't you see me find the clean steps?'

'Yes, Issy; yes, baby.'

'Something felt safe about using the top steps. Something used the top steps every day or night, looking for air on the turret platform. Even looking for sun or people in the garden. It was afraid to raise the little window. And it went down to the bottom of the stairs, too, down to the hall door, maybe even through the door, out into the hall, out into the house. But when it did that, it hugged the wall and made a single, narrow track. That was for safety, that was playing safe. Suppose someone had wanted to come up here, suppose some honest person with an honest reason had unlocked the hall door and looked up the stairs? The narrow track would be invisible, the clean steps would be above eye level. Suppose I'd unlocked the door, alone, and come up here, alone.' I called, 'Who's listening to me? Who's listening?'

'Be quiet,' Mike said. 'Be quiet, now.'

His fingers dug into the mortar, he began at the bottom of the steps and moved up. Joe worked beside him. I stood against the opposite wall and held the light and watched their fingers.

Mike said, 'Got a knife or a nail file?'

Joe's knife went into the mortar up to its hilt. Four steps

218

from the top they lifted a small stone from the wall. Joe put the stone aside, and his hand went into the cavity. A door swung inward, into darkness.

'Get the light.'

Mike took it from my hand. A short flight of steps led down to a stone floor level with the trunk room. A narrow space, a passage to nowhere.

Another light came to meet ours, wavering across the floor. Out of the black behind it, we heard a voice. 'Isobel?'

Then the figure and the face. It was my father, and Tray was with him.

'WHAT there is left of me,' he said, 'is quite harmless.' One hand cupped the burning candles, and the light stripped the flesh from his fingers and turned them red. 'Come down, Isobel. Mike and Joe, come down.'

I think we stood with linked arms. I think we did. We stood with linked arms, on the bottom step. We were in a tunnel between the trunk room and the turret; it widened at the window end, and there was space for a cot and table under the turret stairs. We could see them from the bottom step. My father was buried in a tunnel in his own house. The tunnel was cold.

He backed away from us until he reached the cot. The dog backed away, too, in step with my father, grinning.

'I need time,' my father said. 'Give me a little time.' He was thin and white, and the fire had burned out of his eyes. 'I'm not prepared for you, although I knew you'd come eventually. To-night or to-morrow. I heard you outside, but there was nothing I could do.'

'You can have all the time you want,' Mike said. He kept his hands in his pockets.

'I'm harmless, Mike.' He sat on the cot as if he had come a long way and was tired. The candles were on the table, the dog was at his feet. He had tins of food, tobacco, books. He wore clothing I had never seen before, shoddy but clean.

Not the Harris tweed he died in. A scrap of Harris tweed, singed.

I heard myself say, 'And the candles are yellow!'

Mike's arm tightened against mine. 'A medieval kind of guy,' he said softly to my father. 'Everything but the iron mask. Only yesterday I told Isobel you were a medieval kind of guy. I was trying to comfort her. She said you hated her. I said you didn't. We were down at the shacks.'

My father's eyes met his steadily.

'I said you were a doer,' Mike went on. 'I said if you didn't like a thing, you fixed it in your own way. I didn't know how good I was going to turn out to be. How long have you been here?'

'I came after the car burned.'

'Well, I know this much. I know a man can leave his family and he can't be touched as long as they're provided for. If he's a good provider, like yourself, he can disappear for ever if he wants to. But I don't know how the law feels about a phony funeral. We'll have to check on that. What was it, an insurance racket?'

'I had no insurance. Who is in the house beside yourselves?'

'*Ourselves*. My grandmother, your wife, and her cousins.'

'What mistake did I make? How did you find this room?'

'We saw your light.'

Joe, looking from me to my father, to Mike, was a tall child thrown into battle unarmed. Joe and I were alike. The other two were a different breed; they spoke another language, not with words but with their eyes.

My father's hand went to Tray's head and rested there. Watching that hand go out in the old gesture was like finding a long-lost letter and reading lines that should have been destroyed.

'ARE you going to believe me?' my father asked. 'Are you willing to believe me?'

220

Mike answered. 'We'll wait a bit before we decide that. Tell your story in your own way, Mr Ford. You must have one ready, you've had time enough.'

My father spoke to me. 'Not quite time enough, Isobel, because I haven't reached the end. I'm still waiting and looking for the end.' It was the same voice, grown old, that once had said, 'Always open doors when you hear music.'

Mike said, 'Talk to me, Mr Ford. To *me*. Who was the man in your car?'

He told us; and in spite of Mike, he talked to me. He began with his illness, watching me receive his words, pausing between sentences. He was an anxious beggar, holding out an empty heart. 'I was ill; everyone knew I was ill. And everyone knows a sick man is not a responsible man, he magnifies and distorts. Can you understand that?'

He was a beggar but not abject. He was asking for something, and I thought it was courage. I thought he wanted courage, from me, so that he could give it back. To me. I wondered why I would need it.

One day in the spring, he said, he went to the squatters' settlement. He was looking for someone more miserable than himself. In the lane his car passed a man who staggered under a load of firewood. They talked, they measured each other, and each one liked the thing he saw. That was how he first went to the shack at the end of the row.

'Two men lived there, brothers, as old as I am. Not derelicts, but old, tired men who had forgotten how to hope. The older brother was incurably ill, dying. Death was as close and real to him as I thought it was to me. We were both trapped, the dying man and I; we were both waiting. But he was ready and I was not; he had only one life to lose and I had two. I was afraid that I had two.'

'Afraid you had two lives to lose?' Mike was urbane.

My father said, 'Yes. My own and Isobel's.'

I think it was Joe who made the strangled sound. It must have been Joe. I remember that Mike laughed and I did nothing. Yes, it was Joe.

MIKE said, 'Tell me about the man who had only one life, Mr Ford. He died in your car, didn't he? How did that happen?'

My father talked to me again – not to Mike, to me.

He said they had been drinking in the shack, and the sick man was restless and irritable. He crouched beside the stove and complained of the cold.

'Although the fire was roaring, the poor wretch trembled with the cold. I lent him my jacket. I sent him out to gather wood. He went willingly, he thanked me, I know now that he was too willing. When he failed to return, we went to look for him. We called his name, we heard no answer. You know the rest. We found the blazing car. The surviving brother was terrified, perhaps of me, of my reaction. I don't know. I only know he left me standing at the quarry's edge and I never saw him again.'

Mike asked, 'How did you know who was in the car?'

'We followed the tracks from the field. We went as close as we dared. It was all plain enough. When I returned to the shack and found it empty I told myself I was free. I was dead, if I wanted to be. I was dead in the bottom of the quarry. I was dead and free to live and think.'

'No qualms about letting a stranger's body be found and identified as yours? No conscience about your wife and daughter and what they would have to face?' There was no venom in Mike's voice. I felt his arm grow slack in mine and saw his eyes meet Joe's.

He and Joe talked to each other with their eyes, and my father watched them. He looked as if he understood what they were thinking and wanted to answer, but was afraid. I felt the strength of pyramiding thoughts that were too frail to bear the weight of speech but strong enough to fill a room. I felt Mike's silent disbelief and, over it, my father's fear. My father's story was unbelievable, but his fear was real. Mike's eyes talked to Joe, and my father watched.

'I was ill,' my father insisted quietly. 'Very ill. There was a dead man in my car, burned beyond recognition. His only relative, the only witness, had disappeared. I took what fate had given me, a living release.'

Mike nodded. 'A perfect setup for a man with death on his mind. But suppose the other brother returns? And talks? He knows who you are?'

My father looked at me and turned away. 'I think of that constantly.'

'Then why did you come here?'

'I had to think. I had to see Isobel. I had played in this house when I was a child. I remembered this tunnel. I thought I might stay here for a few days until I had finished my thinking.'

'A few days. You've had a month, more than a month.'

'I'm ready to leave now.'

'Do you think we'll let you?'

'Yes. You're going to marry Isobel; you wouldn't hurt her. This would hurt her. You'd never be rid of it – you, Isobel, your children.'

Mike's nod agreed and approved. My father might have been the lone survivor of a shipwreck and Mike, familiar with the craft and the waters, a sympathetic and understanding listener. It was insane. Insane.

It was insane; there was no sense in any of it. My father was truly the monster of my story. He lived in a tunnel in his own house; he sat on a cot and warmed his hands over candlelight; he talked about two lives, his own and mine. He talked about not hurting me. Downstairs, within reach of my voice if I screamed, were five elderly women, four of them mourning him. My mother –

I thought of my mother wandering through the house she loved, wondering where the spiced and sweetened years had gone, hiding her pride and pain in silence. Breaking her heart in memory of a man who let a stranger fill his grave while he lived between walls like a rat.

'I'M afraid he's mad,' I said. 'Mother must be warned and protected. Suppose she comes here, unprepared?'

223

My father spoke eagerly. 'Isobel is right. I'm afraid you'll be missed. If you will leave me now, give me a few hours –'

'Why?' Mike's voice was mild and soft. 'Why, suddenly, do you want a few hours? So you can run away again? And what's happened to the end you said you were waiting for? The end of your story? Don't tell me you've found it. Don't tell me that one of us has given you the answer to your thinking. What are you afraid of, Mr Ford?'

My father said he was not afraid. He said, 'I am only ill, I am not afraid. Let me go, Mike, now, to-night. Believe me, it's the best thing.'

Mike released my arm. He went to the cot. I waited for Tray's snarl, but he was quiet and absorbed. He was listening, as he always did. 'Soon, soon,' Mike said. 'But first I want to hear more about your illness and the little incidentals of your life in here. Then we can talk about your going. Tell me about your food, for instance, and the books and so on. Where did they come from?'

'They came from the shack; they were originally bought for the use of myself and my friends. I moved them here, later.'

'Later,' Mike agreed. 'After the accident, or suicide, or whatever you want to call it. By the way, what do you call it?'

'I have always called it a release, for both of us. But I had no hand in it. I didn't kill him.'

'No, you didn't kill him. You're no murderer, not you.'

I was not the only one who heard Mike's underscoring. Joe and my father heard it, too. Mike said, 'Not *you*.' The almost whispered words relit the fire in my father's eyes and filled Joe's with wonder. I heard myself echoing Mike. Murderer. Not you. Not you. I heard Mike talking on, not giving me time to think, to probe, to dig deep in my mind and bring up names and faces.

'Do you still go out at night, Mr Ford?'

'Occasionally.'

224

I made myself ask, 'With Tray?'

He looked over my head to the stairs. Joe blocked the way. 'Yes,' he said.

'I want to hear about Tray, too,' Mike said. 'He tracked you here, didn't he?'

'Yes. That first night I tied him in the stable. I wanted him discovered and cared for, not roaming the countryside. But he found me, and I had to take him in.'

'Did you tell him to take care of Isobel?'

'I may have.'

'Where do you get the meat you've been giving him?'

My father looked at the blocked door again.

'Don't worry about the door,' Mike said. 'Nobody goes out and nobody comes in, not until we're ready.'

Joe's hand gripped mine, and his mouth brushed my cheek. He whispered, 'He's stalling; Mike's stalling. I don't know what for, I don't know why. He's stalling and waiting, and I don't know what for. Do you?'

I knew nothing.

'And forget about the meat,' Mike went on. 'I'm a good guesser. If you have an ally in the house, that's okay with me.'

My father said, 'Let me go, Mike!'

'Soon,' Mike promised again. 'Don't you know that I'm on your side, whatever that is? If you still want oblivion, I'll help you get it. I'll help you get away for good, and I'll make Isobel understand. But you've got to help me, too. You've got to stop lying.'

'I'm not lying.'

'You're not talking, and that's the same thing. In this situation, it's the same. If you want to lose yourself again, we'll make a good job of it; but you'll have to sell me on it first. You'll have to prove that you're alone in this cockeyed game of hide-and-seek, that you aren't being hunted and you aren't hunting. If you can do that, you're free. You can start another life anywhere you want to; you can make a comeback if you want one. A little amnesia, tactfully

225

handled, is something to keep in mind. You can turn up, all bewildered, in a hospital halfway across the country.'

My father's hand covered his eyes.

'So,' Mike said. 'Let's go back to the beginning and tie it up. You were ill, too ill to think straight, unwilling to confide in your family or your doctor. Want to tell us what you thought was wrong?'

No answer.

'Sick in body or mind or both, and yet you preferred to treat yourself. That's the first snag in your story, and it's a pretty one. We'll follow it with your decision to play dead. You played dead in the first place because you were ill. Right? Well, you're not ill now, you're thin but you're sound enough, and yet you still want to play dead. Why?'

No answer, no movement, no sound but Joe's small, frightened cough.

'Come on, Mr Ford,' Mike said. 'You've been here a month, you've straightened yourself out physically. What have you been hanging around for? As far as the world knows, you're suitably buried in the family plot, your wife and daughter are well provided for, everything is on the up and up, on the surface. On the surface you're free, free, free. What have you been hanging around for?'

My father filled Mike's pause with two words. He said, 'Please don't.'

'I must,' Mike said. 'For the everlasting peace of everyone in this house. You made a quick and desperate decision on the edge of that quarry, and you got what you wanted: a grave with your name on it. You got oblivion, and how did you use it? You went straight back to the life you ran away from. What for? To think, you say; and to see Isobel. What's wrong with Isobel?'

My father said, 'You don't know what you're asking!'

I BEGGED Mike to let me leave. I begged him to let me leave and take Joe. I reminded him that Joe was only seventeen;

226

I told him we were hurting Joe. 'He's only a baby,' I said. 'Look at him, he's frightened. Let us both go.'

'Nobody goes,' Mike said, 'until we all go together. And I have a hunch it won't be long now.' He turned to my father. 'Now, I can understand a man's wanting to run away; it's not my cup of tea, but I can understand it. "Most men live lives of quiet desperation." One of the bright boys wrote that, I don't know which one, but I can get the point, I can understand it. It's *you* I can't understand. You got what you wanted and came home again. To see Isobel. That's the part I plug, to see Isobel. You'd been seeing her every day for months, but apparently that wasn't enough. You wanted a better view, and you had to play dead to get it. No sense to that unless we cut one word and substitute another. I say you came back to *watch* Isobel, to watch her unseen.'

'Give me until daylight,' my father whispered. 'I want to think. I'm still not sure. Give me a few hours, and I'll talk to you.'

'No,' Mike said. 'Mr Ford, when we found that door and came in here, I was all set to call the cops. But not now, not any more. I changed my mind when I began to smell fear and panic. *Your* fear and panic, and not for yourself, either. For someone else. I want you to tell me what to do. I want to line up on your side, but I don't know how to get there.'

Fear and panic. When Mike called them by name, they went away, as such things do. They fell away before a strange, new warmth. It came slowly, it was tangible, it was in my father's voice when he said, 'Thank you.'

They looked at each other for a long time, in silence; I could have warmed my hands by holding them out to the two quiet men.

Mike spoke first. 'What did you mean, Mr Ford, when you said you were still not sure? Not sure of what?'

My father didn't answer.

Mike went on. 'Who or what has been hurting you, Mr Ford?' His arm lay across my father's shoulders.

Still no answer.

'That man's death gave you a peculiar freedom. Does your death free someone else?'

There was silence again while they read each other's faces.

The silence might have lasted until, in desperation and defeat, we left him. It might have lasted until we closed the tunnel door behind us and left him, until we went down to the others in the library and moved among them, lighting my mother's cigarettes and playing the cousins' games.

But Mike broke it. 'I'm remembering how you refused food,' Mike said softly. 'Isobel told me about that. I'm remembering how you preferred to eat and drink with the men in the shack. What put you off the food in your own house? Were you afraid of poison?'

JOE took my hand, and we crept forward. We walked into the current of my father's voice as if it were the sea.

'I was ill,' he begged. 'I am still ill. Can't you see that? I couldn't think, I'm unable to think now. Look at me. I'm not responsible, for myself or anyone else. Don't talk to me. I'm not responsible for what I say.'

'Bull's-eye,' Mike said, 'And I almost wish I hadn't hit it.' He whispered his questions, and my father fought against their strength.

'Have you proof, Mr Ford?'

'No, no, no!'

'Can you ever prove it?'

'No.'

'But you think you were given poison in your own house?'

'I don't know, I don't know.'

'Now I get the point about the quarry business. It makes sense now, even the tunnel makes sense. You came back here to look for proof, proof of poison or of your own madness. But why did you try to handle it alone? Why didn't you come to me? Between us we'd have licked it, one way or another. You trust me, don't you? You've always trusted me, haven't you?'

'I didn't trust myself.'

'Small wonder. Mr Ford, how does Isobel come into this? You talked about two lives, yours and hers. I don't like that. It can mean anything, and all of it bad. What's Isobel's place in the picture?'

The tunnel room was filled with the sound of breathing, but I heard another sound that wasn't there. It was familiar. I had been hearing it in other places for more than a month, in the house, in the garden, at night. It was the sound of my father's mind churning.

I listened to the sound and heard the pattern change. I heard the end before it came. It crept between us, moved among us like a spectre; nameless, faceless, invisible, but strong enough to stir the air and draw my father to his feet. We were no longer four minds, but five. The new warmth ebbed on a dying tide, and the old cold returned. My father raised one arm in a warding gesture. One arm, outflung, to make a barrier.

Then I heard the footsteps. They were outside the tunnel where the halls form a cross.

I said, 'Tench.'

The steps came on. No, not Tench. Light, clicking, little spool heels.

I said, 'Don't let her see. She'll be terrified. Let me tell her, let me!'

Her voice was faint at first, then it grew stronger. 'Isobel? Isobel?'

My father said, 'Close the door!'

But we stood there, Mike and Joe and I rooted to the floor. The steps came on, and we heard them falter at the open turret door. I was turned to stone; I tried to warn her; my mouth was turned to stone.

'Isobel, are you here? Why are you here?' She was frightened.

My father stood alone and waited. She came on, slowly; we heard the measured rustle of her trailing skirt. She stood in the doorway at the top of the steps, a candle in her hand.

She looked down. One scream, only one. She turned and ran.

She fell twice on the turret stairs; we heard her fall. We were behind her, running, when she reached the main stairs. She turned once and looked back. The others stopped, only I ran ahead. She sent me one look from eyes I did not recognize and flung her body to the stones below. Her candle was an arc of light that fell a second later.

She killed herself because she was a killer.

MIKE met the stream of terrified people that poured into the hall; the cousins, Mrs Barnaby, Tench, Mrs Tench. He held them with lies.

He knew she had killed herself; he didn't know why. But he lied with authority, and now his story is our story. We have tightened and strengthened it, and we will tell it the rest of our lives. He concentrated on the cousins, instinctively choosing the weakest links and holding them together with words.

'He has been ill, out of his mind. The dead man was a stranger, wearing his coat. He was ill, shocked. He doesn't know where he's been. But he was on his way home when we found him at the gates.'

They looked from my father to my mother; my father leaning on the balustrade, my mother on the floor at his feet. They clung to Mike, and he told his thin, loud lies over and over, while Tench led my father to a chair and stood beside him. Anna came from the cottage, summoned by Mrs Tench. I don't know who covered my mother; I think it was Joe. They all stood in a circle around Mike, Tench, and my father, and listened to the story we all will tell from now on. Even Tench, who knew it was a lie, nodded and listened. They believed it, all but Tench and one other. Tray watched from the head of the stairs, his head resting on his paws. Joe tried to drive him back, but he crouched like the brooding gargoyle that looks down on Paris and thinks. He looked as if he were waiting for my mother to move.

Mike told them my mother had fallen. He said she was running down the stairs to tell them the great news. Her little spool heels.

The cousins drank the words, and their eyes never left his face. Those little spool heels, hadn't they always warned her? And running to tell them her great, good news, running to share her miracle. They wept softly, and their old, tired weeping was her only elegy.

We had walked to the road, Mike said, and found my father standing at the gates. We had brought him into the house, secretly, and hidden him upstairs, because we wanted to prepare them. He was not fit to be questioned, not yet.

Mike did not look at me or my father when he talked. He avoided detail and forestalled interruptions. 'We don't know much about this ourselves. Mr Ford will talk to you later, but he must be quiet now. We know he lent his car and jacket to a man who needed them, and you know what happened to that man. The shock was too much for Mr Ford – he was on the edge of a breakdown and the man's death sent him over the edge. He doesn't remember where he's been or what he's done, except that to-night he found himself outside his own gates and knew he was home. Tench?'

'Yes, sir?'

'You and I will handle this. What's the first thing we do?'

It was Tench who called the doctor and the police and sent Anna and Mrs Tench to the kitchen to make coffee. It was Mrs Barnaby who took my father and me to his room, left us alone, and returned to the cousins. Later she drove them home. It was Joe who closed the tunnel door and removed the strips from the windows. It was also Joe who stopped halfway up the stairs and slit the carpet with his pocket knife. He made a ragged tear at the edge, the kind of tear a heel might make. He thought no one saw him, but

231

Tench did. Tench showed the tear to the doctor and the coroner, and they shook their heads. The foolish heels, the trailing skirt, the sudden happiness. Poor lady.

Tench. Tench talking to the doctor and the coroner, giving them coffee, serving them as they had never been served, repeating Mike's story as he had heard it, adding a few things of his own. 'Mr Ford was in bad shape before the accident. Mrs Ford and I often spoke of it and worried about it. He was what you might call a sensitive man, failing in health and sensitive. So it stands to reason, gentlemen, that when he saw the fatal result of his charity – Well, we read of such things in the papers, but we never think they will come to us, do we? Shock, do you say, doctor? Similar to battle shock? Yes, we read of such things.'

The coroner and the doctor were pleased to agree.

TENCH had known for three days that my father was in the house. Later, when we were together, and my father said, 'Sit down, Tench,' he sank into a chair like the tired old man he was. My father covered Tench's hand with his.

Mike and Joe, my father and I, and Tench. My father lying on his bed, covered with an eiderdown. Downstairs the strangers came and went and the lawyer talked to the reporters. The cousins and Mrs Barnaby were gone, and Mrs Tench and Anna had returned to the cottage.

'I knew it all along,' Anna said. 'Didn't I say as much, or something like it? I felt his living presence, that's what I did. He had me dropping dishes. I felt his living presence drawing near. The dog felt it, too, don't tell me he didn't. Dogs always know. It wouldn't surprise me if that dog wasn't trying to tell me all along. The poor man, wandering the face of the earth, not knowing who he was or where he was bound, and all the time his footsteps guiding him home. A death and a life, that's the way it goes.'

Mrs Barnaby said, 'Joe, the allowance cut is restored.' That's all.

And Tench, Tench had known for three days.

232

Before the doctor left, he talked to me. He said, 'Your mother's relatives tell me you were never reconciled to your father's death. That's very interesting. Did you feel from the first that it was – unfinished business, my dear?' I must have nodded, because he talked about prescience. He collects examples of prescience. He said it was far from uncommon. 'You, his own flesh and blood, resisted what others accepted. Instinctively you knew the tie had not been broken. When he came, you were ready for him, waiting. Very interesting, I may use it in a little brochure – no names, of course.' He was pleased with his evening's work; he had been interviewed and photographed and would be quoted.

IN my father's room, with the door closed and the shades drawn, my father told the others what my mother was and why he had sent me away. He had told me before, when we were alone.

My mother wanted to own, to possess, not share. She wanted things and money and people in her own hands; she wanted lives and destiny in her own hands. She wanted to give and withhold, she wanted everything to come through her. Food, clothing, pain, and pleasure, all must come through her. She wanted the power of life and death, and she took it. She almost took it.

Mike and Joe, my father and I, and Tench. And Tray. In a closed room with drawn shades.

'You must remember her background,' my father said. 'Respectable poverty, the great test. She fought it every day of her life, not with work but with dreams. Her cousins denied themselves to give her the things she wanted, and she took what they gave and dreamed of more. Marriage was her goal, not love. A house, a mansion, not a cottage. She'd had enough of cottages. When Isobel was born, even before she was born, I began to be uneasy. Her mother made no preparations for her. And although Isobel started life with a smile on her face it went away too soon. I saw it change to a look of quiet wonder that was ugly and frightening in a child. She looked as if she were on trial, as if she had to placate and please, or be punished. So I sent her to boarding school, as an experiment, and when I saw that she accepted the new life and was healthy and cared for, I kept her there. And I thought I had found the right solution. Her mother was happier during those years, I thought we could adjust our lives eventually.'

I remembered that my mother had never touched me, never smiled at me, until she thought my father was dead. On my rare visits home I would run into the house, looking for her, hoping each time that she would tell me I could stay.

My father said that, in those years, he lived for the day when I was grown and we could talk together as two adults. He thought he could make me understand. He never considered a legal separation – he had nothing to tell in a courtroom. He planned to bring me home when I was twenty-one; he planned to give me the house on my twenty-first birthday. Early in the spring he told my mother his plans.

He said, 'I told her because I wanted to be sure of Isobel's welcome. I wanted us to be three again, not two. I spoke of travel together, of parties and young people, of our courtship and love. She listened quietly, and smiled and nodded; but when I spoke of giving Isobel the house, she shook her head. She said the house was hers; she said it had always been hers. She smiled and cried, "My house, mine! Darling, you know it's mine."

'It was never hers; it was the one thing I had kept in my own name. Throughout the years, I had given her the greater part of my possessions, and I thought I had given them freely; but when she fought my gift to Isobel, I knew I had never given, that she had taken. She had plundered me, using my love and need. She emerged clearly, but I refused to believe what I saw. I didn't want to believe. I fought the truth. I fought it until to-night when she stood at the top

of the tunnel stairs, looked at me, turned and ran ... I'm
hurting you, Isobel.'

I said no.

'Talk to Isobel now,' Mike said. 'Not to me this time,
to Isobel.'

He talked to me. 'When you came home, my illness
began. I mean the physical illness; my mind was already
ill. I began to wonder if I were being poisoned, and I con-
demned myself for such thinking. I took refuge in the
shacks. Throughout those days she was tender and considerate. I convinced myself that I was approaching madness. I know the truth now. You saw her tell me the truth,
without words, to-night, when she chose death. She had been
giving me arsenic.'

TENCH spoke quietly, bitterly. 'I should have guessed from
your looks. We've always had arsenic on the premises, a
large tin, on a shelf in the cellar. We keep it for rats and
foxes. People with country houses can always buy it, and
they can keep it in plain sight and spoon it out as needed.
Spoon it out when they want it and replace what they've
used.'

My father said, 'Replace what they've used. Yes. She
kept her own supply in her medicine chest. I found it last
night when she was away. In a plain jar, ready to play its
part in the long, sad history of unlabelled drugs. Ready for
an accident, a post mortem; for tears and self condemna-
tion. She used to stroke my hand and say, "Poor Marsh, you
are not yourself." If she had won, she would have said, "Poor
Marsh, poor darling, and it's all my fault, my carelessness.
It was an accident, wasn't it? Make me believe it was an
accident!"'

I said, 'It's all right, Father.'

He said, 'Thank you. I think now that she gave it to me in
the breakfast coffee, in the wine we drank at dinner. She
scolded me gently when I complained about the bitterness.
'Poor Marsh, you are not yourself.' And when I improved,

she repeated the dose, always a small one, always a small, tormenting one. She sat by my bed and asked me how I felt and talked about my nerves. I think she was driving me to take my own life; I think she wanted it to be that way. My nerves were fast becoming a legend – she saw to that. She was prepared for suicide or murder. The unlabelled jar, a fumbling, desperate man. Suicide, murder, accident. Can you understand that I still find this incredible?'

Mike said. 'You mean baroque. Baroque is the word for this. You've been having a high old time, haven't you?'

The ghost of a smile moved across my father's face, but Joe laughed out loud, like a child released. Joe said, 'Baroque? Baroque? I could say it more colloquially. I say it's the nuts. Go on, Mr Ford, please. Doesn't anything come next?'

'Isobel comes next. I didn't desert Isobel. I've known everything Isobel has done. I've known everything her mother did. I took no chances. I died by proxy so that I could watch her. When people came to the house, I stood in the upper hall and listened. When Isobel walked at night, Tray followed. And I was never far behind. When I heard she was not well, I waited for the first illness, like mine. I told myself it would never come, that a woman's child is always safe. I told myself again that I was mad, but I was prepared to wait indefinitely, until I was sure. Then I heard talk of a marriage between Isobel and Mike. Marriage would have taken her away – that was one solution, that was what I wanted. After that, I don't know. I didn't plan beyond that. I suppose I would have gone away myself, eventually. And now, in spite of my care, Isobel knows. I've saved her nothing.'

'You did, too,' Joe said. 'You did fine, you did a fine job. But if you ask me, you were plain lucky when you showed that light.'

'My curtain fell, twice. The first time, no one saw it.'

'No?' Joe said. 'Well, anyway, we got away with it.'

236

TENCH cleared his throat. 'Mr Ford,' he said, 'would have got away with nothing more. I had reached the end of my endurance. I think I would have taken steps.' Tench had known for three days. He had seen Tray coming down from the top floor. 'A one-man dog Tray was and is,' he said, 'and not a sign of grief. And what would he be doing on the top floor? I set myself to find out, and three nights ago I caught him at it. He went to one of the turret doors and stood there, waiting. The door opened, from the inside. I knew it was kept locked. I don't mind admitting –' Tench mopped his face, but no one smiled.

'I have known Mr Ford since he was twenty-one. I was steward at his club. I tell you I knew him. I came to him when he married, at his own request, and brought my wife and Anna with me. I served him through the years and minded my own business and kept my thoughts to myself, no matter how I felt about certain things. I identified his car and jacket and believed it was him. I watched his daughter eating her heart out. I felt what she felt – we both loved him, you see. And when I saw that door open and Tray go in, I told myself that what I saw was none of my business. I told myself the world got crazier every day, but praise the Lord. And I bought a little spirit stove and plenty of good ground meat and put it outside the door. When it disappeared, stove and all, I knew Tray hadn't taken it. But the young people worried me a bit when I saw them going up there to-night.'

'You worried me,' Mike said to Tench. 'But when we found that room, I knew you had a hand in it somewhere.'

'Only the meat, Mr Mike. Mr Ford never saw me nor I him. But after that first night I never really worried. I knew Mr Ford, see? What was that word you were passing around? Baroque? I think I know what that means.' He built a monument with his hands. 'It means a large design and sound material, put together in a kind of *style*. I think it's out of fashion, though it's much admired by many people still. Among them, myself.' ...

I am waiting in my room for the last time.

My father and Mike are talking to the lawyer, and when they have finished, we are going to the Barnabys'. After that, I don't know where we will go, but we will never come here again. Some day we three will have another house, with Tench and Mrs Tench and Anna.

Baroque. A large design and sound material, put together in a kind of style. That's what it means to Tench. But it means something else, too. Grotesque.

It means a girl who tied candy-box ribbon in her hair, who wore sapphires – 'under my pillow until the engagement is announced. They are much too grand for my present position, and I will be talked about.' Who said she wanted children. 'Why do you think I love that great enormous house?'

It means a woman who made no preparation for her coming child, and kept a bowl of flowers in the room of the man she tried to kill. Baroque.

After the house is cleaned and closed, there will be nothing left of her unless the cleaners overlook a drop of candle wax in some dark corner. But if my father had died as I thought he did, I would still have something – 'Always open doors when you hear music.'

We always will.